I0730602

BONDS OF BLOOD AND DUTY

JEN A. EGERTON

CRANTHORPE
—MILLNER—
PUBLISHERS

Map artwork by Jenna Richards © Cranthorpe Millner Publishers

Copyright © Jen A. Egerton (2025)

The right of Jen A. Egerton to be identified as author of this work has been asserted by them in accordance with section 77 and 78 of the Copyright, Designs and Patents Act 1988.

All rights reserved. No part of this publication may be reproduced, stored in a retrieval system, or transmitted in any form or by any means, electronic, mechanical, photocopying, recording, or otherwise, without the prior permission of the publishers.

Any person who commits any unauthorised act in relation to this publication may be liable to criminal prosecution and civil claims for damages.

This book is a work of fiction. Names, characters, places and incidents are either products of the author's imagination or are used fictitiously. Any resemblance to actual events or locales or persons, living or dead, is entirely coincidental.

First published by Cranthorpe Millner Publishers (2025)

ISBN 978-1-80378-329-1 (Paperback)

www.cranthorpemillner.com

Cranthorpe Millner Publishers

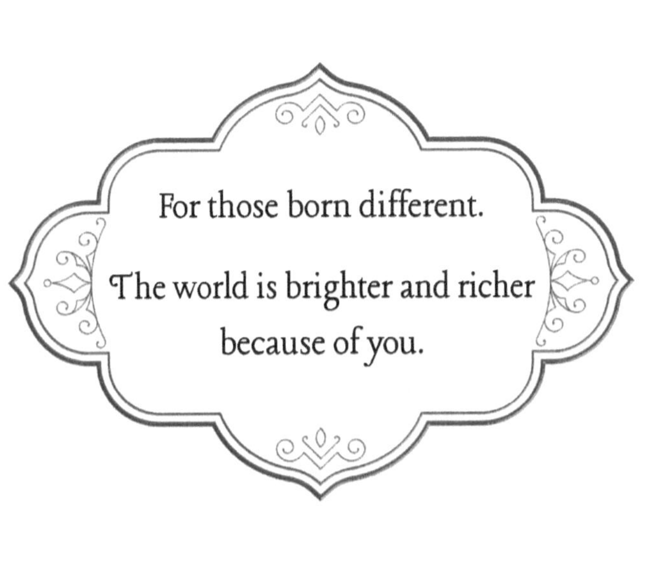
For those born different.

The world is brighter and richer
because of you.

What Was I Made For? – Billie Eilish

Safe & Sound – Taylor Swift, Joy Williams and John Paul White

Running With the Wolves – AURORA

Princesses Don't Cry – CARYS

Lost Boy – Ruth B

I Found – Amber Run

Like Real People Do – Hozier and Allison Russell

Yellow Flicker Beat – Lorde

War of Hearts – Ruelle

All I Want – Kodaline

AVATHAIR

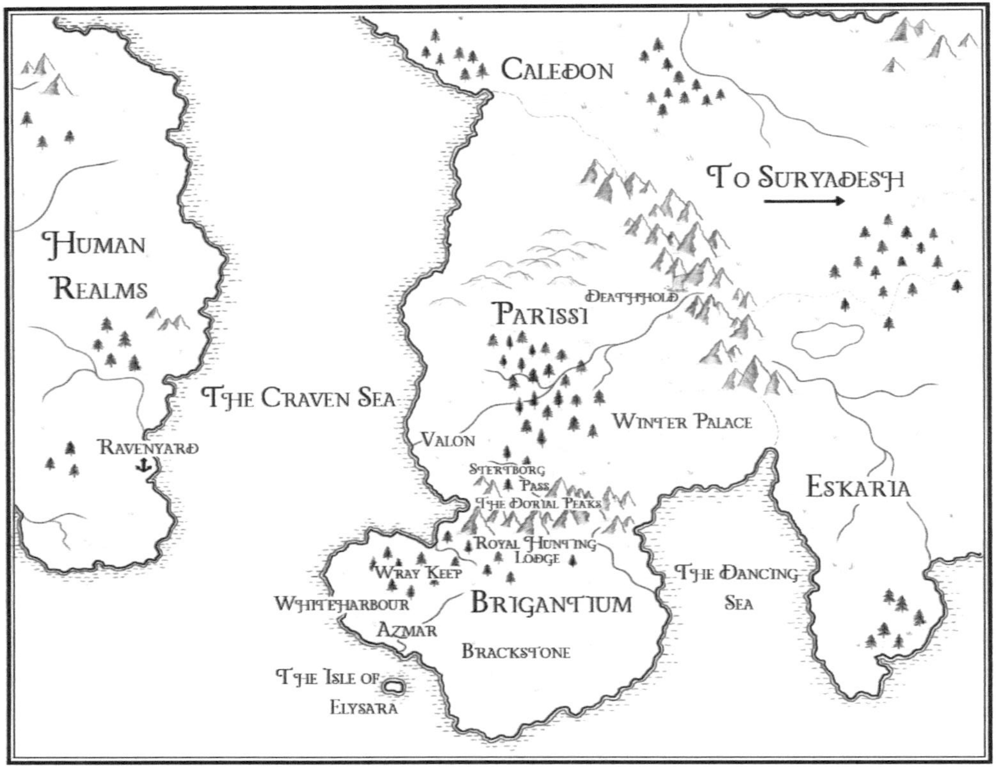

Caledon
To Suryadesh
Human Realms
The Craven Sea
Parissi
Deathhold
Winter Palace
Valon
Ravenyard
Stertborg Pass
The Dorial Peaks
Eskaria
Royal Hunting Lodge
Wray Keep
Whiteharbour
Brigantium
Azmar
Brackstone
The Dancing Sea
The Isle of Elysara

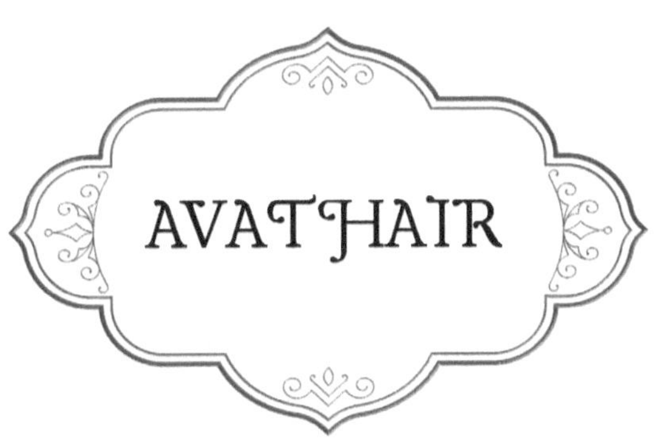

CHAPTER ONE

EVELIN

Royal Hunting Lodge, Kingdom of Brigantium

Evelin bit down hard on the thin linen fabric of her sleeve, muffling the scream that tore from her lips. Where the hell was Agnes?

The Princess of Brigantium wrapped her hands around the post of the wooden bed frame as the pain bent her in two. Her breathing was shallow and rapid, each breath pulling her heart into her throat.

It was too soon.

Too soon.

Too soon.

The words swirling around in her mind were the only things that Evelin could focus on. The pain of childbirth was not new to her, but this time felt different. Something was wrong.

"My lady, what is the—" Agnes' strong, clear voice cut through the fog of panic overwhelming her. Light footsteps hurried over and a hand began rubbing gentle circles on Evelin's back. "When did it start?"

Speaking was out of the question – just remembering to breathe was effort enough – so Evelin merely shook her head, her long strawberry-blonde hair falling onto her face. Sweat poured off her brow, turning her hair the colour of a dying fire.

Evelin rocked her hips from side to side, trying to ride out the contraction. When the swell finally began to subside, she yanked herself upright and turned to face her lady-in-waiting. The older woman's wrinkled forehead was furrowed with concern, her slate-grey eyes narrow. Evelin wanted to throw her arms around Agnes and let out the flood of tears that pricked her eyes, but she wouldn't. If she gave in to her fear, she would be lost.

"How often are the pains coming?" Agnes asked, gripping Evelin's hand tightly. Although advanced in years, Agnes' small frame belied a woman of formidable strength and courage.

"Every couple of minutes." Evelin swallowed hard.

Agnes reached out for Evelin's swollen stomach, prodding carefully. "And when did they start?" she asked, repeating her earlier question.

"About five or six hours ago," Evelin admitted, looking away at the specks of dust floating in the hazy light of dawn which seeped through a crack in the thick curtains. They bobbed and eddied upwards in the direction of the heavens, dancing on the breeze.

Agnes' eyes shot open, deep lines creasing her brow. "Why didn't you send for me sooner, my lady? We could have tried to halt the progress, but it is far too late now. You should have—"

"I know that!" Evelin snapped. The child wasn't even born and she was failing it already. "I thought it was just false labour. The baby isn't due for months."

Agnes nodded and tied her long, silver-grey hair into a plait with deft hands, then rummaged in the leather satchel slung over her thin shoulder. Glass bottles clinked together as a series of vials were pulled out and inspected. She nodded, seemingly content with her choice, and sprinkled their contents liberally around the stone chamber. The clary sage and geranium were meant to aid with the delivery of children, but their scent was oppressive. Cloying and sickly, they smelled of death made flesh.

The room swam before Evelin. It was the height of summer and it promised to be another sweltering day. Even at dawn it was warm and the air in the room was treacly thick.

"I'm going to be sick," she muttered, doubling over, vomit rising in her throat.

The screech of the long, damask curtains being drawn open made her wince. She closed her eyes against the flood of light. Counting her breaths, Evelin tried to focus on the reassuring firmness of the wooden floor under her bare feet.

One. Two. Three.

A cool breeze began to lick at the bottom of her long white shift; the nausea started to ebb away.

"Drink some water," Agnes commanded, holding out a pewter goblet.

Evelin managed a small sip before thrusting it back. "Please… help me. Just make it stop," she begged through ragged breaths. Another contraction was coming. They were now so frequent there was barely any respite.

"You know I cannot stop this; it has gone on too long, but I will do what I can to relieve your pains."

Agnes was one of the fae who was blessed with the gift of healing. She held her hands over Evelin's swollen belly and closed her eyes. Beneath softly wrinkled palms, a pale blue-green light appeared and spread in ripples over her rounded stomach.

Evelin's breathing began to ease. The pain wasn't gone, but it had lessened slightly.

"Get on the bed, my lady. On your hands and knees," Agnes instructed, yanking back the sweat-soaked sheets.

With shaking legs, Evelin did as she was commanded.

Agnes moved her long, slender hands down the length of Evelin's back, stroking gently. Fear lurked in her dark, watchful eyes; as a fae, Evelin was stronger than her human neighbours across the water, but childbirth was still perilous.

"Get off. Get off. Please get off," Evelin hissed at the older woman. The touch of another person was too much to bear. She felt like a wild animal caught in a trap, pinned and desperate to be free.

A new wave of pain began to sweep through her. She dug her fingers into the edge of the mattress and clenched her jaw tight. She had no idea how long the contraction lasted for, but once it had released its fiery grip, she collapsed onto her forearms, panting whilst Agnes examined her.

"When the next one comes, you must push, my lady," Agnes said firmly. "The baby will not wait. If you do not begin pushing, I fear we may lose you both. You know the dangers of childbirth well enough. I couldn't save your mother when she brought your brother into the world, and I will be damned if I lose you in the same way."

Evelin had known something was wrong with this pregnancy. It had felt different from the start.

She kept her eyes firmly shut, not wanting to look at Agnes before she spoke softly of the fear that had been devouring her the past few months. "What happens to William if I die, Agnes? If this birth kills me I can't let him be raised by Marcellus. What kind of a man would he become? I can't leave him."

Agnes tutted and gave her a hard stare. "Come now, that won't happen. You mustn't think that way, my lady. The baby might be coming early, but there is still a chance for you both. You are young and strong, but you need to push when you feel the pain build again. You must fight."

Evelin let out a derisive chuckle; she hadn't felt strong in a very long time. Years sequestered away in the hunting lodge in the middle of nowhere by Marcellus, the fae lord she had married, had weakened her. Nerves ate away at her, sapping the vitality which once drove her. Evelin's time was spent wrapped in anxious thoughts, and worst-case scenarios were constant shadows even on the brightest of days.

But Agnes was right. She had to try. She had to fight for her children's sake.

The pain mounted once more and Evelin screwed her green eyes closed, gritted her teeth, and pushed. She bore down again and again on Agnes' order, breathing on command for what felt like hours until the baby came with one final effort. She fell forwards onto the pillows, any strength utterly spent as Agnes wrapped the baby up in the prepared linens. Her limbs were still shaking from her efforts as she twisted into a sitting position and looked around for her new child. Surely, there should have been a cry by now?

Something *was* wrong.

"Agnes. Agnes? Is it…? Is the baby breathing?" Evelin asked, hardly daring to breathe herself. Panic threatened to consume her. Her heartbeat whooshed in her ears, her vision blurring at the edges. Why was the woman taking so long to reply?

Suddenly, a cry filled the room, loud and plaintive.

Relief flooded through her. "Thank God. Thank you, Agnes," she whispered, tears flowing freely down her face.

The baby was obviously hungry and ready to be fed, but Agnes remained still.

"What is the matter? Please give the child to me, Agnes."

Her companion remained silent.

"For God's sake, give me the child!" Evelin exclaimed, attempting to swing her shaking legs over the side of the bed. She needed to hold her baby in her arms; the pull was overpowering.

Agnes turned to her, the woman's tanned face drained of colour, her expression inscrutable. "My lady…" Agnes' voice faltered as she looked at the princess. "The baby… He…" Agnes stepped slowly towards Evelin and passed her the bundle.

"A boy?" Evelin asked as she looked down at the tiny child squalling in her arms, forcing down the flood of love that rose within her. Not yet. She had to know that he was all right. Her eyes scanned him rapidly. His skin was a good colour, pink and healthy, and another heir for the kingdom of Brigantium was no bad thing. Evelin didn't understand Agnes' hesitation. What was wrong?

Agnes knelt down and slowly pulled the swaddling sheets away from the baby's head.

Evelin looked down. A small gasp escaped her lips. "He… his ears… Agnes… what has happened?" Fingers trembling, Evelin gently traced the outline of her baby's ears. Unlike her own, and every other fae's in the land, his ears were small and rounded.

The baby didn't look fae.

He looked human.

CHAPTER TWO

UNKNOWN

Valon, capital of Parissi

Two years earlier

The ball celebrating the spring equinox was already in full swing at the Summer Palace when the man entered the ballroom and carefully adjusted his black mask. The setting sun had burned a fiery red on his short walk from the docks, and even he had marvelled at the delicate grandeur of both the palace and the city. A haven by the sea, the City of Valon and its palace were beloved by the citizens of the kingdom and those drawn to it from the other fae realms. The streets were clean and orderly, and the shops bustled with merchants selling their wares to city folk and traders alike.

The palace was the main residence of the King of Parissi and his court. As such, it mirrored the virtues extolled by its inhabitants: intelligence, artistry, and beauty. Tonight's celebration was no exception. Soul-crushingly beautiful music filled the air and the smell of various Parissi delicacies wafted towards the man as the two-dozen, elegantly dressed fae servants wove between the guests.

His gaze was drawn upwards to the intricate roof, delicately lit by faelights. The palace's blue and gold dome soared even higher than the spires of the Academie, where the most talented fae honed their abilities under the expert tutelage of the Fellows. But tonight was not one of the formal Academie dinners, dictated by traditions passed down through the ages; tonight was one of pure joy. King Silas' balls were – by reputation, at least – always magnificent, festive occasions, and invites were often hard to acquire. However, it was rumoured that this ball would far surpass its predecessors for not only its entertainment and libations, but also its guest list. For the king had not just invited some of the most powerful, talented, and beautiful fae, but also a select number of humans.

For millennia, fae and humans had not mixed. The history books told of various wars and struggles, but over time, a quiet and accepted order had gradually developed. With a large body of water separating the two, the human lands and fae realms had become peaceful, if watchful, neighbours.

In recent years, King Silas had even decided to open up the ports of Parissi to human traders. They had come sparingly at first, sensibly wary of the faster, magical fae, even the least skilled of whom could perform small magic – lighting fires without flint, healing cuts, setting simple wards. Yet their fellow men had overcome this fear when they saw the riches those who ventured first returned with: cloths that shone with a light of their own, foods bursting with flavours that danced on the palate, and even fae-made weapons with edges that never dulled.

The humans were skilled craftsmen, producing all kinds of articulated and mechanical devices that were highly prized by the wealthier fae. Soon, there was a flourishing trade between Parissi and the closest human port city of Ravenyard, and tonight, King Silas had invited the richest of these traders and the Archduke of Ravenyard himself to celebrate in the palace.

Despite the masks that the revellers wore, the man could easily make out which of the guests were not fae. For one thing, their scent was completely different. Children of both species tended to smell much the same, yet after puberty, humans had a distinct, but not unpleasant odour: earthier, and more metallic. They also tended to be a couple of inches shorter and their movements were far less graceful and swift. He knew from experience that there were many humans just as beautiful as the fae, male and female alike, but the most obvious difference was their ears, which were rounded, unlike the delicate points of the fae's.

This evening, King Silas himself sat next to a few humans on the raised platform by the windows, which looked out to the sea. His handsome bearded face smiled benevolently at the guests. They were overwhelmed; their heads turning this way and that, taking in the wonders that surrounded them.

As the band began to increase the tempo of their music, King Silas turned away from talking with his guests and gently inclined his head. One of the few guardsmen in the room banged his staff on the marble floor in two quick raps. As one, the fae guests began to form lines for the first dance.

The revellers stepped in perfect formation, swirling around each other, their tunics and gowns mirroring the smooth steps of their agile bodies. The band played on and on, faster and faster, with not one fae missing a beat. Their masks shimmered as they spun. The sight was entrancing, and the man could see the humans on the dais transfixed by the display before them.

When the music began to fade, the king rose to his feet, smoothing his crimson tunic. The dancers turned to the ruler and waited expectantly.

"Citizens, visitors, and honoured guests," he started. The king's clear voice boomed sonorously across the hall, and the fae servants meandered once more between the guests, handing out glasses of a sparkling drink that shimmered under the lights.

"We come together tonight to celebrate the new bonds formed with our dear neighbours across the water. I hope you will join me in a toast! To new friends, shared wealth, and future joy!" King Silas took a long drink from his glass and smiled at the crowd as they mirrored his action. "Another song, would you not agree?" the king put to the crowd.

The musicians swiftly began another raucous tune and the dancers began their exertions again, twirling around each other on the marble dancefloor.

The man edged carefully around the dancers and made his way towards the dais. His black cloak snagged on a female's headdress when her partner dipped her backwards, and he bit back a snarl as he yanked the cloak back and stepped away from their overly dramatic performance. The dancers had lost all semblance of order now and had either split off into pairs or twirled around alone.

Mere feet from the platform, the man reached into his pocket and pulled out a small, blue velvet pouch. Loosening the neck, he cast its contents to the floor in one swift movement. At once, complete darkness swept through the room, and a hush descended. The man sensed movement on the dais and a voice rang out through the dark.

"Lux."

A ball of white light appeared between King Silas' outstretched hands. The ruler threw his arms wide and the light flew across the hall, pushing the darkness towards the numerous windows that graced the hall's perimeter. The fae and humans looked around in wonder, their eyes readjusting to the brightness. Without warning, a guttural scream pierced the silence; a young woman – fae – was lying prone on the floor, her silver gown soaked in blood, ebony hair spilt around her. Gasps and shouts of panic filled the room, and the nearest fae knelt to tend to her. A crowd gathered around, whispering and jostling. From the corner of his eye, the man spied a subtle movement.

In tandem, the fae servers glided through the crowd, angling their bodies between the dancers, and silently removed the blades that had been strapped beneath their cloaks. They stood behind the guests, reached out their long, nimble arms and pulled their blades back, all in less than a breath. Fae blood, with its purplish tinge, sprayed across the dancers, who barely had time to scream before the servants spun round and stabbed at them with horrifying precision. The Kingsguard rushed forward to protect their ruler, but before they could reach the dais and shield him from attack, the man leapt forward. His strong legs propelled him right in front of the king.

King Silas had already drawn his longsword, Lightwielder. Its blade glowed and the king readied himself, shifting his weight onto his back leg. The man didn't draw a weapon. Instead, he raised his right arm and slowly rotated a gloved hand. Between his long fingers, a dark red ball of light flickered and grew. He thrust his arm outwards towards the king, flinging the sphere in his direction with breath-taking speed. It hit King Silas in the centre of his broad chest, disappearing beneath his crimson tunic.

Silas' brow furrowed as he looked down at his chest. Seeing nothing, he lunged forward towards the man, who took a quick step backwards.

"Coward!" Silas bellowed, pulling his weapon back, ready to mete out a killing blow.

As he did so, the centre of his tunic glowed red, the light spreading across his chest. Silas' handsome face froze, pain and fear flashing across his eyes. Lightwielder slipped from his grasp and he clutched at his chest and throat, gasping for air. Sinking to his knees, his gaze turned to the black-clothed man in front of him.

"Why?" he gasped.

The man did not reply; the blood traitor didn't merit one. He turned back to the dance floor and looked across to the doors that led to the two wings of the palace. From the two adjoining corridors, members of the Kingsguard surged to aid their ruler. Two of the fae servants were carefully casting wards on the doors, sealing them shut at their bronze frames. The frenzied bangs of the guards behind them were just audible over the screams that continued to fill the room.

On the dais, the humans cowered from the man, backing behind the gilt chairs. Suddenly, a burly human with ash-blond hair, holding a wickedly sharp dagger in his hand, sprang forwards. Just as the cloaked man was about to summon up another ball of red light, there was a sharp tug on the back of his left ankle. The dying king's fingers wrapped around his leg and squeezed into his flesh, drawing his attention. In that moment, the human's dagger caught him across the cheek, slicing through his flesh.

Stinging pain radiated out across his face, yet it only encouraged him. He stepped forwards, out of the clutch of the dying king, and knocked the dagger from the human's hand with a swift chop to the forearm. He gripped the human by the neck as red light emanated from his hands. When he released his grip, a ring of red encircled the human's neck, spreading through the body as it had with the king.

The servants had made swift work of the rest of the people in the room, fae and human. Bodies were cast across the floor, their blood glistening in dark pools; any survivors of the initial attack had been quickly dispatched. The man strode to the windows behind the dais and flung them open. He shot a single blast of light up into the centre of the dome which arced down, fading away. Upon the signal, the servants followed the man to the windows. They launched themselves out into the dark night, falling the thirty or so feet to the ground and landing adeptly. Anyone looking from the windows of the Academie next door would see the black-clad figures scatter into the city once they were through the palace gates, casting off their masks into the bushes of the front lawn as they went.

The man turned and looked back to the palace. Was that a movement in the ballroom? A shadow shifting against the faelights? No survivors – that had been the order. He was about to return and ensure all life had been extinguished when he heard the seal on the doors break. The Kingsguard would be entering now. The chance was lost. The risk wasn't worth returning, so the man continued on towards the dock where a small boat was waiting with a lantern lit, the boatsman ready. He slipped aboard and pulled his hood closer over his head as the sailor pushed them onto the open water. A small droplet of blood fell onto the wooden boards beneath him. He frowned and raised a hand to the incision across his cheek – that would need healing when he returned.

A warm breeze filled the sails, driving the boat forwards and carrying the screams that sang through the night as word of what had happened spread through Valon.

Royal Hunting Lodge, Kingdom of Brigantium

Present day

Agnes frowned as she pushed away loose strands of hair with the back of her hand, palms still stained with blood from the birth.

"What in God's name have you done?" she gasped, confusion turning to anger as she strode towards Evelin, who was sitting on the bed cradling her new child.

Evelin knew what Agnes was implying and indignation filled her. "Agnes, nothing has happened. I have been shut up in this Godforsaken lodge for over three years. How the hell could I do anything?"

"Then explain to me how you have just birthed a human child! This doesn't just *happen*."

"I don't know!" The shaking had returned to Evelin's limbs. She clenched and unclenched her fingers, trying to regain control.

Agnes reached for a shawl draped over one of the few wooden chairs in the room and wrapped it around her. The mattress sagged slightly as she sat beside her. The older woman always had a comforting smell – milk thistle, chamomile, and eucalyptus. The scent calmed Evelin as she pulled the shawl tight around herself.

"Agnes, I have not bedded a human. Where would I even find one? You know as well as they do that they are not welcome in Brigantium anymore. They haven't been for a long time."

Agnes looked down at the child and stroked the soft pink curve of his cheek. "Maybe… maybe he is fae. Perhaps his ears are some sort of genetic throwback? Your parents didn't have any human ancestors that I know of, but perhaps on his father's side…?"

"Do you think so?" Evelin asked hopefully. "He doesn't look even *part* fae, though, and he's just so tiny." The baby squirmed in her arms, his mouth and nose twitching, blindly searching.

"Well, there is a way we can be certain, but for now, I think the child needs feeding."

Evelin loosened the front of her shift and angled the baby at her breast. She surveyed the tiny figure nuzzling at her and was filled with the same love as when she had first held William. Whether he was fae or human made no difference.

This child was hers to protect.

The sun had just reached its peak when Evelin opened her eyes, sight bleary.

"Good, you're awake," Agnes said from her sentinel post next to the bed as she gently rocked the wooden cradle next to her. "Here, eat something."

Evelin reached for the platter handed to her; it was piled high with gleaming peaches and plums, so ripe that she could smell their sweetness before even taking a bite. How long had it been since she had eaten something? Her stomach grumbled as she picked one of the plums and bit into it, sticky juice bursting from its flesh. She ate greedily, but her eyes never left the swaying cradle.

Once her hunger was abated, her mind returned to what Agnes had said before. "You said there was a way to tell if the baby is part fae. What is it?"

If there was a way to find out, to prove that the baby was part fae, it might make things easier to explain to her husband. She had never lain with another man, human or otherwise, but convincing Marcellus of that would be impossible if he even slightly doubted the parentage of his new son.

"I'm afraid you won't like it, my lady, but the method should give us an answer either way. You know the basics of how fae healing works; our magic calls to the magic in others and uses it as a conduit to accelerate or bolster the body's own healing. However, fae healing does not work on humans, as they have no powers of their own. What I suggest is that we make a small cut on the child's foot... and then see if my magic heals it."

"No! Agnes, he's only a few hours old. That's just cruel," Evelin protested, rising to look at her sleeping infant. He had a good head of hair, light golden strands so unlike the dark locks of Marcellus or the deep auburn of his older brother. Her heart caught in her chest when his perfect little nose twitched, as if he could smell her approach.

"Come now. It will be the barest scratch, and all being well I will close it just as quickly. Let us do it now." Agnes rose to her feet and picked up the battered leather roll she carried everywhere. Slowly, and with the utmost respect, she laid it on the bed and unfurled it. Inside was a vast selection of tools and implements. Her hand hovered over them before she selected a tiny golden blade. "Hold the child in your arms and keep him steady."

Evelin reached into the cradle and gently picked up the boy with the greatest care. It felt strange to hold a newborn once more, to be responsible for something so precious and fragile. She sat down and began to unwrap his feet from the blanket she had swaddled him in. Agnes knelt beside them and clasped the boy's ankle firmly. The baby mewled in protest, his face turning puce with frustration. Swiftly, the old woman made a small incision on the base of his foot. The baby let out a pitiful scream that pierced Evelin's heart, and she stroked the silky-smooth skin of his face, hushing him.

Agnes placed her hands over the injury and began to summon her magic, calling to the boy's own.

Nothing happened.

The light blue glow between her fingers flickered and died.

This couldn't be.

Evelin held her breath, her eyes wide. "Try again. Please, Agnes," she said quietly, swallowing to fight back the tears that threatened to spill down her face.

The older woman attempted the healing once more, but the light faded again, even faster this time, as if it too recognised that the task was impossible.

No.

No, no, no.

"My dear, the boy has no magic," Agnes said gently. "What I say now is not meant to hurt or scare you, but his ears are rounded, and he is so much smaller than any other fae baby I have ever seen. Moreover, your pregnancy was far shorter than normal. I believe him to be fully human."

"But how? How?" Evelin's stomach was churning; she wanted to vomit. Her eyes searched the baby, up and down, looking for any sign that Agnes was wrong.

"I have absolutely no idea," Agnes murmured. "Even if you had lain with a human— "

"I've already told you, I haven't!" Evelin snapped, anger rising to replace her fear.

"My lady, I said '*if*'. If you say you haven't, I believe you. Besides, such a joining would have resulted in a part fae child. They are rare, but not unheard of. This… this is unprecedented. I have been healing fae and attending births for well over a century, and I have never even heard of a human child born to a fae mother." The lines in Agnes' forehead deepened and there was nothing but worry in her slate-grey eyes. "We need a plan."

"What do you mean?" Evelin asked. She was still bone-tired from the birth and her mind refused to follow a coherent train of thought.

"This is a dangerous situation for you both," Agnes explained. "Your husband is a man with a quick and vicious temper. You, of all people, know his intolerance of humans. When he finds out about the child, there will be a reckoning."

Evelin knew Agnes spoke the truth. She had only married Marcellus at the request of her brother, just a few short months after he became king. Otto had been so unhinged in the days following their father's death; she would have done anything to ease his suffering.

Now, all she felt was regret.

Azmar, capital city of Brigantium

Six years earlier

Otto's relationship with their father had not been an easy one. Both men had formidable tempers, and their interactions often ended in arguments so loud it felt like they might bring down the walls of the castle with their force.

Before she went to the Academie, and during her summer breaks, Evelin had taken on the role of peacemaker, sanding down the rough edges of their words with calming interjections. Her father had doted on her; often all it took was a pleading look or a small smile from her to calm his ire. They had been so close, yet it was Otto who had been broken by the news of his death. Evelin hadn't even cried. From the moment she'd received the news, she began simply floating through her daily existence at the Academie. Nothing felt solid or real anymore. Not until she was home, back in the castle at Azmar, and flung her arms around her brother.

The tears racked his slim frame as he struggled for breath, head buried in her shoulder.

"I know. I know," Evelin whispered, softly stroking his long copper hair. "I miss him too." She wanted to do anything to bring solace to him. It was just the two of them now – all that remained of the royal house of Brigantium. "Tell me how I can help… please." Perhaps she could make the funeral arrangements, or send out some ravens? She needed to feel useful. She needed a way to help her brother.

Otto lifted his head and looked at her with tear-reddened eyes. "There's one thing you could do, Eve." He swallowed hard. "Make a match."

"What?" She blinked. Her father had just died. Marriage was the last thing on her mind.

"Yes," he replied, his eyes darting across her face. "You know that I can't marry. I won't. People are already talking about it… If you marry and have sons, the line of succession will be safe."

What he was asking for was too much. Whilst her father lived, Evelin had enjoyed a level of freedom unheard of for most royal women. Such an early marriage, especially an arranged one, was not something she had ever considered. She had a life in Valon, at the Academie. She had friends… hopes… but she knew that Otto preferred the company of other men.

Evelin took his face in her hands, the scruff on his jaw damp from tears. "Change the law, Otto. You are king now! Who cares if you want to be with a man? You speak like this is the last century. Love who you want and let the rest be damned."

Otto shook his head. "You've been away from Azmar for too long, sister. This is no Valon; no liberal paradise. The vultures at this court are already circling, looking for any weakness to strike – to take the throne Father left me. If you make a good alliance, our house will be secure. We are at our lowest now and we need the support of a strong match behind us. Please, *please* do this for me. For us."

Otto fell to his knees. He looked so small, so fragile, just like the little boy who had run to her each time he skinned his knee. The unbearable weight of responsibility pressed down on her.

Evelin pinched the bridge of her nose, trying to push away the headache that was blooming there. "Otto... I can make no promises, but I will consider a match."

His face lit up – not with a smile, but with the smallest flicker of hope.

Otto began his efforts to find her a match immediately, drawing up long lists of possible suitors. Her heart skipped not one, but *several* beats when a particular name on the list caught her attention: Lord Trystan, nephew of the King of Parissi. He was one of her closest friends at the Academie and she had always nursed a not-entirely-platonic affection for him.

Otto caught her staring. "Ah, yes. I forgot you know him. My chancellor suggested his name, among many, but I think we can do a little better for the Princess of Brigantium, don't you think? The son of King Silas' youngest sister, with little personal power and no wealth from that wastrel of a father, plus no military background to speak of? I think not. My sister deserves the best."

Otto struck through Trystan's name with a flourish that cut into her heart as surely as a dagger would have.

"I have invited some candidates with slightly more... *potential* to a dinner on Saturday. I think you will be impressed, sister."

Evelin forced back the sigh rising in her chest. She doubted any of these candidates would be suitable, but she had promised Otto that she would at least consider them... however dull they might be.

The dinner that weekend was a lavish occasion. Part of the official state mourning, the meal was for notable guests from Brigantium and those who had journeyed from the other fae realms to pay their respects to the late king.

Evelin was dressed in an onyx gown with a matching cape and long billowing sleeves that fell to the floor. She hated wearing black. It reminded her of the awful, restrictive dresses she was forced into for what felt like years after her mother's death. There had been so little colour anywhere in her life at that time. The dress weighed her down with the expectations now placed upon her, just like the grief that was woven into her heart.

Lost in her thoughts, Evelin ran her fingers over the beading on the impractical sleeves, unaware that a man had sat down beside her. It wasn't until Otto coughed and inclined his head towards her neighbour that she saw him.

He was tall, even for a fae, with jet black hair that formed beautiful, spiralling curls that fell loosely around his ears. His eyes were equally dark, and they bore into her with a strange intensity as he introduced himself.

"It is so good to meet you at long last, princess. I am Lord Marcellus of House Ashburner," the man said with a deep, buttery-smooth voice.

"At last?" she asked, momentarily forgetting the formalities required, lost in those beautiful eyes. They were so dark that they drew in the light around them and held it there, imprisoned in his gaze.

"Don't tell me that Otto hasn't spoken about me?" Marcellus chuckled. The sound turned heads and earned him a few disapproving glances from their fellow dinner guests, but it was a glorious thing to Evelin. "Oh, he is a rogue! We have been training together at Brackstone. I'm one of the junior officers."

Ashburner. Evelin knew the name. One of the lesser noble families of Brigantium, with little ancient pedigree and only a few members gifted with particular fae arts, but filthy rich. They provided one of the largest groups of soldiers for the army; no wonder Otto had wanted her to sit next to him.

"I'm sorry, my lord. It must have slipped my mind. It has been a trying time. The weather has been turbulent of late. I hope the journey here was not too arduous?" she asked, taking a bite of the small salad in front of her.

"Do you really wish to talk of the weather?" Marcellus leaned in conspiratorially. "I'd rather know all about what it is like to study in Valon."

Marcellus was so engaging and charming that, for the first time in weeks, Evelin felt the darkness inside her lift and a smile curled the corners of her mouth upwards. The conversation flowed easily, and she found herself able to talk freely, her tongue no doubt loosened by the copious amounts of wine he poured for them both. Sat next to him at that dinner, Evelin had blushed under his intense gaze and felt sparks run up her arm when he grazed her hand as he reached for his goblet.

At her father's funeral, Marcellus had taken the same hand and stroked it gently. That small gesture filled her heart with gratitude. After that, they met every day for walks in the castle grounds.

Marcellus spoke of his far-flung travels before commencing his military training, beguiling Evelin with stories of mystical lands and wondrous sights. She could almost smell the spices he spoke of. He even offered to take her with him to show her all of the fae realms. This possibility hadn't even occurred to her as being an option for a princess. She had been afforded a large measure of freedom by studying at the Academie, yet nothing on that scale.

Growing up, Evelin had hoped that she would be free to choose a husband, but if she had to wed someone else's choice, Marcellus did not seem a poor option. He was handsome and intelligent, and marriage to him would give her a greater deal of freedom than she had enjoyed even whilst her father had lived. When he proposed in front of the entire royal court at Otto's coronation ball, Evelin accepted immediately.

The young couple were married within the fortnight. Otto was delighted, and spared no expense on the wedding celebrations, even summoning their Aunt Katyana to bless the union as High Priestess. At the reception that followed, Marcellus whirled Evelin round the dancefloor, lifting her in the air before kissing her gently. After the band played a final song, he took her by the hand and led her to his room.

The wedding night was not what Evelin had expected. Once in the privacy of his own chamber, Marcellus became oddly cold and detached. Their coupling was brief and uncomfortable at best. Agnes had told her that this was often the case, so Evelin had hoped that, as they became more acquainted with each other, pleasure would accompany duty.

Over the following months, she spent hardly any time at all with her new husband. He was off hunting with her brother, studying maps in the library, or drilling the regiments that Otto had made him commander of as a wedding present. Their coupling did not improve, at least for her. Marcellus came to her room frequently, but she never felt loved in those moments. His kisses were not tender, his touch pawing and grasping.

All Evelin felt was alone.

A couple of months into their marriage, Evelin decided enough was enough. She was determined to forge some sort of connection with her husband. Catching sight of him heading out on a walk one blustery morning, she grabbed her cloak and hurried off after him.

"Marcellus?" she called.

He had just reached the rear gates of the palace that opened out onto the headland. His head whipped around, suddenly stiffening at the sight of her half-running through the grounds in pursuit of him.

"May I join you on your walk?" she asked, panting slightly from the effort of catching up with him.

Marcellus' dark eyes narrowed questioningly, but he nodded and held out his arm to her. She took it gladly, enjoying the intimacy the gesture implied. Maybe this would be a turning point for them? Perhaps it was simply the pressure of his new role that had created this distance between them.

Repeatedly, Evelin tried to engage him in conversation, asking questions about how his regiments were doing and what it had been like completing his military training at Brackstone. But no matter how gentle her nudges, his answers remained stilted, and he asked her nothing in return.

Before long, the wind had whipped itself into a frenzy and it became too difficult to talk at all. She clung onto her hood, trying in vain to keep her hair dry.

"Shall we go back?" she shouted over the howling squall.

"You go back if you wish to, wife," he replied. "I intend to venture down to the beach." He indicated to the small inlet, which had just about come into view.

Evelin desperately wanted to return to the warmth of the castle and get out of the worsening weather, but was determined to make the marriage work, so she put her head down and pushed forward.

Marcellus had rushed on, leaving her to navigate the sharp descent on her own. Her clothes were drenched and ice cold by the time she had manoeuvred her way down the rocky path to the beach. Sand got into her shoes immediately and she was half-tempted to kick them off. Leaning over to empty them out, a lumpen shape by the water's edge caught her eye.

Marcellus must have seen it too; he sprinted over to the shape and recoiled. Following behind, Evelin soon realised what had shocked him. The shape was a person.

A human.

She knelt down in the wet sand, small waves licking at her dress. It was a man. No, he was little more than a boy. His face was deathly pale and his eyes were shut, but she could see his chest rising and falling, just a fraction. Panic rose inside her.

"We've got to get help!" she shouted to Marcellus. The poor boy. How on earth had he washed up here?

"Do not fear, wife," he replied. "I will handle this."

Before she knew could say another word, Marcellus drew a dagger from his belt and pulled it swiftly across the youth's throat. Blood sprayed over her face, stinging her eyes and filling her mouth. A scream tore from her chest. No. *No.* This couldn't be happening. Her panic turned to horror and confusion.

"What have you done?" she gasped.

Marcellus wiped his dagger on the boy's tunic. "What needed to be done to that human scum."

"But he was no threat to us... Why? Why would you do such a thing?"

Marcellus made no reply and just stared out to sea, scouring the horizon.

"Answer me!" she cried. "What have you done?"

Marcellus rounded on her and raised his arm, bringing his palm down harshly across her cheek so hard that she was knocked into the shallows. Tears blinded her and she struggled to right herself, her face stinging with the force of his slap, but through her blurred vision she could just about make out Marcellus looming over her as he gripped her chin in his hand.

"Never presume to question me again," her husband hissed in a venomous whisper, before striding back across the beach, leaving her sobbing next to the body of the young man, the waves tugging at them both.

Who was this monster she had married? How on earth could anyone do that to another living being, human or not?

Royal Hunting Lodge, Kingdom of Brigantium

Present day

Evelin's attention was pulled back to the present by another wail from her new baby, his tiny face screwed up with anger.

Something within her snapped. "I don't care what Marcellus thinks or does, Agnes. I don't love him, and I never will – I should have divorced him years ago."

"My lady, be that as it may, it is not safe for you to tell him. You know your husband… I fear he will hurt you or the child if he finds out about the baby's… condition."

Evelin paused. "You're right. He can never find out the truth. Agnes, who else knows that I have birthed the child?"

"Only me and Bessie, the chambermaid. She heard your cries when she came to bring the breakfast this morning."

"Good." Evelin took a deep breath. "I think I know what we need to do."

CHAPTER SIX

EVELIN

Azmar, capital city of Brigantium

Five years earlier

Evelin didn't know how long she sat on the beach for, her fingers gripping tightly to the fabric of the human boy's tunic as the waves pulled at their clothes. She couldn't leave him to be washed out to sea; he was someone's son. Humans preferred a cremation; she had to at least assure him of that dignity.

The muscles in her arms burned as she dragged the young man's body up into the sand dunes. His clothes kept catching on the rocks that covered the beach, but she kept going. She had to keep going. When she had finally pulled him to the driest part of the inlet, she gathered up what driftwood she could find that wasn't sodden from the morning's rain and laid it around the body. She closed his eyes gently, muttering a short prayer to speed his soul to heaven.

"I'm sorry," Evelin whispered, the words accompanied by tears which streaked across her face, falling onto her hands which were coated with blood and sand. Gathering up what little strength remained, she used her magic to light a fire and kept it burning until the funeral pyre was fully lit.

Once the grisly deed was done, Evelin headed back up the rocky path. Anyone who saw her storming hellbent to the castle would have thought she was some vengeful demon made flesh, cloaked in smoke and blood.

By the time she returned to her chamber, she could barely open the door, but the uncontrollable shaking was only partly from the cold. She ripped off her clothes and hurled them across the room, before washing herself more thoroughly than she had ever done in her life.

Dressed in clean, dry clothes, Evelin stormed down to her brother's study. She could not live in this marriage for another moment. Marcellus both disgusted and terrified her. Otto would understand. He would never expect her to remain with Marcellus once he knew the sort of man he truly was. He would arrange for the marriage to be dissolved, Evelin was certain of it.

When their father had been alive, she and her brother had been encouraged to spend as much time as they pleased amongst the books in the ancient study, but the cosy, wood-panelled room had been far more to her taste than Otto's. However, since becoming king, her brother had been tied to his desk more than ever. She was sure to find him here.

As soon as she crossed the threshold of the study, the sight before her stopped Evelin in her tracks. She blinked, unable to comprehend what she was seeing. Marcellus was leaning against the large, hexagonal table in the centre of the room, wrapped in an embrace with her brother, their hands roaming each other's bodies. The two men broke apart. Otto looked aghast, but Marcellus simply turned to her, smiled a wolf-like grin, and began to relace his trousers. Her husband slunk away without a word.

Otto's shock turned to rage swifter than the tide, but Evelin was equally furious.

"What gives you the right to enter my study without knocking?" Otto yelled, still fumbling with his laces.

"I'm sorry, but that is the least of the wrongs here. You were kissing my husband! I only married him at *your* request." Evelin had given up everything, *everything*, that was good in her life to help him solidify his rule, and this was how he repaid her?

Otto sagged onto a window seat, head in his hands.

"Why? *Why* Otto?"

"Because I love him," her brother replied. "I have done so ever since we completed our training together in Brackstone."

"It's been going on for that long? You knew that he preferred men and you still married me off to him?"

Otto looked away. "I didn't know… I mean, I always hoped but… I needed him, and I needed you to continue our line. I thought I could just have him near and be a friend to him, but as soon as I saw him again, I couldn't help myself. I'm sorry, Evelin. I'm so sorry."

"Why encourage me to marry him if you wanted him? I could have married any one of your list of suitors. Why offer me to a man who would never want me? Did he tell you what happened on the beach today?"

Otto nodded, but he still didn't look at her.

"I can't stay married to him, Otto. This *thing* between the two of you only makes that even more obvious. I love you and I always will, but I cannot stay here. I am going to Whiteharbour. Whilst I am gone, I expect you to make arrangements for a divorce."

A shadow passed over Otto's face. "He won't like that," he whispered. "Your marriage has brought him status that he never held before."

"I am your *sister*, Otto. You will do this for me," Evelin demanded, rising.

She didn't wait for a reply, and left the city with Agnes the next day.

Evelin's joy at discovering she was pregnant later that month was tempered by sadness and loneliness. She missed life at the Academie and wished to God that she had never married Marcellus, but she knew her life was no longer her own.

When word reached Otto of her pregnancy, he wrote to Evelin and informed her that if she chose to continue divorce proceedings, she would be cut off financially and her child declared a bastard. Alternatively, she could accept the situation as it was, and her baby would be named heir.

She chose the second option, even though she hated herself for it. What could she offer a child without the wealth of Brigantium? She didn't even have a home of her own. The Brigantian throne followed the male line of succession, and all wealth was retained by the crown.

When William was still little, Otto ordered them to move to the royal hunting lodge, as it offered better protection being further from the coast. She had been stuck there ever since. Evelin hadn't seen her brother apart from at William's naming ceremony. He had held his nephew in his arms and looked at him with such tenderness that the ice-cold rage she felt had thawed momentarily, until Otto had ordered his guards to take her and William straight back to the lodge after the celebrations.

Marcellus paid her irregular visits, turning up at the lodge a couple of times each year. On each occasion he took her to his bed. Evelin despised herself for going, for allowing herself to be touched by a man she reviled, but Marcellus had threatened to take William back to Azmar with him if she failed to do her wifely duty. Apparently, one heir was not enough to secure the royal line.

Evelin was stuck. Stuck in a marriage without love to a man that she loathed. Stuck in a home that might as well be a royal prison. Stuck in a life with no choice.

33

Royal Hunting Lodge, Brigantium

Present day

Throughout the summer, Evelin was unable to shake a lingering fear. Like ominous grey clouds on the horizon, the worry of what might happen if her plan did not work eked away at the joy she felt whenever she held her sons. For the last three months, she had secluded herself and the baby in her chamber. Agnes had told the staff that Evelin was experiencing cramping and would be confined to her bed for the last few months of her pregnancy. The Kingsguard that Otto had stationed at the lodge were forbidden from coming anywhere near the family rooms in case they startled the fragile princess, and Evelin had cast wards herself to prevent the sounds of the baby's cries drifting through the lodge and grounds. Though she had not finished her training at the Academie in Parissi, she was more proficient than most in the use of the different fae arts.

All fae were able to perform some magic, but the vast majority had to use an enchanted object or potion to cast more than the most basic of spells. It was rare for a fae to be born with more potent magic, but they did exist, and only the most gifted or wealthiest fae were granted a place at the Academie. Females rarely applied, discouraged by the festering misogyny among the fae, and even fewer were accepted.

Once enrolled, students were trained by the Fellows for two years in the more common fae arts, before specialising in their strongest disciplines for a further two. The most common arts included healing, light magic, telekinesis, and glamouring, but there were also other, more subtle forms of magic that could be mastered if one had the natural inclination.

Some fae remained at the Academie for many years, honing their skills, yet Evelin had left part way through her third year, when word reached her of her father's death. She had always regretted not having the opportunity to finish her studies.

How had this become her life? She loved both her children with a fierceness she worried might one day consume her, but to be living in constant fear, caged between the lodge's walls, was unbearable.

The first few days after Gabriel's birth had been the most fraught. Casting wards whilst trying to feed the tiny infant with her engorged breasts had almost broken her. Even as a newborn, Gabriel had been far more wilful than his brother, turning himself red with his persistent screams. Eventually, they had settled into a comfortable sort of rhythm, and the day Evelin saw his first little smile made all the sleepless nights, pain and the fear worth it.

Yet she knew that this peace was not to last.

Watching the sun sinking low over the horizon, burning the sky an orangey pink, Evelin heard a knock at her chamber door.

"Enter," Evelin commanded, tearing her eyes from the sprawling woods below.

The bright greens of summer were shifting to burnt oranges, golden yellows, and fiery reds. She loved this time of year; it felt as though the trees had stored up all the heat of the summer and were releasing it in a vibrant, final show of colour.

Bessie kept her eyes low and proffered a wooden plate, upon which a small, tightly-wrapped scroll had been placed. "A raven has just arrived, my lady," she said, bobbing a neat curtsey.

Twisting the note over in her pale hands, Evelin tried to stop her fingers from shaking as she recognised the black seal. Two hawks facing each other: Marcellus' crest. She swept her thumb underneath and uncurled the letter. Her heart thumped in her chest so loudly she worried it would wake the baby.

My lady wife,

I trust this letter finds you and my son in good health. I believe you will be nearing the birth of the new child.

Your brother and I have determined that, since your attention will soon be directed towards the new babe, it would be an excellent time for William to return to Azmar. As Brigantium's heir, it is high time he began his studies. Rest assured, I will collect him myself and personally escort him back to Azmar.

I will be arriving at the lodge a week tomorrow. Please ensure a chamber is prepared for me.

Regards,
Marcellus, Duke of Brackstone

The words swam on the page as overwhelming panic threatened to envelop her. This was not the plan. She thought she had more time. Marcellus had not visited for months after William's birth.

"Will there be any reply, my lady?" Bessie asked tentatively, lingering by the door.

Evelin tried her best to conceal the tremor in her voice. "Please would you ask Agnes to come here directly?" She turned back to the window. The first few stars had peeked out as darkness took hold, their faint light poking holes in the fabric of the sky.

It seemed like she had only taken a few breaths before the door handle clunked open.

"Bessie said you needed me, my lady?"

Evelin said nothing, simply handing the letter to Agnes. Her companion squinted at the neat, precise writing, her older eyes struggling in the fading light.

"Our plans must change. We cannot wait." Evelin twisted the fabric of her sleeve. "I had hoped we would have longer to prepare before Marcellus arrived, but my glamours will not hold long enough."

Evelin had spent every moment of the past three months, when she had not been caring for the boys, honing the art that she had begun to specialise in at the Academie: glamouring. It was a notoriously difficult art to master, but she had revelled in the challenge at Valon. Glamouring worked by using one's own magic to create an altered image in the eye of the beholder. It required intense concentration and willpower to build a picture that was both convincing and long-lasting. Evelin had been pushing herself to the limit in an attempt to create a glamour that would make her baby appear fae, but it had not worked. The glamour faded too quickly, or holes began to emerge, his humanity pressing through.

"You must not torment yourself. You have done more in these few months than anyone would have thought possible," Agnes reassured her.

"But I haven't done enough," Evelin responded flatly. "We must change course. Marcellus arrives in a week and I cannot have him see Gabriel in his true form. Moreover, I will not allow him to take William. He is too young to be away from me. God, he hardly knows Marcellus. Even when he visits, he pays no attention to the boy. He needs me. I will not lose him. I know Marcellus might well kill us both when he discovers what Gabriel is, so we have to leave."

"What? Leave? Where would you go?" Agnes asked, her nostrils flaring. "You are the Princess of Brigantium. No one will harbour you in these lands, not at the risk of the king's wrath."

"We won't be staying in Brigantium," Evelin informed her, resolve ringing clear in her tone. "We are going to Valon."

"Valon? My lady, I would strongly advise that you reconsider. I have heard the new king to be a fair and tolerant ruler, but you must remember what happened to those humans in Valon two years ago. The king may be just, but would he be willing to protect a human child?"

"Trystan *is* a fair and tolerant ruler, Agnes. Moreover, he is my friend. We studied at the Academie together. He will not refuse me if I beg for sanctuary."

"That's a grand assumption, my lady. Are you willing to bet your life, your sons' lives, on his leniency? You haven't seen this man in nearly seven years. What if he has changed?"

"What else do you suggest, Agnes? Do you have a better plan?"

Agnes bowed her head in defeat.

"I thought not. I am going to take the children at first light. I won't ask you to come with me, I know it is dangerous—"

"Where else would I be but by your side?" Agnes insisted, a tight smile on her lips. "First light, then. I will speak with Bessie now – she will know the best way out past the guards."

The oak floorboards creaked underfoot as Evelin paced her chamber. Three small bags sat neatly arranged upon her still-made bed. She had packed lightly: the horses would be carrying enough with the two women and children. Luckily, it was still warm enough not to require too many layers, but they would need as much food and water as they could carry. With William and Gabriel in tow, their journey would not be fast, and it was at least a two-day ride to the border, after which they would have to navigate the treacherous mountain pass. From there, Valon was another day or so in the saddle.

Evelin twitched the curtains. Above the tops of the tallest trees the sky was glowing a burnt umber. It was time.

Evelin lifted Gabriel as gently as possible, trying not to wake the sleeping infant. She cocooned him in the sling strapped around her chest; it was imperative that he remained asleep and silent for as long as possible. Whilst the wards she had placed over her chambers were effective, they would not work once they were in the main part of the lodge.

The door opened, making her jump, but it was simply Agnes, leading a tired-looking William into the room.

"Mama?" he said, rubbing his eyes. "Why are we going out in the dark?"

"What a good question, darling! We're going on a little

adventure. Are you excited?" She wondered whether the forced cheeriness in her voice was obvious to her son?

"Yes, yes!" William exclaimed.

"Good. Now, you must do everything that Agnes and I say. We're going to play a little game of hide and seek with the guards first. We need to be very, very quiet because they are keeping an eye out for us."

"Do we have to be super sneaky?" William asked, a small smile on his face, his eyes bright.

"That's right, little one, and I know that you can be the sneakiest of us all," whispered Agnes, grabbing two of Evelin's bags before she led William down the spiral staircase just outside of the room.

Evelin followed, stepping swiftly but carefully.

The bottom of the stairs opened out onto a long corridor, which bisected the main building of the lodge. It had been built centuries ago, before Brigantium even had a king, but over the years it had been added to here and there, so that it was now a warren of passageways. Agnes led the small group, heading for the rear gatehouse, which would not be watched at this time in the morning. Bessie had told them that the guard stationed there took his breakfast in the kitchens once the cook arrived to start baking the bread for the day ahead.

The gatehouse wasn't far now. Evelin's palms were coated with so much sweat that she was worried her bag would slip through her fingers. Adjusting the handles, her pointed ears strained to listen to every sound. She froze. Someone was breathing outside the strong, iron-bolted door, their breaths sluggish; raspy. Agnes stood stock-still beside her, the older woman's body as motionless as the River Azmar in the dead of winter.

Ever so gently, Evelin placed her bag on the ground. She nodded briefly to Agnes and brought her hands together, placing her right slightly over her left, interlocking her thumbs. She exhaled as smoothly as her galloping heart would permit and a faint green light began to emerge from beneath her palms. She closed her eyes and tried to still her racing mind. Even though she couldn't see it, Evelin sensed the light deepening to an emerald green. At the exact moment the magic reached its peak, she raised her hands above her head and brought them down in a graceful, sweeping motion. The glamour was set. She hoped it would be enough.

Evelin reached for the bolt on the door and pulled it back, the metal bar shunting into place with a harsh clank. She stepped out into the cool morning air and gestured with her hand for Agnes and William to follow. Agnes placed a slender finger to William's lips. The boy smirked at her, but kept silent.

"Morning. Cook's sent us to get some braeberries from the garden. Apparently, her ladyship's been craving them," Evelin said and gave an exaggerated roll of her eyes.

The guard was short; portly too, unlike most fae. He let out a bellicose laugh. "Ah, you women do get demanding when your time's near!"

Evelin went to step around him, but the guard turned and raised his eyebrows theatrically.

"Think you could put a few of those on the side for me, love?" he asked, waggling his overly bushy brows.

Evelin needed the conversation to be over. There was no telling how long the glamour would hold: altering the appearance of two people and masking the children was at the top end of her abilities.

"Yes, yes," she said hastily. "I'd better be getting on now, don't want Cook getting vexed, do we?"

"No, we don't, love. Indeed, we don't," the guard replied, stepping aside for her.

Picking their way across the dew-laden grass, Evelin turned to Agnes. "We're going to have to head for the kitchen garden, so he doesn't suspect anything, but there's a gate there that opens onto the woodland." They hurried onwards, the damp darkening the bottoms of their gowns.

There, across the walled garden, was the gate. It was old and rusting – such a rarity for a fae-made object – and locked with a ward. Thankfully, it was one that would open if touched by a member of the Brigantian royal line.

Evelin wrapped her hand around one of the intricately swirled bars. A blue haze shimmered over the latch and the gate swept open on silent hinges. They hurried through, Evelin waiting until Agnes and William had crossed before closing it gently behind them.

To the right of the gate were two horses tied to a fallen tree: a palomino and a bay, both strong, healthy-looking beasts. Bessie had done well.

"How long do you think the glamour will last, my lady?" Agnes asked. Her long, straight hair wafted around her, caught in the breeze.

"A few more minutes at most. I'm losing my grip on it already." The effort of holding the glamour was taking its toll, her breaths becoming increasingly laboured.

She cast her eyes around, trying to get her bearings. She hadn't been outside the main building of the lodge for years. Her father had taken her hunting here on occasion, but that was many years ago, and her memory was playing tricks on her. *There should be a path to the left*, she thought, rubbing at her temples as her gaze shot from one tree to another. *Damn, damn, damn. Where the hell is the path?*

"Do not let the glamour drop. Hold on for as long as you can; we can still be seen," warned Agnes, quickening her pace.

The force of the words broke into Evelin's panic. "We need to head south-west," she told the older woman, before slowly circling the silver-oak nearest them. Towering thirty feet above, its red-brown leaves dappled the morning light that cascaded through them.

Her fingers traced over the white bark of the trunk, searching. *There.*

Dark green moss. It only grew on the south side of silver-oaks.

A memory suddenly came back to Evelin as clear as if it were playing out in front of her. She was walking through a glade, holding her mother's hand.

Isabel knelt down and pushed back Evelin's unruly locks. '*And how can we tell which way is south when the stars aren't out?*'

'*We look for the moss on silver-oaks, Mama,*' Evelin heard herself reply.

Yes. This was the way.

"Agnes, the path is just beyond that rock to the left. It will take us in the direction of the mountain pass. It's should allow us to avoid most of the villages between here and the border."

This was it. There would be no turning back now. It was one thing to plan their escape, but another entirely to act upon it. Yet it had to be done.

It was the only way to keep her boys safe.

The first two days of travel passed smoothly, without encountering a soul. Not that Evelin had expected to this far from the road. Still, something about the woods made her feel uneasy. She saw nothing amiss, heard nothing to cause alarm, and yet Evelin felt a strange, crawling sensation under her skin. It was worse when the sun set. When they made camp at night, she could barely sleep; her body in a state of constant alarm, all her senses firing continuously.

William, at least, seemed to be enjoying the journey. He chatted nonstop, pointing out the various animals and plants that caught his attention. Everything was new and exciting to him.

Oh, to see the world through his eyes, Evelin thought as he shrieked with delight at the sight of a deer skittering through the trees.

Gabriel was content enough as well, beaming at her from his sling. They stopped frequently to give the boys time to rest and Evelin loved watching the tenderness William showed his little brother as he brought over leaves and other trinkets he had found to show Gabriel.

The Dorial Peaks had been looming in the distance ever since they had picked their way through the borderlands, the snow-capped mountain tops glistening like an icy crown against the bright blue autumn sky. On the third day, they reached the mountain pass through which they would cross the border into Parissi. The Stertborg Pass itself wasn't particularly challenging to traverse, but few people took this route, preferring to travel by ship straight from Valon to Azmar. Those who did make it through often regaled their friends back home with tales of bandits and other nameless but far more sinister threats.

It will be fine, Evelin assured herself. The so-called horrors of the Stertborg Pass were simply the products of drunken bravado. All they had to do was get through and remain unseen until they reached the woodlands just across the border. They would all be safer then.

The small group travelled cautiously through the pass, following the winding route as it twisted this way and that like the glistening trail of a mollusc. On either side of them, the mountains soared upwards, their jagged peaks piercing the clouds. Evelin held her breath around every bend, fearful of what might be lurking just out of sight, but there was no one to be seen. Only once the majority of the pass was behind them did Evelin finally begin to breathe more easily.

Until she sensed something behind them.

"Do you feel that?" she whispered.

Agnes nodded, tightening her grip on the reins as she scanned their surroundings. "We'd best make haste."

They dug their heels into their horses' flanks, urging them onwards, but the beasts refused to move.

"Come on," Evelin pleaded, leaning down to stroke her mare's silky, chestnut nose. The poor horse's heart thundered beneath her palm, its eyes wide with fear. "We have to keep going."

A low keening sound filled her ears.

"Golow wisps," Agnes breathed.

Dusk was settling quickly, and through the evening mist, a

faint, pulsing white light emerged behind them. It couldn't have been more than a hand's breadth across. Evelin strained her eyes, watching in horror as three more appeared in the grey ahead.

Golow wisps were scavengers; small, insubstantial creatures. During the daylight, one would think they were little more than a swirl of luminous smoke. Yet they were deadly. Using their glow to lure their prey through the dark towards the edges of cliffs, they would hover just over the drop. Once their victims had fallen swiftly to their deaths, the wisps would swoop in en masse and feast.

"We have to dismount," Agnes insisted, raising her voice over the nickering of the horses. "Leave the animals here; we'll continue on foot."

Evelin nodded. It wasn't worth the risk. William protested at having to walk, but seemed to recognise that something was amiss, and dutifully hurried onwards. Sticking close to the path, the two women kept their eyes fixed on the meandering route beneath their feet, wary of being lured astray.

The light from the wisps grew fainter as they walked, yet Evelin's heart remained leaden. She knew the horses would have fallen prey to the wisps regardless, but she still hated leaving the beautiful creatures behind.

The border with Parissi was barely half a mile away, but with the darkness of night now surrounding them, and a rough path underfoot, their journey was slow going. Unable to risk lighting one of the lamps, for fear of attracting the wisps, the group plodded onward, treading carefully. Agnes soon ended up carrying a tired and frightened William, making the last stretch feel unbearably long.

Finally, in the distance, Evelin spotted the great stone column that marked the border.

"Thank God," she murmured.

They had made it.

She could only hope that Parissi would offer them the sanctuary they so desperately needed.

Gesturing to the dense woods to the left of the track, she turned to Agnes. "Quick, let's get off the path and make camp."

Nodding, Anges carried William towards the woodland, and the two women quickly set up camp. Whilst Agnes gathered wood for a fire, Evelin nursed Gabriel and told William his favourite story to settle him to sleep. He was overly tired and nestled into her warmth as she recounted the tale of the first fae.

"Many years ago, when the world was still new, the first fae lived a life of magic and peace. There was Xoros, who could conjure light, and his wife Igraine, who mastered the art of telekinesis. Xoros used his light to keep them safe in the darkness, whilst Igraine used her powers to build them a beautiful home, a strong dwelling made of glimmering white rock.

"Soon, Igraine came to be with child. The couple were blissfully happy, until one day, Igraine became very ill. Xoros feared that she and the baby might die, so he travelled to the most potent shrine in the land and prayed to God to intercede and save them. He heard no answer, and Igraine continued to worsen.

"One night, when all hope seemed lost, Xoros awoke to see a blue light glowing from Igraine's swollen belly. Within minutes, Igraine felt stronger. The sickness had passed. Not long after, their son was born, and the pair named him Rafael, meaning 'God has healed', so they would never forget the blessing God had given them.

"The couple went on to have many more children, each with a unique and powerful gift of magic. This is how the race of fae began.

"Many centuries passed in peace, but as time went by, some of the fae grew greedy; dissatisfied with having dominion over only one skill. As Xoros had done all those years before, they too visited the shrine, but this time, they went to beg God for even more power.

When nothing happened, the fae became angry, and razed the shrine to the ground in protest.

"But God had heard them, and as punishment for their greed and violence, He took away their gifts. And thus, the first humans were created."

Before she had even finished, William's eyelids drooped, and he curled up next to her in slumber, the fire crackling to life before them.

"Agnes," Evelin whispered, a hard knot forming in her throat. "Do you think what happened to Gabriel is a punishment from God? That it's my fault he's… different?"

Her eyes began to prick as her darkest thoughts came to light, and she had to fight back the tears that threatened to spill out. How many nights had she lain there, looking at her human child, wondering whether she had done something to cause this? The pain – the not knowing – threatened to break her daily.

Agnes turned to her and shook her head. "Come now, my lady, don't allow such foolish thoughts to burden your mind. You know those stories are simply to teach us right from wrong; you have not done anything for which God might curse you. Look at your son – this child is no curse." Agnes grabbed Evelin's hand tightly. "Look at him, Evelin! He is a blessing."

The sob which had been building in her chest broke free and Evelin let her tears run down her cheeks. Agnes' words of kindness and the release of having spoken her worst fears freed something inside her. She rubbed the sleeve of her dress across her face, attempting to mop up the tears before they fell onto William's head.

Evelin cleared her throat, embarrassed by her lack of composure. "Of course, you're right. I don't know what I was thinking. Thank you, Agnes. I think I'll try to get some sleep now."

Ever since childhood, she had been taught never to reveal her vulnerability; that it was a weakness easily used against her. Even with only Agnes as her witness, her skin prickled still at the lapse. Princesses didn't cry.

Carefully placing Gabriel next to her, she settled down on the hard ground, curling herself around her two sons.

A soft crack sounded amongst the trees.

Evelin shot upright, shielding her sleeping children with her body. Squinting into the darkness, past the glow of the fire, her eyes scanned for what had made the noise.

From between the trees on the far side of the clearing, a tall, dark shape emerged. It was a man – fae – heavily armed with a longsword sheathed at his side, a dagger strapped to his belt, and a bow across his back. He looked appraisingly at the two women and slowly withdrew his sword. The metal scraped against the leather of its scabbard.

A smile curved his lips upward, but it did not reach his eyes. "Well, well… what do we have here?"

CHAPTER TEN

TRYSTAN

The Summer Palace, Valon

Trystan lounged languidly in his high-backed, wooden chair, flicking through the papers that had landed on his desk earlier that morning. He ran a hand through his light brown hair and sighed. Bureaucracy was so damned tedious.

The sky was the colour of cobalt, the air was exceptionally crisp, and the sun was shining brightly. What he wouldn't give to be out there, hunting and enjoying what was sure to be one of the last fine days of autumn before the frost set in. Unfortunately, he was king, and this was what kings did, or so he had been told by Ceinwyn during one of her interminable lectures just the other week.

His chancellor had come to seek him out when he had not arrived for their weekly meeting, only to find him in bed with a woman whom he had met in one of the most notorious inns in Valon the night before. Ceinwyn had given the pair a withering look, frightening off the poor woman, and proceeded to shout at him about his responsibilities for what had felt like hours. God, it had been worth it, though. The woman had been magnificent: beautiful, lithe, and particularly athletic. Trystan made a mental note to seek her out later. That was, if he even made it to the old town this evening. He had to make some sort of headway with these papers first.

Begrudgingly, he had to concede that Ceinwyn was right. His uncle would never have missed important meetings to indulge in such a way… not that he had known him particularly well, but Silas' dedication to his kingdom was often spoken of by his former subjects and courtiers.

Trystan had been raised in Eskaria, his father's homeland, and had only come to Parissi to enrol at the Academie. He had met his uncle on a few occasions, but had never spoken more than a couple of formal words to him. The only exception had been the time Silas had summoned him to the Summer Palace, after Trystan and his friends had played a rather wicked prank on one of the Fellows at the Academie. Not that he had been given the opportunity to say much then, either. As the son of Silas' youngest sister, he had remained mostly beneath the king's notice. Still, Silas had been a good king, and Trystan knew he should try harder to live up to his uncle's legacy.

Returning his focus on the papers before him, he studied the documents from supplicants asking him to intercede on their behalf, reports on the progress on latest recruits' military training, and a newly proposed trade treaty with Parissi's uneasy ally of Brigantium. None of them were particularly gripping, and his attention soon drifted once again, his eyes drawn magnetically back to the large windows of his study. Perhaps he should leave the papers for today… after all, Ceinwyn was far better at dealing with these matters. She was whip smart, intuitive, and could even be diplomatic when not berating someone. Trystan hadn't made many good decisions as king, but appointing Ceinwyn as Chancellor had been an excellent choice.

He had met her at the Academie; she had been a Fellow when Trystan was studying there. Only a few years older than him, Ceinwyn was one of the most gifted fae in the art of glamouring.

Despite her obvious love of learning, she had readily accepted his invitation to lead his court, and he valued her advice. Not that Parissi had much of a royal court these days.

Since the massacre, there had been no celebrations within the palace walls, and visits from courtiers and members of foreign nobility remained rare. All the pomp and parties had seemed so pointless in the wake of the slaughter. When he had first walked through the palace in the early days of his reign, it felt like the ghosts of those slain still haunted the walls. How could he be expected to host dinners when the shadow of that night still hung like a shroud over the place? A shiver ran down his spine at the memory of those first few weeks.

Yes, Ceinwyn would know exactly how to respond to these supplicants. He would have one of the servants take the papers over to her directly. In the meantime, he would see if Nikolas fancied taking a ride; he knew his commander wanted to test the abilities of a new mare. Ceinwyn wouldn't be happy with him abandoning his duties so early in the day, but that was a problem he could deal with later.

Dusk was settling over the city by the time they returned from their ride. Trystan was pleasantly tired; his muscles were aching slightly, but the pain still felt far better than the restlessness that had hounded him after a day trapped in his study.

The old town was still bustling, even at this late hour. People milled around the streets of the city, some seeking a last-minute bargain from closing shops, others in search of an inn with lively music. The palace could be seen from most streets in the old town, its dome glistening in the sky above. It still felt strange to call it home; to call it his.

Loping up the steps towards the main doors, he entered the foyer, pulling off his brown leather gloves. He was about to yank off his boots when the Captain of the Kingsguard entered.

The man clicked his heels to attention and saluted smartly. "Sire, one of the border guards has arrived back from the Stertborg Pass and begs an audience with you."

Damn. He could do without this right now: his stomach was rumbling and he desperately wanted to sink into a scolding hot bath. Still, it was unusual for a guard to ask to speak with the king. Perhaps the golow wisps were massing again; in small groups, they were only a hazard to those foolhardy enough to attempt the pass without proper protection, but in larger numbers they had been known to venture down from the mountains. There had been tales of them luring animals and even children away from the settlements near the border.

It was probably nothing, but he would hear the man's report quickly and clean up before dinner.

"Send him in, Captain. I'll be in my study," Trystan responded.

The man nodded and strode off in the direction of the guardhouse.

Trystan barely had time to sit at his desk before a sharp rap sounded on the door. "Enter."

"Sire, I… I…" the guard stammered, swallowing hard before restarting, "I was in the woods by the pass and I apprehended some intruders."

"Intruders?" *Really?* This wasn't something he needed to deal with, was it? "I think this might be best discussed with your captain, unless they are numerous?"

"Sire, one of the intruders demanded an audience with you."

"Demanded?" Trystan scoffed incredulously. "You didn't bring them here, did you?"

The guard looked for all the world like he wished the ground would swallow him whole. His cheeks flushed, but he kept staring straight ahead. "She wouldn't take no for an answer, sire."

That caught Trystan's attention. There were often fae who attempted to cross the border from Brigantium into Parissi, but they were usually smugglers, trying to avoid the taxes at the ports. For a female intruder to demand an audience with the king? That *was* unusual.

"It can wait until morning. I am holding my weekly supplicant meeting then. The woman may make an appointment during that time to speak with me." The situation may have been a bit out of the ordinary, but Trystan's patience was wearing thin.

"Forgive me, sire, but I think you might want to speak with this particular woman sooner rather than later."

Trystan sighed. So much for a relaxing bath. "Fine, fine. Let's get this over with. Send her in and go down to the kitchens. Ask the cook to prepare you a hot meal. By the looks of things, you've been out by the border for a while and could do with some decent food."

The man wilted with relief and backed out of the room, thanking him as he went.

Trystan glanced at his desk, currently topped with a pile of papers placed neatly in the centre. The towering stack was crowned with a folded note.

I think you mislaid these in my study, C.

He chuckled, but his gaze was swiftly pulled away by the sound of the door reopening. Trystan blinked repeatedly, trying to clear his vision as a woman entered. Surely he was seeing things?

Long, strawberry blonde hair fell in loose waves down to the curve of her waist. The woman took a small step forward, the movement shifting the hem of the cerulean gown, the colour accentuating the deep green of her eyes. Her skin was pale and dewy, and her blush red lips pulled up in a tentative smile as she looked at him.

"Hello, Trystan."

"Evelin."

His words came out as little more than a breath, the sound of her name on his lips taking his mind back to a place long forgotten yet achingly familiar.

Her movements were precise as she stepped closer, stopping halfway across the room and sinking into a deep curtsey. For what felt like aeons, Trystan couldn't think of what to say; how to respond. He hadn't seen Evelin for nearly seven years, not since the Academie, and now she was here, without any notice, standing in his study. His mind had gone blank and he struggled to think, a situation made far harder with Evelin looking up at him through those long, dark lashes.

He shook his head, trying to force his brain into action. "Please rise, Evelin. Old friends need not stand upon ceremony, especially when those friends are also of royal blood. Unless," he joked, trying to regain some of his usual confidence, "this is you finally conceding to my superiority at chess?"

Evelin rose to her feet, keeping her head bowed. At the Academie, she had always been so composed, so controlled. Now, Trystan noticed that she couldn't seem to stop running her fingers over the seam in her gown, and even from behind his desk, he could hear her heart racing.

"It's so good to see you, Trystan. It has been far too long." Evelin's smile was wide, but didn't quite reach her eyes.

"The pleasure is all mine. May I offer you a drink? Some wine, perhaps?" He rang a small bell, attempting to regain control of the situation.

"Some water would be very much welcome. Thank you," she said as a servant arrived at the door.

"Let us sit whilst the drinks are fetched. I think I might have something a bit stronger than water." Trystan nodded to the servant, who promptly disappeared.

Leading Evelin towards the large wing-backed chairs by the fire, he gestured for her to take a seat, wincing as he once again recalled his mud-spattered clothes. He had no doubt his uncle would never have met with another royal dressed in such unsuitable attire.

Trystan cleared his throat. "Please do not mistake my questions for displeasure – I'm delighted to see you, especially after all these years – but I cannot help but wonder *why* you are here, Evelin? The guard told me he found you at the border. Is all well? Has something happened in Brigantium?"

As Evelin's lips parted in reply, the door swung open, and his chancellor swept inside, her burgundy gown flapping behind her. Ceinwyn's delicate frame was offset by her shrewd gaze, her dark brown eyes narrowing as they flicked from Evelin to Trystan, attempting to ascertain precisely what the pair had been discussing before she had entered.

Trystan rushed to speak before his chancellor could make any of her usual, acerbic remarks. "Ceinwyn, may I introduce Princess Evelin of Brigantium. Evelin, Ceinwyn is my chancellor."

Ceinwyn let out a dry chuckle. "You forget that I taught the princess at the Academie. You were specialising in glamouring before your early exit, were you not, Evelin?"

If the princess was surprised by the Chancellor's informality, she didn't show it. "Yes, it was my strongest art. I am only sorry that I did not have the opportunity to study under your tutelage for longer, Chancellor."

A courtier's response, Trystan reflected. It had been so long since he had seen Evelin; he'd forgotten the grace and measure of her formal interactions. He was grateful to have known her better, beyond such niceties. He had seen her release that guard of propriety she held over herself like a shield. Evelin might keep her light hidden from most, but when she truly let herself be free, she was like fire made human; within her burned a soul brighter and fiercer than the sun.

"You returned to Azmar, I believe," Ceinwyn continued. "May I ask what you are doing so far from home?"

Evelin's eyes widened and Trystan ground his teeth in frustration. His chancellor was being particularly challenging tonight. Whilst he also desperately wanted to know what had brought his friend to the border so unexpectedly, he disapproved of the conversation taking on such a combative tone.

"I—" the princess stammered, before Trystan swiftly interrupted.

"Ladies, as you can see, I am in desperate need of a bath and some clean clothes. Evelin, from what I've been told, you have also had quite the journey. Perhaps we should freshen up first, and discuss the reasons for your visit over supper?"

Not waiting for a reply, he rang the bell for the servant once more and asked for Evelin to be shown to one of the guest chambers.

As soon as the door closed behind the princess, Ceinwyn turned her glare on him. "Do you have any idea why she's here? This is highly unusual."

"No. I haven't heard a word from her since just after she left the Academie. Nevertheless, she was once my friend, and I expect you to treat her as such. We will find out more at dinner. I'm going to bathe and change."

As he promptly left the room, Trystan's mind whirled. Why

was she here? Did it even matter? He exhaled deeply. God it was good to see Evelin again. Until now, he hadn't fully realised how much he had missed her. The past years had done nothing to dim her beauty; if anything she was more stunning than ever. Yet... *something* was different. She seemed even more cautious; less sure of herself than she had been at the Academie.

Whatever ailed her, he was determined to find out.

CHAPTER ELEVEN

EVELIN

The guest chambers were tastefully decorated, the four-poster bed calling out to Evelin's weary limbs. Its thick, fluffy duvet and plump pillows looked like the perfect place to rest her aching muscles. She was bone-tired, but she knew she could not sleep. Trystan had invited her to supper, and if she wanted to remain here, she needed him to grant her and the children sanctuary. This might be her only opportunity to plead her case.

Trystan had seemed pleased, if surprised, to see her, but the Chancellor had been less than welcoming. Evelin recalled Ceinwyn well from her time at the Academie; she had been one of the sharpest, toughest Fellows, but she had also been a remarkable teacher. The pair had developed a bond of sorts, being two of the very few females at the Academie, though that friendship clearly hadn't lasted the test of time.

Evelin wondered how much sway the shrewd academic had over Trystan? The King of Parissi was exactly how she remembered. He had always exuded confidence, and becoming king hadn't changed that. Nor had it dulled his ridiculously handsome physique. With toned muscles that shifted supply every time he moved and golden brown hair that fell casually into his face, often obscuring his hazel eyes, he'd captured the interest of every girl that laid eyes on him during their time at the Academie, courting one after the other. The man she'd known had left a trail of broken hearts in his wake, drifting through life from one woman to the next.

Not that there had ever been anything like that between the two of them. She had been nothing like the girls Trystan was interested in – girls who found making conversation so incredibly easy; who always knew what to say and managed to look effortlessly beautiful. Evelin had only ever been his friend, and he *had* been a wonderful friend: charming, funny, and always able to pull her out of her seriousness.

She shook her head. There was no point living in the past, pining over what never was. She grabbed one of the gowns that had been dug out of storage for her. It was slightly too small, pulling tight across her chest, but it was better than her travelling clothes.

Staring hard at the mirror, Evelin appraised the woman staring back at her. Clean and tidy; good enough for supper, at least. Raising her chin slightly, she practised a carefree smile. God, it looked like someone was torturing her.

She was about to try again when the dinner gong sounded. A small sigh escaped her. This would have to do.

Seated at one end of the long silver-oak table, Evelin made an attempt at small talk while Trystan's servants poured wine for the three of them. Despite the intensity of Ceinwyn's expression, the Chancellor somehow managed to resist asking what she really wanted to, and the conversation remained fixed on decidedly neutral topics, such as the weather and what was going to be served for dinner. When the small talk ground to a juddering halt, Trystan broke the awkward silence and made a short toast to friends, near and far, before joking casually with a servant about him never being on time for a meal.

It was a relief to be in Trystan's orbit again. He was always such relaxing company, knowing exactly the right thing to say to put everyone around him at ease.

When the servant left to bring the first course, Trystan turned to face her, the flecks of amber in his eyes glinting in the candlelight.

"Evelin, please forgive me for being so direct, but I must know what brings you to Valon without prior word. It's been years since we last spoke. What has happened? Are you in danger?"

Evelin swallowed, her mouth suddenly bone-dry. She took a long sip of wine, wrinkling her nose at the burn in her throat. "Trystan, I… I have come here to ask for your help. I know this is unorthodox, but I must request—"

"Evening, Trys. Ceinwyn."

Stalking into the dining room was a towering wall of a man, dressed in hunting leathers that clung to his muscled body. Everything about him suggested barely contained power simmering beneath the surface. Obsidian hair fell in waves a few inches past his strong jaw, which clenched tightly as his eyes landed on Evelin.

The man scraped back a chair and sat down next to Ceinwyn, before reaching for the wine and pouring himself a large glass. His tanned skin shone with sweat and his forearms were flecked with dirt. Evelin was fighting the urge to frown at him when surprisingly bright blue eyes met hers as she took in the stranger opposite.

He nodded to her and raised his glass. "Greetings, princess. My men informed me of your arrival. I hope your journey wasn't too… arduous?" He raised one eyebrow, an expression that seemed far too much like a challenge.

Unsettled by the stranger, Evelin struggled to regain her composure.

Trystan seemed to sense her discomfort and turned to her, his expression gentle. "Evelin, you were about to tell us how you came to be here."

As the stranger opened his mouth to interject, Trystan gestured for silence. The man obliged, running his tongue over his teeth.

"Yes, well, as I was saying, I came here because I need your help, Trystan. I truly would not have come if I had anywhere else to go, and I know this is unprecedented, but I must request sanctuary in your kingdom for myself, my lady-in-waiting, and my two children. Marcellus, he… I'm afraid he will do something when he… when he finds out about…" She cleared her throat, staving off a sob. "Gabriel's only a baby and I… I just can't…"

Her friend's eyes burned with concern as he stared at her and Evelin felt the rest of her words tumble away, the speech she had carefully prepared over the past few days dissolving into a rush of garbled half-sentences laced with panic.

Stuttering through the events of the past few months, she let the truth spill from her lips gracelessly. When she finally paused, having finished her story with a recount of meeting the guard at the border, she risked a glance at the king. All the certainty she had felt when convincing Agnes to leave the lodge had disappeared as she spoke, the enormity of what she was asking of Trystan finally taking hold. Why had she come here? How could she expect this of someone she had not seen in years, who had his own kingdom to think of?

Trystan reached out a hand across the table, as though he was about to take her own in his. Her skin tingled in anticipation of the touch, but just before their hands met, he paused, looking across at Ceinwyn and the other man.

The king opened his mouth to speak, but Ceinwyn cut in. "You mean to tell us that you have not only *taken* the heir of Brigantium outside the realm without your king's permission, but you have also brought a *human* child – *your* human child – into our midst? What in God's name were you thinking?"

Ceinwyn's dark eyes were filled with such raw fury that Evelin felt herself recoil in her chair. Her gaze darted to the stranger, who said nothing, wariness and something akin to anger etched across his face. His eyes burned with a cold intensity that unsettled her even more than Ceinwyn's words.

After what felt like an age, Trystan spoke, his firm tone softened with understanding. "Evelin, as you are no doubt aware, this is no easy decision. I must think on what you have said and speak with my advisors. You have had a long journey and I am sure you are exhausted. You said the boys and your companion are still in the guardhouse? I imagine you will want to see them. I will send word with one of the servants for them to join you in your chambers. My housekeeper will attend to everything you need. Please rest tonight. We will speak again in the morning."

Evelin couldn't stop herself from trying to explain further; to gauge what her friend was thinking. "Trystan, I know what I'm asking of you, but I swear I—"

"It is late," he insisted, his words dousing the kernel of hope flickering in her chest. "We will speak tomorrow. Sleep well, princess."

The formality stung her as he turned away and walked towards the windows, which looked out over the lights of the city below. Evelin hurried away, a furious look from Ceinwyn searing into her back as she retreated.

Her ears were ringing when she stepped into the corridor and tremors ravaged her hands. Nausea rose in her throat. It had been so horrible; seeing the confusion, pity, and fear on her friend's face was almost too much to bear.

Evelin had to get a hold of herself. Her boys needed her, and she needed them. She needed to hold them in her arms and see them safe and happy. That was why she was here, after all, and why she had put her friend in this situation. As unbearable as it had been, she would do it a thousand times over if it meant keeping her children safe here in Valon.

But how long would they be able to remain?

CHAPTER TWELVE

EVELIN

Later that evening, when the boys were safely tucked up in bed and she had planted soft kisses on their smooth brows, Evelin paced her chamber. Agnes was already in a deep but troubled sleep, which only compounded Evelin's rising guilt. She realised that she hadn't considered how selfish her actions were when she'd decided to leave Brigantium; she hadn't even thought about what danger her presence in Valon might bring to Trystan.

Evelin had to speak with him. She had to apologise and beg for his forgiveness. It was the right thing to do, but that dark, selfish part of her knew that it might mean the difference between him offering sanctuary and turning them away.

Silent as a golow wisp, she slipped out of her chambers and made for the dining room. With any luck he might still be there – alone this time – and she would have the chance to express herself more clearly. That stranger had put her on edge. She had to try again.

The cold, smooth stone of the floor stung her bare feet as she walked down the corridor, until raised voices drifting from a study stopped her in her tracks. The door was ajar, pools of light spilling out into the corridor. Evelin was about to hurry on, anxious not to be caught scampering around the palace at night, when she heard a familiar voice.

"When someone asks for help, we answer, you know that!"

Trystan snapped.

"She's not just *someone*, though, is she?" a voice retorted, one Evelin presumed to be Ceinwyn's. "This puts Parissi in an extremely dangerous position. To harbour royal fugitives is bad enough, but the baby? I don't even know if what she told us is possible—"

"Well, I believe her." Trystan paused. "You know the motto of my house: *the light that shines in the darkest night*. We protect those that cannot protect themselves. What else would you have me do? Cast her and the children out onto the street?"

No response came.

Evelin pressed her back against the cool solidity of the wall, willing herself to remain silent.

"You've been quiet, Nikolas," Ceinwyn mused. "Surely you have something to say on the matter? You are the commander of our armies, after all…"

Nikolas. The man at dinner, perhaps?

His voice, strong and resonant, filled not only the room but the whole corridor. "Trys, you were there with me in the days after the ball. Do you remember what happened? The humans and fae slain that night? To offer the princess and her sons shelter here is madness—"

"Don't. Don't go there. You know I remember exactly what happened. She… they need me, Nik. What is the purpose of being king if I cannot assist those in need?"

"*She* needs you? That's what this is about, isn't it?" Nikolas laughed, the sound echoing. "You're thinking with your cock again, Trys."

Evelin's breath caught in her throat.

"Watch yourself." Trystan's tone was harsh as granite. "You may be my oldest friend, I am still your king."

Evelin knew she should go back to her room. Trystan couldn't find her here, eavesdropping.

"Trys, let me take them back to…" The commander's voice was low, pleading.

Evelin could not stand to hear a second more. She turned on her heels, hair whipping out behind her, and ran as lightly as she could back to her chambers. Her mind was a maelstrom, each thought spinning too fast to pin down.

Ceinwyn wanted her gone; Nikolas, whoever he was, wanted her gone. But Trystan… Trystan wanted to help.

He cared.

Evelin didn't believe a word of what that foul-mouthed commander had insinuated, but she knew that Trystan was a good man. He was still the man that she had been fortunate enough to call her friend all those years ago. What she had overheard tonight was evidence enough of that. He would help her if he could, or at least, that was what she told herself as she lay in bed unable to sleep.

She hoped to God that it was true.

CHAPTER THIRTEEN

TRYSTAN

Trystan had spent the morning searching for Evelin, carefully avoiding Ceinwyn's office and the guardhouse where Nik would be receiving his daily report. It was bad enough feeling like an imposter without having them berate him once again. He valued their advice and the skills they brought to his court, but he would not be pushed on this; he had to make the decision himself.

Just before noon, he finally glimpsed a flash of red hair sweeping past the windows of the ballroom. Crossing the floor to the balcony beyond, Trystan realised Evelin was running from something, her skirts hitched up to her knees. Instinctively, he reached for where Lightwielder usually hung at his waist, but he was unarmed. Panicked, he was about to charge outside when her pursuer came into view: a young boy with auburn hair, his face full of joy and determination.

Evelin's son.

Trystan shook his head. Ever since the massacre, his mind always assumed that danger lurked around every corner. A creak in the night would have him wide awake, sitting bolt upright and drenched in sweat. The only thing that made him feel any better was training with Nik and his men, channelling the rage and fear into something productive.

He took a series of deep breaths, his heart slowing gradually with each exhale. The feelings of terror and powerlessness had imprisoned him for too long. How much more of his life would he allow to be ruled by fear?

He would act.

He had to.

CHAPTER FOURTEEN

EVELIN

Evelin collapsed on the blanket beside Agnes and Gabriel, laughing between gasps for air.

"He's gotten fast," Agnes observed.

"Yes, he'll be able to outrun me soon!" Evelin chuckled. She twisted round to pick up Gabriel when the rasp of someone clearing their throat sounded nearby.

Trystan stood behind her, hands clasped at his back. "Evelin, may I speak with you?"

"Of course," she replied, suddenly flustered.

She had no idea what he would say; his expression was inscrutable. There had been a time when she had known what every flicker of emotion on his face meant, but seven years had rendered him a stranger to her.

The king led her towards a walled rose garden, the flowers somehow still blooming despite the lateness of the season. The smell of sweet, rich perfume was almost overwhelming.

As they reached a bench in the centre, Trystan stopped, turning to look at her with those deep hazel eyes. Every time she saw them, they were a slightly different colour. It was easy to see why women lost themselves in his gaze.

"I want to help you," he said, his expression so earnest that it pained her. "But there are two things I must know in order to do so. Your baby… you said Marcellus doesn't know of the child's existence?"

"No, he doesn't. My pregnancy was shorter than expected, and we told no one when Gabriel arrived early."

The tension in Trystan's shoulders seemed to ease slightly. "Good. Ceinwyn will glamour him to appear fae, for now. She can teach you how to check and strengthen the glamour each day. We will tell no one of his true nature. It is no longer safe to be human in Parissi, despite our best efforts."

Evelin was about to speak, to thank him, when he continued.

"I'm afraid the other matter will be far more difficult to resolve. Evelin, you must realise your very presence puts Valon, Parissi itself, in a most precarious position. You are the wife of Brigantium's commander, the sister of the king, and you have smuggled Otto's heir out of the realm. You know your brother far better than I, but I doubt he or your husband will react well to this. For us to offer you sanctuary could be seen as an act of war."

Evelin blinked away the tears that burned her eyes. "I won't pretend that I didn't know how dangerous this would be for you all. But you must understand that my boys are my priority now. I couldn't risk Marcellus finding out about Gabriel. I have to protect him."

"I won't send you back, Evelin. Any of you," Trystan reassured her, his voice sincere. "But I can't promise that this will be easy. As things stand, it would be best for you and the children to lie low. You are welcome in my kingdom for as long as you need to be here, but I have no idea what will happen if and when they find out. The longer we can delay the inevitable, the safer everyone will be."

Evelin stared up at him, tears brimming in her eyes again at his words. "Thank you. Thank you, Trystan."

She reached out to take his hand, but he stepped back,

looking away into the distance. Evelin quickly withdrew her outstretched fingers, brushing invisible dust from her skirts.

Clearing his throat, Trystan nodded. "Parissi will not abandon you, princess, and neither will I," he informed her graciously, absentmindedly tugging at a bandage wrapped round his left hand. "If you'll excuse me, I have much to discuss with Ceinwyn and Nikolas." He gave another polite nod and strode off in the direction of the palace, his head high, back straight as a pine.

Evelin sank to her knees and tried to control the tears that still threatened to fall. She had asked for refuge and Trystan had answered. Relief washed through her, but it was marred by the guilt churning in her stomach.

When Marcellus and Otto found out about her escape, there would be hell to pay.

And Parissi would be the one to pay it.

Suffice to say, Trystan's meeting with his advisors had not gone well, but they had reluctantly accepted his decision. After a lengthy argument, Ceinwyn had begrudgingly agreed to glamour the child and start training Evelin in the spell's maintenance. Nik had looked as though he was ready to bring down the walls of the palace, and had stormed off, slamming the door behind him with a strength that shook the walls. Trystan had been disappointed but unsurprised, knowing his commander needed to process his frustration, and would not let rage rule him for long. Sure enough, barely an hour later, he had received a note from Nik, curtly apologising for how he had left and reassuring Trystan that he could count on him to carry out any order, as always.

Trystan tossed the note into the golden flames that crackled beside him. He hoped that he would see Evelin at dinner again. An invitation had been extended to her and her companion. His chest tightened as he recalled how he had left things that morning; she had looked so hurt when he stepped out of reach, but he needed to keep his distance. The feelings she had stirred in him last night had been unexpected, and frankly rather troubling.

Evelin was his friend – his *married* friend. It didn't matter that she had left Marcellus to protect her children. She belonged to another man, and he'd had enough experience getting embroiled with married women over the last few years. Besides, Evelin was vulnerable. He would be the worst sort of man if he pursued her now.

No, he would be polite but nothing more, even though the mere sight of her had set his every nerve-ending on edge. In the years since they had last seen each other, she had become striking in a way that stole his breath from his lungs.

He released a deep, juddering sigh. He needed a cold bath.

CHAPTER SIXTEEN

EVELIN

Evelin dressed herself in the gown that had been left for her, though this one was a much better fit than the last. It almost appeared brand new... had Trystan ordered something to be made for her? How had he known her measurements? One of the maids must have asked Agnes for them.

The evening dress was made from a sumptuous moss-green velvet. The sleeves and skirt were cut loosely, with delicate gold trim, but the bodice was tight, and the neckline grazed her collarbones. Agnes had braided sections of her hair to form a circlet around her head, whilst the rest cascaded down her back in loose waves.

Yet, as she studied herself in the mirror, all Evelin could focus on were the dark circles under her eyes and the dull pallor of her skin. It had been a long time since she had dressed for dinner, or made any sort of effort with her appearance.

"Ready, my lady?" Agnes asked. Her lady-in-waiting looked stunning in a gown of midnight blue, against which her long, pin-straight grey hair seemed to shimmer.

Evelin shrugged. "I suppose so. You know this is going to be terribly awkward, Agnes. I've put Trystan in a horrible situation. He doesn't want me here, and Ceinwyn and that commander *certainly* don't."

Agnes rested a hand on her shoulder and gave it a quick

squeeze. "That may be, but I will be with you, and we both need to eat. Let's go and make the best of it."

Evelin blew the children a kiss, before giving a thankful smile to the housekeeper who had offered to watch over the boys. Gabriel was already curled up in his bassinet, a cap covering his ears despite a glamour already being in place. She would not run the risk of someone realising his true identity.

Walking through the palace, Evelin took in its immense beauty. Built by some of the most talented masons and craftsmen the fae had ever produced, the walls of Valon's Summer Palace seemed to sing. The smooth moon-pale stone gleamed in the twilight that flooded in through the many windows. Priceless pieces of art graced the walls, and lush green plants were dotted around, their vines spreading like cobwebs up to the ceiling.

It was so different to Azmar. The capital of Brigantium was more of a fortress than a palace, designed to withhold a long siege, not long parties. Though Brigantium enjoyed a milder climate than its northern neighbour, the castle had felt far colder in comparison. Any furniture was purely functional, decorations were scarce, and where they did appear, they were faded or ill-placed.

Trystan and the others were already in the dining room when they arrived, chatting by the large bay window that looked out onto the Academie next door. His back was to them, but as they entered, Trystan turned and offered a warm smile, melting some of the fear that had iced Evelin's blood. Ceinwyn raised her glass in recognition, and even the commander jerked his head in greeting, before turning back to his conversation.

Dinner passed smoothly enough, all of them once again sticking to the neutral topics of music, fashion, and food. Trystan must have warned his friends to be on their best behaviour, and Evelin was grateful for it. Though she hated how guarded

Trystan was around her. She understood – he was king now, after all – but the invisible wall between them felt stifling, so much so that she found herself relieved when their meal came to an end.

Drifting towards the vast windows that looked down over the Academie, Evelin was so lost in her memories that she didn't notice Ceinwyn approach.

"You miss it, don't you?" the Chancellor asked, breaking her reverie.

"Very much," Evelin replied with a melancholy smile. "Do you?"

"My work here is far more important," Ceinwyn replied.

Half an answer – it was so typical of the woman who had taught her that Evelin had to hold back a laugh at the familiarity of it all.

"I do miss my students, though. The Fellows… not so much. Sanctimonious old devils, most of them."

Evelin almost spat out her wine as she failed to stop a laugh from escaping

A mischievous grin tugged at the corner of the Chancellor's mouth. "You know as well as I do that half of them were up their own asses. Their attitude towards women definitely needs some work." She paused, her typical intensity returning as she addressed Evelin directly. "I hear I am to acquire a new student. Or, I should say an old one?"

Evelin ran her fingers up and down the cool stem of her glass, nodding in confirmation. "Trystan suggested you would be kind enough to teach me how to maintain the glamour on Gabriel. I am beyond grateful for your help, Chancellor. Really, thank you."

"Don't mention it," Ceinwyn replied, her dark eyes darting over to Trystan. "He is my king, after all, and I serve at his pleasure. Would tomorrow morning suit for our first lesson, after breakfast?"

"Of course. Where should I meet you?"

"My study will be large enough. I'm going to retire now, but I will see you and your son tomorrow. Goodnight, Evelin."

Ceinwyn swept from the room, nodding to Trystan, who was deep in conversation with Agnes. The commander, who was nursing a drink by the fire, scowled into its flames.

Since she had no desire to speak to the brooding commander, and didn't particularly want to interrupt Agnes and Trystan, Evelin slipped out shortly after Ceinwyn. She would need to sleep well tonight. The now-Chancellor's lessons had been challenging enough at the Academie – she would need all her energy tomorrow if she was to avoid disappointing her former tutor.

Evelin was woken by the sound of thunder rolling through the skies. Although it was morning, the storm clouds were so grimly dark that the faelights still flickered. It was an ominous start to the day.

After breakfast, Evelin gathered Gabriel up into her arms. The baby smiled broadly at her and tried to pull at the loose strands of hair that fell down across her face.

"Ah, ah," she chastised tenderly. "Mama has an important lesson this morning. I don't want to look completely dishevelled."

She tried not to focus on how tiny he still was, or how rounded his ears were, as she kissed him softly. Those thoughts were buried away with the others, deep and locked in a box that would remain hidden. She needed to focus today; she couldn't let her mind drift.

Despite having asked the housekeeper for directions the

night before, it was a challenge to find Ceinwyn's study. Evelin did not want to run the risk of getting lost, or turning up late and facing Ceinwyn's wrath, especially when the Chancellor was doing her a favour.

"It must be here somewhere," she muttered distractedly, more to herself than Gabriel as she traversed the basements of the palace.

It was cooler below surface level, and the lack of natural light seemed to mute even the sounds of her footsteps as she passed through the maze of corridors.

Turning a corner, she discovered a door left slightly ajar, behind which Evelin found the Chancellor sitting at a desk, piled high with papers.

"Right, let's make a start," Ceinwyn said without any further greeting, her dark eyes surveying Gabriel as he wriggled in Evelin's arms.

Reaching out, she plucked the white linen bonnet from his head, inspecting his ears curiously.

"Hm." She lifted her eyes to Evelin's with such a penetrating look that it felt as though the Chancellor was reading her soul. Ceinwyn must have approved of whatever she found there, for she promptly continued. "Let's begin. Try to keep him as still as possible while I construct the glamour."

Ceinwyn brought her hands together and breathed deeply as a strong green light emerged. She raised her slender arms high above her head before bringing them down slowly, the light radiating from her fingers and reaching out towards Gabriel in thin tendrils.

The changes occurred at once. His ears began to elongate into small peaks, and his whole body became larger; longer. Within the space of a few breaths, the glamour was complete. Relief tempered with shame, for wishing her child to be anything other than he was, swirled in her chest. Ceinwyn was visibly pleased with the results as she cast her eyes over the infant.

"As you know, glamours only last a limited time. The more powerful the illusion, the faster it will fade. You will need to tend to this one every morning and evening. I will periodically check it as well. But before we get ahead of ourselves, I think it is best to go back to the theory."

Ceinwyn passed Evelin a thick leather-bound tome, and they spent the rest of the morning talking through the laws of glamouring, the rules that must be obeyed, and the best way to maintain a glamour without pushing oneself to the brink of exhaustion.

When she eventually got up to leave, Ceinwyn spoke gently. "You *will* be able to maintain the glamour, Evelin. You were one of my most talented students before you left. You may be of royal birth, but you would have earned your place at the Academie outright."

Evelin's heart soared at the words. She had always wondered if she had truly deserved to study at the Academie or whether her father had exerted his influence to get her enrolled.

Leaving the study, she felt stronger and more capable than she had in years.

CHAPTER SEVENTEEN

TRYSTAN

Trystan squinted against the morning sun's brightness as he strode out to the stables, his boots crunching across the frosted grass.

Winter had arrived in Valon.

Nik sat by a small brazier, talking amiably with some of the cavalry troops who were seconded to palace duty. The men sprang to their feet as Trystan approached, rubbing his hands together against the cold. Nik's two large hounds weaved amongst the men, deft noses trying to ascertain who would break first and throw them a treat.

"I thought we weren't meeting until later?" Nik queried, tilting his head to the side.

"I've come to hear your report, commander," Trystan replied, indicating for the men to return to their seats.

Once the two of them were out of earshot, Nik furrowed his brows. "I've sent out some riders to survey the border and word has been sent to our agents within Brigantium. We will know soon enough what the situation is and how much they know."

"Good. That's good," Trystan replied, a melee of thoughts battling for supremacy in his head. "Come to me directly when you have word. Otto will have agents here in Valon too. As soon as Marcellus finds out that the princess and her children are missing, you can be sure Brigantium will reach out to their spies."

"With any luck, we have a couple more days before they discover that she is here… though I still think there is a better course, Trys. Have you given any more thought to my suggestion?"

Trystan clenched his fists tightly, the leather gloves he wore straining under the force. When he spoke, his voice was edged with steel. "You know I haven't, Nik. I have made my decision. For now, we do nothing. We watch and we wait to see how Brigantium responds."

His mind had been set, and he was getting frustrated at his friend's lack of cooperation. Nik had been sullen at dinner last night, but had toed the line.

Even after two years as king, Trystan still found it difficult to pull rank on him. They had known each other since boyhood, and Nik had even been his superior officer when Trystan had completed his military training at Deathhold. Having to enforce his wishes on Nik made him feel all the more isolated, cut off from the people he loved best.

"Have you got time for a bout of sparring practice?" Trystan asked, softening his tone and giving his friend a cocky smile. "I haven't had the chance to wipe the floor with you in a while."

Nik slapped him on the shoulder and released a deep chuckle. "You always did live in dreamland, Trys. Never fear, I've always got time to set your imaginings straight."

After barely an hour of training, Trystan was aching from head to toe. The muscles in his arms hummed and he was coated in sweat. As fit as he was, he was no match for Nik's physical power and unparalleled skill with a blade.

Sparring always helped to focus his thoughts, and his mind was now clearer than it had been in days, prompting him to check in with Ceinwyn to see how her tutorial with Evelin had gone.

Walking down the dim corridor to her office, he could hear Ceinwyn speaking, though her voice was softer than usual.

"No, that was better. You see how there was less fraying at the edges? When you summon the magic, keep the whole image that you wish to conjure in your mind."

A green glow spilled out into the corridor from inside the office. She must be working with Evelin on glamouring.

"Like this?" Evelin also sounded different from the last time they had spoken; her tone was light, but focused, drawing Trystan's mind back to the day they had first met.

It was the start of his second year at the Academie, and walking through the cloisters, he felt a surge of relief at being back. He had barely scraped through his first year examinations, having spent far too much time off hunting, drinking, and carousing with his friends, and not nearly enough time studying.

Back home in Eskaria, his mother had been a tempest of maternal discontent when she found out. She had berated him for hours about his laziness, poor attitude, and irresponsible nature. He had weathered it silently, knowing that any attempt to justify his actions would only infuriate her further. When she had finally exhausted her anger, his mother had coldly threatened to remove him from the Academie and send him straight to military training if he didn't brush up his act.

So, as Trystan made his way to the first tutorial lecture of the new term, he promised himself that this year would be different. He would be more focused and attentive to his studies.

Regrettably, his resolve was to be tested earlier than expected. Just as he was about to ascend the worn stone steps up to the lecture hall, a clear voice rang out across the quad.

"Trys! So brilliant to see you! How was your summer?"

It was Bryce, a friend whose father was an advisor to King Silas.

Trystan smiled broadly at the stocky, ruddy-faced man. "Tedious, Bryce. Have you ever travelled to Eskaria? It's deserted in the summer; it's far too hot for anyone with any sense to remain, so there was an absolute dearth of society."

"You'll be damned glad to be back, I should wager?" Bryce said, grinning. "Why don't you join me and the lads? We're going to ditch lectures today and go hunting. There's this amazing inn in the old town with the most voluptuous barmaid you ever saw. How about it?"

Trystan sighed. He shouldn't, but then again, he had done a bit of reading this summer, and none of the Fellows ever said anything important the first day back… or so he imagined.

"Go on then, Bryce. Let me ditch these books and I'll meet you by the stables. I do need to be back by four, though. I've got a tutorial with that female Fellow – Cerys or something – scheduled."

Later that afternoon, as he staggered back through the old town, Trystan began regretting that last ale. When he finally made it back to the Academie, the tutorial had already begun. He knocked smartly on the door to the tutorial room and arranged his features into what he hoped was a winning smile. Without waiting for a reply, he sauntered into the room to find two women sat on soft armchairs by the fire, deep in conversation.

Trystan knew the one closest to him; she was the youngest of all the Fellows, only a few years his senior. The woman had a reputation for being a battle-axe, so he opened his mouth to deliver the charming apology he had been rehearsing in his head on the walk over.

Before he could speak, the Fellow waved her hand dismissively at him. "I'm afraid we've already started. Perhaps you could join us next week, if you are punctual." With that, she turned back to continue her conversation with the other student.

Trystan couldn't make the younger woman out, her face silhouetted by the glow of the fire, but he saw her shoulders twinge in embarrassment on his behalf.

He cleared his throat. "Apologies. I'll return next week," he replied, before turning on his heels and making his way back to his rooms.

Unfortunately, Trystan had hardly made it across the quad when a tidal wave of nausea swam through his body. He turned and retched into the bushes.

A while later, he was still sitting in the quad on one of the benches, head clasped in his clammy hands, when a tentative voice asked, "Are you okay?"

Trystan grunted in reply, looking up to see the young woman from before, carrying a precariously tall stack of books, which she placed carefully on the ground before sitting beside him. She pushed strands of long, wavy hair away from her face and looked at him with a furrowed brow, her moss-green eyes concerned.

"Would you like some water?" she asked, removing a flask from the satchel draped over her shoulder.

He nodded and took it gratefully, long sips of water cooling the burning in his throat. He released an uncontrollable groan at the delightful sensation.

"Sorry, I'm afraid I rather embarrassed myself. I'd promised my mother I'd behave this year, as well. Apparently well-behaved young men study hard and don't get raging drunk before dinner," he muttered, slurring slightly.

"Ah. Well, if you'd like, I can catch you up on what Ceinwyn covered in the tutorial today?"

Trystan gave her a grateful smile. She seemed kindly and studious. Perhaps it wouldn't be the worst thing to be friends with someone a bit more serious who could help him improve his grades.

God knew he could use all the assistance he could get.

"Thanks, that would be amazing."

She gave him a small smile, straightening. "Shall we meet in the main library after lectures tomorrow?"

He nodded briefly, and she picked up all of her – probably quite unnecessary – books and swept off across the quad. Watching her walk away, Trystan's vision still blurry from drink, he realised he hadn't even asked her name.

Never mind. He'd find her tomorrow when he was sober and able to focus.

A gasp of frustration dragged Trystan back to the present and he smiled to himself. Evelin could get quite short-tempered when she struggled to master something quickly. She was a perfectionist and fiercely intelligent; he had been lucky that she had taken pity on him that day in the quad.

They had soon become firm friends, and, with her patient help, he had acquitted himself well in his sessions with Ceinwyn. He didn't have Evelin's natural aptitude for glamouring – his affinity was with light magic, like many of his House – but he did well enough to pass.

Trystan liked to think that he had been a good friend to Evelin, drawing her out of herself and showing her some of the world outside of the Academie. Although he had still seen his old friends frequently, enjoying some of the more visceral pleasures Valon had to offer, he'd always looked forward to seeing Evelin, as well as her roommate, Lianna, a bubbly woman with boundless energy and an infectious laugh.

The three of them had spent hours together in that second year. Apart from Nik, he had never had close friends like that before. Those days at the Academie had been some of the happiest of his life, and he had felt Evelin's absence like a physical ache deep in his soul when she had returned to Brigantium at the start of their third year.

Despite the complexities and danger surrounding her return to Valon, Trystan was grateful to see her again, though he couldn't deny that Evelin's reappearance had awoken the same feelings that had so often plagued him at the Academie. He had always been careful not to blur the line of friendship with her. She was his friend, after all, and even then, he knew his track record with women. It was all very well bedding women from the city, but Evelin was a princess who would be expected to make a good match one day. Trystan wasn't one for maintaining long-term relationships – the very idea of them made him feel claustrophobic – so he kept a respectful distance. He hadn't wanted to run the risk of ruining everything just for one night, no matter how exquisite he imagined that night could be.

The same rules applied now, but just because he refused to act on whatever old desires remained, that didn't mean he couldn't be Evelin's friend. He made up his mind to speak to her later, and turned back down the corridor, leaving the pair to their session.

CHAPTER EIGHTEEN

EVELIN

Evelin was drained from the tutorial with Ceinwyn, but it was a pleasant kind of tiredness. It had been a long time since she had used her brain or powers like that, and the challenge was refreshing.

It had been hard to take time away from the boys – they had both become so accustomed to spending every waking moment with her – but Agnes had been invaluable in arranging for a tutor to take over William's teaching and had taken charge of Gabriel's care herself. Evelin didn't want to run the risk of anyone else spending that much time with him until she was sure that she could keep the glamour in place at all times.

She was relaxing in one of the informal sitting rooms, reading one of the books Ceinwyn had lent her, when Trystan entered. She pushed herself up straight as he walked in and sat down next to her, feeling like she had been caught doing something she shouldn't. It had been days since she had last laid eyes on him: the Summer Palace was vast enough that two people need not spend any time in each other's presence if they did not wish it, and to be truthful, Evelin had taken great care to avoid him.

"You know, I found myself reminiscing earlier about the day we first met," Trystan began. "I was in a bit of a state, wasn't I?"

Evelin laughed, the sound breaking the tension between them. "I'm still surprised you managed to get to your lectures the next day. Your head must have been in agony."

"Well, I couldn't make things worse by missing even more, could I?" he chuckled. "Besides, you had been kind enough to offer to help me catch up. I could hardly have turned up and told you that I had stayed in bed all day and needed even more help. What a way to return your kindness that would have been!"

"I think you are doing more than enough to return my small kindness now, Trystan. I know I've said this a thousand times, but I cannot thank you enough for helping us. You truly are a remarkable man."

Trystan turned to face the fire, a faint colour tingeing his cheeks. He shifted awkwardly in his chair and tightened the bandage on his hand before looking back at her. "Evelin, please forgive me for asking this, but are you sure Marcellus would have reacted badly if he had seen the baby? He is your husband. Surely he would have at least given you the chance to explain?"

Evelin swallowed hard. "Marcellus... he isn't... he makes no secret of his distaste for humans, and his temper can be... unpredictable." *He isn't like you*, she wanted to say.

"But his love for you must surely outweigh any doubts he might harbour?" Trystan pressed.

Evelin looked down at her hands, twisting her fingers around each other, again and again. She didn't want to tell Trystan about Marcellus' relationship with her brother. It would be too humiliating to admit that she had been manipulated by Otto and trapped in a prison of a marriage.

Shortly before her wedding, she had written to Lianna and Trystan, informing them that she would not be returning to the Academie as she was soon to be married to '*the most accomplished and fascinating man I have ever met*'. She cringed inwardly at the words she had written, back when she had been infatuated with Marcellus and hopeful for a life of adventure.

"Trystan, I don't think I can explain Gabriel's condition to myself, let alone my husband," she said, trying to avoid her friend's line of questioning whilst still speaking the truth that she had come to acknowledge more and more. She had no idea why she had given birth to a human child, despite having come up with countless ridiculous theories.

"I've been thinking about that," he admitted, shifting in his chair. "Why don't we go to the Academie and speak to some of the Fellows? I imagine at least one of them will have heard of this happening before? Maybe they can shed some light on the matter?"

Evelin's eyes widened. "You're right, of course! One of them must know something."

"I need to speak with the Dean about another matter anyway, so we can ask him tomorrow. We will have to be cautious, though. Gabriel's condition must be kept a secret for now. It still isn't safe for humans in the fae realms." Trystan stood, tugging down the hem of his tunic, looking pleased to have made a plan. "Shall we meet after lunch?"

Evelin nodded and reopened her book. "I'd better get on with some of this reading Ceinwyn has set me. I swear, it's just like being back at the Academie."

Trystan smiled again, filling her heart with a warm glow as she watched him leave.

Alone once more, Evelin slumped back in her chair, letting the book fall open in her lap.

Would tomorrow bring the answers she craved?

CHAPTER NINETEEN

EVELIN

When Evelin arrived at her tutorial the next morning, Ceinwyn took one look at her and gestured towards the steaming pot on the side table, from which emanated a rich, nutty aroma.

"You look haggard," the Chancellor remarked. Ceinwyn had never subscribed to the niceties of polite conversation.

"Gabriel was up half the night," Evelin explained, pouring the glossy brown liquid into a mug. "I think he's finding the change in routine difficult."

Ceinwyn gave her a tight smile. "We can leave today's session if you want. The techniques we had planned for today do require a lot of work."

"No, no," Evelin insisted. "As soon as this sinks in, I'll be fine. On the plus side, I did manage to do all of the reading while I was up during the night."

Ceinwyn settled back in her leather chair. "Excellent. Then you will have no problem talking me through the theory of blending…"

The session was just as difficult as the Chancellor had promised, and by lunch, all Evelin wanted to do was take a nap. But after popping in to check on William's studies and giving Gabriel some milk, she made her way to the entrance hall to meet Trystan.

The king was already there when she entered the grand room, clearly designed to inspire visitors. He stood tall, rubbing the back of his neck with his hand.

"Bad night's sleep?" Evelin asked as she approached.

He chuckled. "No, tough training session with Nik this morning. You'd think he would take it a bit easier on me now that I'm king, but apparently not."

Evelin had no desire to talk about the commander who so clearly wished her gone, so she quickly changed the subject. "The Dean is expecting us?"

"Yes, I forewarned him that I would be bringing a guest with me, but I haven't told him what our audience is in regard to," Trystan confirmed.

With that, the pair walked out of the palace and down the gleaming white steps – passing by the Kingsguard at the gate, who smartly saluted as they stepped aside – before heading towards the old town.

Evelin's head span, taking in the sights and smells of Valon. Crowds bustled around them, the people of the city sometimes doing a double take when they saw Trystan, but it was as if they couldn't quite place him. It was unusual for a monarch to roam the streets freely, with no accompanying guards, and she had been surprised when no one followed them out of the palace. Then again, Valon wasn't like other cities, and Trystan wasn't like other monarchs. Valon was vibrant, accepting, and open to all... or at least, it had been until the massacre, and Trystan... well, Trystan was Trystan, and he shared all of the best qualities of his capital.

Walking the streets with him brought back a waterfall of memories, setting Evelin's skin tingling with the anticipation of stepping foot in the Academie again. Her time there, though brief, had been joyous. To be allowed such freedom and to focus solely on learning had been one of the greatest privileges of Evelin's life. A life made all the more rounded by her companions. She remembered the wonderful times they had shared, and she had to physically stop herself from linking her arm through Trystan's as she had done so many times before. Things were different now. They were both different.

Evelin's reverie was interrupted as they passed through the porter's lodge at the front of the main Academie building. The stout gentleman behind the desk shot to his feet when Trystan entered and he bowed deeply, moustache quivering. When the porter looked up at her, Evelin thought there was a flicker of recognition in his eyes, but she hurried on, thinking better of stopping for conversation.

She quickly checked the glamour that she had placed over herself; it was still intact. She must have misread his expression. It had been seven years since she had last entered this wonderful place, but there were still many here who would remember her, if only vaguely, and Trystan had warned her against revealing her true identity. He had always been suspicious of some of the Fellows, not completely trusting that their research would lead in the best direction for Parissi.

It didn't take long for them to reach the Dean's quarters, which were the most opulent amongst the already fine buildings. They entered through a vast doorway and discovered that the Dean was waiting in the foyer for them. A painfully thin man, he looked all the more austere due to his precisely groomed obsidian beard, trimmed to a sharp point an inch below his chin. He wore the black robes most of the Fellows donned in the Academie, but his were of a far richer material. Golden chains of office gleamed against the dark fabric, and his narrow eyes assessed the pair appraisingly.

"My king," the Dean said obsequiously, barely nodding his head in a perfunctory bow. "May I offer you some refreshment?"

"No, thank you," Trystan replied, firmly but politely. "I am afraid we have much to discuss and not too much time, so we had better make a start." Trystan gestured towards Evelin. "My secretary will be taking notes."

The pair followed the Dean into his private office, a wood-panelled room crammed with art and rare curiosities, though there was not one book to be seen.

Evelin sat beside Trystan on one side of the Dean's huge oak desk, clutching at the notebook she had brought. Her stomach was aflutter at the prospect of some sort of answer to the question that had been haunting her for so many months.

"First and foremost, I am pleased to say that the Treasury have approved your grant application," Trystan began. The Dean's mouth curled in a greedy smile, but before he could speak, the king continued. "However, half of the money will be going towards setting up two scholarships for students who would not otherwise be able to afford the exorbitant fees charged by the Academie."

The smile never left the Dean's face, but his beady eyes narrowed slightly. "Your highness is far too generous."

Evelin didn't doubt the double meaning behind his words.

"You are most welcome, Dean," Trystan said, with a quick look across at her. "I was also hoping that you might be able to help me with another matter."

Trystan had explained to Evelin on the walk over that they were not going to tell the Dean the whole story; he did not trust the man who had come to this position of power shortly after the massacre. The previous Dean, under whom Trystan and Evelin had both studied, had been a giant in the field of scholarly research and had pushed for greater access to the Academie for all classes of fae. The post's current holder was still somewhat of an unknown entity, and Trystan was unsure where his true allegiances lay.

"An interesting quandary has been presented to me, and I would like to seek the advice of one of your Fellows. With whom would you suggest I speak regarding fae heritage?"

The Dean's dark eyebrows shot upwards. "Well, that would be Master Draxus, sire, but perhaps I may help? I have some reputation in these matters..."

"I think we've already taken up enough of your valuable time, Dean," Trystan replied smoothly. "We will seek an audience with Master Draxus directly."

Trystan stood and gestured Evelin towards the door, allowing her to lead the way.

"I neither like nor trust that man," he whispered as they exited the Dean's chambers. "Let's hope that Draxus is someone of integrity and honesty. Have you any idea where his office is?"

Evelin nodded. "I had to take some books to him once for Ceinwyn. I believe his office is in the Elden Quad."

They found the staircase easily, and as Trystan raised his strong hand to knock, a faint voice from inside called out impatiently.

"Oh, will you just come in already!"

Trystan glanced down at her, eyes wide, as he pushed the door open. The room was dark and filled with the aroma of a spice that Evelin couldn't place; it was at once familiar and oddly like nothing she had ever smelled before. A fire raged in the hearth, with a cauldron sitting directly in the flames, and a small man with flowing white hair stood hunched over it, stirring with surprising vigour for someone of his advanced years.

The Fellow made no attempt to turn around, seemingly fixed

on his task.

Trystan cleared his throat. "Master Draxus? I was hoping that we might ask you some questions."

"Hm," came a disgruntled reply. "In a minute, boy. I am in the middle of a most important concoction. One false move and—" He gestured violently with his spare hand.

Trystan looked down at Evelin again, giving her a perplexed look. Not knowing how to proceed either, she simply shrugged. Running a hand through his hair, Trystan strode over to the chaotic desk in the corner of the room and picked up the nearest book to hand, beginning to leaf through it. Evelin simply waited, trying to work out what the Fellow was doing. She was about to approach when a bloom of purple smoke rose out of the cauldron and spiralled up to the ceiling. This seemed to please the Fellow, and he nodded excitedly.

With that, he finally turned to the pair. "Sire… Princess Evelin. It is a pleasure to see you both after all these years. May I ask what has brought you to see me today?"

How does he know? Can he see through my glamour?

If Trystan was as shocked as she was, he somehow managed to keep his surprise hidden. "Master Draxus, a matter has been presented to me of which I have no knowledge. I was hoping that you might be able to provide us with some guidance."

"Of course. I will endeavour to assist in whatever way I can," the old man replied, sinking into an overstuffed armchair.

"Word has reached me of a child born to a fully fae mother and father. The child itself appears to be completely human. Have you ever come across such a case before?" Trystan asked.

Evelin wrung her hands behind her back, unable to settle.

"A human borne of fae?" The Fellow's expression was one of curiosity as he looked into the fire, seemingly searching the darkest recesses of his memory. "I am afraid that I have never come across such a being in my lifetime, nor in any of the texts I have studied."

Evelin felt her heart sink. Trystan's eyes were burning into her, but she couldn't bring herself to look at him. She was never going to get answers, was she? She loved Gabriel so deeply, but every time she looked at him, she felt like she was just waiting to see if something would happen; if he would suddenly become fae. It wasn't fair on him, to have a mother who doubted his very nature.

Just as Evelin's thoughts began to suck her into their dark abyss, Master Draxus spoke again. "Hmm… there was something… the Priestesses of Igraine, I believe. Their written records are few, and what remain have been poorly translated, but I do seem to remember a visitor to their shrine many centuries ago making mention of a fae-borne human. Perhaps they might be able to shed light on this matter?"

This was it, what she had been waiting for. It wasn't the clearest answer, but it was at least *something*. Evelin stood, eager to leave so she and Trystan could discuss what they had heard.

Master Draxus heaved himself upright and stepped towards her, grasping her hands in his. "Princess, I wish you every fortune. It has been a pleasure to see you in the Academie once again."

"The pleasure has been all mine, Master Draxus," Evelin replied. "May I ask how you recognised me? I believe my glamour is still in place."

The Fellow chortled and leaned in close, his voice so quiet she had to focus hard to hear his words. "It was the way the young king looks at you. He was quite the presence around the Academie during his time here. He may not have noticed me, but I certainly noticed him strutting about the place. The way he looks at you has not changed, princess. Not in all these years."

It took all of her years of training in the ways of court to maintain her composure in that moment. First the commander, now Master Draxus. What did they see that she could not? Clearly they were all mistaken, but she could not help the feeling of warmth that blossomed in her chest at the thought of them being right.

She was so caught up in her thoughts, she almost failed to recognise the feel of something cool and solid between her palms. As the Fellow released her hands and moved to farewell the king, Evelin realised the old man had placed a small glass vial in her hands. Swiftly pocketing it – certain that, whatever it was, she should not be seen carrying it around the Academie – she promptly followed Trystan back towards the porters' lodge.

Just as she was about to mention the strange vial to Trystan, he stopped and turned to face her.

"How about a drink at the Crossed Swords before we return to the palace? Do you think Agnes will be okay with your boys for a bit longer?"

Evelin smiled. "That sounds perfect."

CHAPTER TWENTY

EVELIN

The Crossed Swords was a favourite haunt of students from the Academie, but since there were a few more hours before lectures finished for the day, the inn was practically empty when Trystan and Evelin slipped inside. They both wore their hoods up, but as the owner approached, it was clear from his excited expression that he had recognised Trystan.

"You wouldn't happen to have my usual table free, would you, Pierre?" the king asked, passing the man a weighty gold coin.

Pierre bowed deeply, waving them to the far side of the bar and showing them to a booth with blood-red leather seats. Trystan took a seat opposite Evelin, ordering a bottle of Eskarian red. The owner looked around furtively before interlocking his fingers and pressing them against the right-hand side of the booth. A green glow rippled across to the left – a sign that a glamour had been set.

"I thought this might give us a bit more privacy," Trystan explained, gesturing to the glamoured booth. "The citizens don't tend to recognise me much in the street, but you know how often I came here when we were at the Academie. They often want to chat, bend my ear about something or other. I usually don't mind, but I don't think it would be wise at the moment."

Evelin shook her head, relieved to be able to release the

glamour she had set on herself. "This is perfect. It's been so long since I was last here. It hasn't changed."

The inn was cosy and inviting, with an open hearth blazing in the centre of the large room and a long bar to one side. Behind the bar were shelves neatly stacked with bottles of all different shapes and sizes, containing liquids of a vast array of colours. Some shimmered, iridescent, but others looked dark, almost treacly. Evelin knew enough to avoid those ones; she had suffered the worst headache of her life after having only a couple of glasses one night many years ago.

A woman sat by the door playing a battered-looking fiddle, her green hair streaked with black. The music was soft and lilting, and many of the patrons were tapping their feet in time. Some were Fellows in their customary black gowns, others were city dwellers, but all looked to be entranced by the tune.

"Evelin?"

Trystan's voice pulled her away from watching the musician. He was looking at her intensely, his sandy brown hair falling in front of his eyes.

"What did you make of what Master Draxus told us about the Priestesses of Igraine?" he asked.

"I don't know what to think. I suppose part of me is disappointed – I was hoping someone would be able to explain Gabriel's situation to me today. But at least we have *something* to go on."

Pierre returned with a crystal bottle filled with a ruby liquid and two pewter goblets. He poured them a drink each before silently backing away, his eyes checking the strength of the glamour.

Evelin took a sip of the wine, savouring the taste of cherries, plums, and cinnamon dancing on her tongue. "I'll write to the Order when we return. My aunt is a priestess. Perhaps they'll be more inclined to help if there is a family connection."

Trystan cocked his head to the side, assessing her. "I'd have thought you would be more enthused by this discovery. Doesn't this bring you hope, Evelin?"

"Of course it does, I just… I'm sorry, I don't mean to be so melancholy. I *am* grateful that we have a path to explore now. I've just been so terrified these past few months. Not understanding why Gabriel was born human, worrying for him, for what his condition might mean for William, and what Marcellus might do to Gabriel, to me, if he finds out…" Her voice began to quaver, a sob threatening to surface. "Forgive me, I just need a moment." She fixed her gaze on the worn wood of the table, breathing deeply, focusing on calming her rioting emotions.

Once she was sure she had regained tenuous control of her body, she dared to glance up at Trystan. He was fidgeting in his seat, unsure of what to do with himself. He reached out a hand, paused for a second, then made a grab for the bottle.

"You needn't apologise," he reassured her, his eyes finally meeting her own. "I know this has been a difficult time for you, but you've always been such a strong person. I am certain you will get through this."

Evelin knew his words came from a place of kindness, but she found herself forcing down a bitter retort. He *didn't* know, not really. As a man – a king, no less – he would never truly know how difficult her life had been in recent years. She hadn't felt strong in a long time. Beaten down by Marcellus and her forced isolation, she had lost that part of herself.

Trystan frowned at her silence, concern evident in his gaze, before glancing towards the grandfather clock on the far wall. "We had better head back before dinner. Agnes must be wondering where we are." He beckoned to Pierre for the bill, pushing the unfinished bottle away.

Shame crawled under Evelin's skin and she quickly drained her glass. The liquid burned her throat and she fought back a cough. That was twice now she had almost broken down crying in front of Trystan, and she hated admitting her weakness. What had happened to her? When had she turned into such a fragile, snivelling wreck?

She clenched her fists tight, nails digging into the soft flesh of her palms as she shimmied out of the booth. Standing behind Trystan, she raised her hood with care before hurrying past him out into the street. She didn't have the energy to glamour herself again – Trystan's presence and her cloak would have to suffice. Hopefully the fresh air would re-energise her.

Above the spires of the Academie, the sky was caught in a battle between the burned orange of the setting sun and the inky black creeping towards it. The evening was turning cold, and Evelin's breath swirled as she blew on her hands for warmth.

The door behind her creaked open and Trystan stepped out, a tentative smile on his face.

"Shall we?" he asked, gesturing down the street in the direction of the palace.

They walked in silence, Evelin too worn down by her emotions to make small talk, and Trystan no doubt unsure what to say given her reaction back at the inn. She shivered, the light cloak she had picked out this morning entirely unsuitable for the current climate. Winter was setting in fast and she hadn't expected to be out so late. Her teeth chattered as she rubbed her arms.

"You're cold," Trystan observed, resting his hand on her arm and swiftly guiding her down a side street. "Here."

Evelin found herself on the dockside, the sweet smell of smoky applewood drifting through the air from the glowing braziers that lined the water. She hurried to the closest one, savouring its warmth as she looked out over the unsettlingly calm sea.

"It won't be too long now before the port is frozen," Trystan noted, seeming to read her thoughts. "It is predicted to be a particularly harsh winter this year. We'll need to acquire a warmer cloak for you. Are you feeling any better?"

The cold still stung her hands, but she nodded regardless. "Yes, much, thank you. Shall we continue?"

If she was honest with herself, Evelin desperately wanted to be back in her own rooms and have this interaction over with. Their friendship wasn't like it had been. Seven years of distance was bound to do that. She simply needed to accept it and be grateful for what remained.

They turned down a poorly lit alley, darkened further by the overhanging houses lining each side. Evelin was about to apologise to Trystan yet again when she felt something whip past her face.

An arrow protruded from a wooden window frame just ahead of them, still quivering.

Trystan's body shifted instantly, his right hand darting for the sword strapped to his side. With his left, he grabbed her shoulder and pushed her backwards against the rough cold wall of one of the houses, keeping his back to her, sword poised to strike. He was too tall for her to see beyond him, but she heard three more arrows whistle through the air, followed by the sound of splintering wood.

Unable to read his expression, all Evelin could do was tune into his heartbeat, the organ pounding like a war drum. Footsteps sounded nearby, but no more arrows came. Were they safe now? What was happening?

Trystan turned back to her, his expression filled with fear and something Evelin couldn't place. His eyes scanned her whole body, rapidly moving back and forth as he brushed her hair off her face with his free hand, checking for injuries.

Her own heart was beating the twin rhythm to his, blood pounding in her ears as she felt his touch, tender yet assessing. The king cupped her cheek and moved in towards her, still not taking his eyes off her. His broad chest was barely a hair's breadth from her own; his face angled down towards her. Evelin lifted her chin a fraction, looking into his eyes as he stood over her, still not saying a word.

Every thought left her mind. There was only Trystan, standing tantalisingly close, his eyes locked with hers. In that moment, all she wanted was to pull him in towards her and feel the press of his body against her own. His gaze burned into her, the intensity sending her heart racing even faster. She raised a hand to his sword arm, gently tugging at his elbow. She needed to close the small distance that remained between them. His hand moved slowly down to the side of her neck, pushing back her hair further and stroking along the bare skin of her shoulder where her cloak had fallen away. The slight touch sent a jolt coursing through her body; every inch of her skin suddenly alert to the fabric between them.

"Sire!" a strong, clear voice echoed down the alleyway.

Trystan released her so quickly she almost fell forwards, turning in the direction of the voice. Three members of the Kingsguard rushed towards them, swords drawn.

"We heard reports of an attack, sire. Are either of you hurt?" the foremost guard inquired.

"We are fine, thank you," Trystan replied. "But we would appreciate you accompanying us back to the palace. Come, Evelin, let's go."

Trystan waited until Evelin was safely inside her chambers before finally relaxing the muscles that had remained tightly coiled, ready to spring, since the first arrow had flown past them. He leaned heavily against the wall of the corridor, in desperate need of its solidity – too many thoughts jostling for his attention.

He had barely touched Evelin, and his glove had remained in place, yet it felt like her skin still sat beneath his left hand, smooth and soft. The tips of his fingers tingled at the memory. He shook his head, continuing down the corridor to Nik's office, located beside the guardhouse. He would conquer this. He had to.

"Trys," Nik started, rising from his chair as Trystan entered without knocking. "My men just reported—"

"It was nothing. But it could have been far worse. How did the guards where to find us?"

"They were on patrol by the docks. A passer-by saw a group of armed men running through the streets, so they rushed over."

"Was it Brigantium? Have you heard anything?"

"Still nothing. With winter setting in, fewer ravens are coming and there is barely anyone sailing or crossing the border now." Nikolas shook his head. "I doubt Otto would risk an attack in the middle of Valon, but who knows about that commander of his. All my intelligence says he's an impulsive prick."

"What if the attack wasn't meant for me?" Trystan fumed, pacing the small office. "You need to contact our agents. How many times must we be taken by surprise?" He gripped the back of the other chair firmly, so hard that the wood began to cut into his palms.

"I'll sort it, Trys," his friend assured him.

"Make sure that you do," Trystan ordered, stalking out of the room.

He was sick of waiting so long for everything he wanted.

Back in the quiet of the corridor, he knew exactly what – exactly *who* – he needed right now, but he was determined not to break his promise. He had come far too close tonight; he could feel his resolve slipping. He could not ruin a friendship, nor his friend's reputation, by acting on his lust. That was all it was, all it could be; he didn't want a relationship. They just complicated things.

Sighing, he stepped back into the office. "Nik, I'm going out. Is it beneath the commander of my armies to escort his king to the nearest inn?"

Nik laughed. "Probably, but I've seen your performance in the training ring – you definitely need the back up." With that, he grabbed his cloak and followed Trystan out into the night. "Are we in search of wine, women, or both, my liege?"

"Both. Most decidedly both," Trystan said, steel piercing his words.

CHAPTER TWENTY-TWO

EVELIN

The raven perched patiently on the sill, its velvety black wings gleaming in the early morning light, as Evelin tied the note to its leg. She gave the bird a gentle stroke before it took off into the crisp air, buffeted by the cold winds sweeping in from the sea. Hope and anxiety rose in her chest, mirroring the bird's flight.

She watched until it was out of sight, disappearing into the thick bank of clouds. There was nothing to do now but wait. It would take a while to hear back from her aunt Katyana. Still, that knowledge did nothing to ease the nervous tension that zipped through her veins, though she had to admit, that wasn't *solely* a consequence of waiting for answers.

Ever since the attack of the previous night, Evelin had been unable to stop thinking about Trystan and the sensation of his body pressed so close to hers. She had lain awake for hours in the night, her skin burning despite the cold that even the generous fires of the palace couldn't keep at bay. Trystan hadn't spoken a word to her during the walk back, but had kept shooting quick glances in her direction. Upon reaching her rooms, he had merely bid her a terse goodnight and strode off.

Maybe the king hadn't felt the same charge she had. Maybe he hadn't wanted to embarrass her further by rejecting her outright. How would Evelin know unless she asked?

Sending the raven to her aunt had fortified her. Searching

for knowledge about Gabriel might be out of her hands for now, but at least she had *done* something. She was so tired of being passive, of letting life simply happen to her. It was doing her absolutely no good sitting here and trying to analyse Trystan's every look; his every word. No matter how he felt, surely it was best to know the truth?

Evelin walked purposefully towards his rooms, not entirely sure what she was going to say. All she knew was that she had to see him; to hear his voice. Turning the corner of the corridor that led towards the royal apartments, she stopped as a door clicked open. From within emerged a stunningly beautiful woman, her tawny skin flushed, her dark hair tousled and unbrushed. The woman tipped her head back and let out a delicate laugh in response to some comment from within, before raising her hand in farewell and heading in the opposite direction.

Colour flooded Evelin's cheeks, burning. She needed to leave. Trystan couldn't find her here. God, how stupid was she to think that he might desire *her*?

"I imagine our king is resting after his night-time exertions. May I assist you with anything, princess?" a deep voice enquired from over her shoulder.

Evelin spun around and nearly slammed into the commander's chest. He was looking down at her, a smirk plastered across his stubbled cheeks. A faint whiff of ale surrounded him, and his cerulean eyes looked startling against his olive complexion.

"No, thank you, commander," Evelin replied tightly, scanning his body from top to toe with an arched brow. "I doubt that *you* would be able to."

He looked momentarily taken aback, and Evelin couldn't help but feel slightly proud of herself. She brushed past him, the weight of his gaze following her down the corridor. It was a relief to finally turn the corner, out of sight.

CHAPTER TWENTY-THREE

EVELIN

Evelin and William had spent the morning making a snowfaerie with the first white flakes that had fallen overnight. The snow wasn't deep, yet the hem of Evelin's iris-blue dress was soaked, and her hands were aflame from the cold. She should definitely have worn gloves.

Stamping the snow from her boots as they entered the foyer, she crossed in the direction of the stairs.

"Evelin? Would you mind joining me in the drawing room?" Trystan's voice echoed across to her.

It was the first time the king had spoken to her in days, and she wished he hadn't noticed her entrance. She was still burning with humiliation after the commander had found her in the corridor. It had been made abundantly clear that Trystan didn't feel the same way she did, the attraction on her part completely one-sided.

Evelin had no idea if his friend had told him about seeing her there, but if he had... oh, that would be so much worse. He probably thought she was some love-addled stalker, waiting around in the hope of 'accidentally' bumping into him.

His friend, that was all she was. All she would ever be. She had to remember that.

Sighing heavily, she followed the sound of his voice.

The wood-panelled drawing room had been painted

tastefully in ivory-white, with deep blue curtains draped at the windows. Plush armchairs and chaise longues in various shades of blue were gathered in neat circles around the long space. It was beautiful, though a little chilly, the single fireplace not producing much heat. Why hadn't Trystan and his small circle of advisors decamped to the Winter Palace, closer to the heart of Parissi? It surely must be better suited to this time of year?

Trystan stood by the fire, one arm resting on the mantle. The warm light of the flames brought out the tones of gold in his hair, making Evelin's heart tighten.

"I've been thinking about our conversation the other night," he said, his eyes fixed on the fire. "About everything that has happened; how overwhelming it has all been for you."

Embarrassment roiled in Evelin's stomach; she hated that Trystan hadn't forgotten the words she'd spoken in a moment of vulnerability.

"I told you, I'm fine. Truly," she replied, her voice cracking slightly, despite her best efforts.

Trystan turned and stepped towards her, stopping just a foot away. He looked down at her appraisingly. "I thought you might benefit from a reminder of how strong you are."

An icy draft wafted through Evelin's hair as the door behind her opened, revealing a woman, her golden-brown skin glowing in the faelights. Large amber eyes mirrored the warm smile on her full lips.

"Lianna!" Evelin exclaimed, rushing into the open arms of her friend.

The taller woman hugged her tightly, then pulled back to plant a gentle kiss on her brow. "It's wonderful to see you, Eve. You're looking so well! How's your new little one?"

Evelin stepped back, assessing her friend warily. "Trystan told you about Gabriel?"

Lianna grasped her forearms reassuringly. "Don't be mad at Trys. He's been worried about you. Besides, you should have told me yourself! I would have been there as fast as I could," she scolded, before crossing the room to Trystan and wrapping him in a tight hug. "You may be king, Trys, but I'm going to have to ask you to clear out for a bit. I've got some catching up to do with my best friend."

Trystan chuckled. "As you wish. I'll leave you two alone. Take all the time you need."

"Oh, Trys?" Lianna called, just as he reached the door. "Can someone bring us one of your best bottles of wine and a couple of glasses?"

"Of course, *my lady*. Anything for you," Trystan replied, giving an exaggerated bow as he left.

Lianna pulled Evelin over to the sofa closest to the fire and wrapped her strong hands around hers. "All Trystan has told me is that you had your baby early and you came here because it wasn't safe for you at home. You only have to tell me what you're comfortable with, but just know that I am here for you, no matter what."

Evelin struggled to hold back the sob that threatened to break forth at her friend's words. Telling Trystan had been a relief, certainly, but there was nothing quite like unburdening one's troubles to a close female friend.

Lianna already knew that she hadn't been particularly happy in her marriage to Marcellus, and had visited her at the hunting lodge a couple of times, but this time Evelin told her the full story: the truth about Otto and Marcellus, Gabriel's birth... everything.

"... and four nights ago, when we were on our way back from the inn, we came under arrow fire. It was only a few arrows, but there *is* something I don't understand," Evelin continued.

"Trystan was ready to protect us, and I didn't think much of it at the time, but he only drew his sword."

"What do you mean?" Lianna asked.

"He didn't summon the light. We were in a dark alley, under attack, and he didn't use his magic. It doesn't make sense."

Her friend sighed. "Trys hasn't used his magic since the coronation, though I'm afraid the whole story is not mind to tell. You'll have to speak with him, if you wish to know more."

"Of course, forgive me, I didn't mean to pry. I didn't know."

Evelin hesitated. She desperately wanted to tell Lianna about the moment between them after the attack, about seeing that woman leave Trystan's room the morning after. Yet something held her back. It had always been the three of them at the Academie… to tell Lianna about her growing feelings for Trystan would feel like breaking some unspoken rule.

"Would you like to see the boys?" she asked instead. "William is a lot bigger than when you last saw him, and I know Gabriel would very much like to meet his godmother."

"Godmother?" Lianna threw her arms around Evelin in delight. "I adore you. Of course I want to see them, I can't wait!"

Smiling brightly at her friend's joy and affection for her sons, Evelin sent for them both, watching on fondly as Lianna spoke animatedly with William and cooed adoringly over Gabriel. As her friend held the little boy in her arms, Evelin knew there was something she had to do.

"I want you to see him truly, Lianna," she said, raising her arms and drawing back the glamour.

Tears welled in her friend's large, dark eyes. "Oh, Eve. He is beautiful. Just like his mama."

Smiling softly, Evelin watched as Lianna cradled her baby, nodding whilst William recounted to her all about his snowfaerie. She had not felt this at peace for a long time.

No matter Trystan's feelings, he knew her well enough to know that she needed to see Lianna, and had made that reunion happen. He cared about her, and her boys, and she would not risk that care and kindness for anything.

CHAPTER TWENTY-FOUR

EVELIN

"You've not told me much about what *you've* been up to recently, Lianna," Evelin mused as she walked arm in arm with her friend towards the stables.

They had decided to go for a short ride that morning before the next snow fell, and she was grateful for the warmth the fleece lining of her riding leathers provided against the cold.

"There's not much to report." Lianna shrugged. "I've been doing a bit of travelling, and I visited my parents this summer."

"How are they?"

"Same as always. My mother is desperate to find me a match, and my father is still grumbling that I chose telepathy as my specialty. He's always viewed it as '*a conniving art and beneath one of our House*'. I think he's just worried that I'll use it to find out what he's thinking."

Evelin squeezed her friend's arm in consolation. "I'm sorry, that must be tough."

"Ah, I've decided to not let his antiquated attitudes bother me anymore. I'm lucky that Trys lets me stay here so much, even if I do have to put up with that cocky friend of his." Lianna grimaced. "I don't understand how Trys has put up with Nik for so long. He acts like he's God's gift, swaggering around the place. Just because he's handsome and a good fighter, doesn't mean he has to keep *reminding* us all of the fact."

"Lianna, I think that might be the nicest thing you've ever said about me," the commander commented as he pushed open the stable door. "If I'd known you prized my physique so highly, I would have made myself available to you during your last visit."

"Eurgh, shut up Nik!" Lianna snapped. "We're taking two of the horses for a ride."

"Well, if you're ever looking for something else to ride—"

Lianna back-handed his broad bicep in retort, but Nikolas merely chuckled, sauntering off across the yard with two large dogs bounding after him.

"See what I mean?" groused Lianna, her face thunderous.

"Forget about him," Evelin soothed. "He's trying to wind you up. Let's just enjoy our ride."

It felt incredible to be out riding again, the wind biting against her skin. Evelin's father used to take her and Otto out riding when they were children, and she had many happy memories of those times.

Evelin's mind turned to Otto. What was he doing right now? Surely Marcellus would have learned of her absence by now? Was he behind the attack in the old town? The possibility unsettled her. A reckoning would be coming sooner or later; neither man would accept her taking the children out of the kingdom.

Evelin's train of thought was broken by a braxhawk's piercing call echoing through the icy woodland. One was circling in the sky directly above them, its rusty red wings flapping gently as it searched the ground for prey. Braxhawks were greatly prized among the fae nobility for their hunting skills; they were highly intelligent birds with an unending loyalty to their keeper. Their wingspan was unsettlingly large, with the biggest males reaching over five feet across, and their cunning eyes were the colour of gold. Legend had it that they were once much larger, and the first fae would ride them into battle, bird and rider soaring through the sky as one.

What would it be like, to soar amongst the clouds, looking down upon the world beneath? There had been many times at the lodge when Evelin had wished she could fly away; free herself from the constant supervision and tedium of the place; choose when and where to go, answering to no one. It had sounded like heaven at the time, and as scared as she was now, riding through the woods with her best friend felt like a small slice of that paradise.

A shrill whistle sliced through the trees and the braxhawk swiftly spun around, heading for the noise. Evelin followed the bird's flight as it dived rapidly downwards before landing softly on an outstretched gloved hand. The keeper stroked its head gently, the bird nuzzling into the touch, before passing it a morsel of food, which it gulped down quickly.

"That's a gorgeous bird, Trys. Is it one of your uncle's mating pair?" Lianna's voice rang out across the clearing.

Trystan nodded, smiling down at the bird, who was pulling at his glove, eager for another treat. "I thought she'd like to get out for a bit, before the snowstorm sets in later."

"Fancy joining us for the rest of the ride?" Lianna asked. "We're aiming to get out past the old temple."

Trystan's eyes darted straight to Evelin, and her cheeks warmed despite the cold. She loved that he had asked Lianna to come, and had known exactly what she needed, but she still felt awkward around him. Evelin hoped that the king would decline the invitation and looked down, suddenly fascinated by the reins in her hands.

"Yes, I'd like that," he replied.

Damn. Evelin gripped the reins more tightly as Trystan gently guided his mount round to join them and the trio fell in together. With a jerk of his arm, he sent his braxhawk off into the sky, the bird soon becoming just a fleck of red in the grey vastness.

Her friends chatted aimlessly, but Evelin remained quiet, contemplating both her surroundings and how best to deal with the situation with Trystan. She longed to return to the easy companionship of their time at the Academie, but was unsure of how. Should she make a joke about reaching out to him in the old town? Ignore it and carry on as before? Though their relationship hadn't exactly been easy before that anyway. How could it be when she had turned up on his doorstep, begging for sanctuary after not speaking to him for years?

"You up for it, Eve?" Lianna's question shattered through Evelin's spiralling thoughts.

"Sorry, what?"

"I bet Trys that my horse is the fastest and I can make it to the temple before him. Want to join in on our little race?" Lianna had a teasing expression on her face.

Evelin definitely did not want to race – as accomplished a rider as she had been in her youth, she hadn't ridden in years, and was still getting acquainted with the horse she rode now. Still... maybe this was her chance to return to some sort of normalcy. At the Academie, she had been continuously embroiled in Lianna and Trystan's stupid bets, throwing herself in with their laughter.

"Go on then," she responded, trying to look casual and confident. "What does the winner get?"

"Everlasting glory!" Lianna yelled, before digging in her heels and spurring her horse forward. Trystan was less than a breath behind her, urging his grey mare onwards. Evelin swallowed and followed in their wake, whispering an encouraging word to her mount.

Her hair whipped at her face, lashing her already frozen cheeks, the ivy-green riding cloak she wore billowing out behind her. Trystan and Lianna were already twenty yards ahead, but Evelin was desperate to keep up. She galloped through the woods, thankful that they had picked a fairly wide path with few overhanging trees. Trystan turned in his saddle slightly, assessing where she was, his eyes bright. He shot her a cocky smile before leaning further forward, focused on catching up with Lianna.

Evelin was finally beginning to enjoy the race, adrenaline coursing through her, when the forest began to thicken, the dark greys and browns of the trees growing closer together. Her focus sharpened, using the reins and her thighs to guide her horse more precisely as it sped forwards. She had lost sight of her friends, too focused on not careening headfirst into a tree.

A dense thicket was coming up quickly ahead and she steered to the right, towards a wider path. A flash of red caught her eye. Suddenly, Trystan's braxhawk sailed downwards at terrifying speed, its keen eyes trained on some small mammal scurrying across the forest floor right in front of her.

Evelin cried out as her horse whinnied in shock. Spooked by the missile-like bird shooting across its path, the beast tried to stop, but the path beneath was icy and its hooves began to slide. The braxhawk spat a warning cry, frightening the horse further.

It's eyes wide with panic, Evelin's mount reared on its hind legs. She tried desperately to hold on, but her icy fingers were stiff, and the muscles in her legs were no longer strong enough to grip the saddle. As her horse continued to flail in the air, Evelin was thrown backwards, her shout of surprise echoing through the woods and startling the braxhawk into flight once more.

She landed painfully in a bank of snow, winded but otherwise unscathed, the snow having cushioned the worst of the fall.

Relieved, she pushed against the ground to stand, only for the earth to give out beneath her, leaving her tumbling down the steep bank of a stream.

As her body slid into the icy waters below, the cold stole her breath, her ankle cracking against something hard. Hands trembling, she scrambled towards the shore, reaching for her leg to assess the damage. Pressing gently on the bone, a jolt of pain shot through her, making her whole body shudder. She screwed her eyes shut and tried to stand on her good leg, struggling against her sodden clothes, but promptly fell back into the water.

Two strong hands hooked under her arms and hauled her out of her frozen misery.

"Are you alright? Can you stand?" Trystan asked frantically.

"I'm fine, it's just my ankle," she said through gritted teeth.

Lianna slid carefully down the bank and grasped her left arm, Trystan taking her right, and the pair eased her back up to the path.

"Eve, you're bleeding!" Lianna's gentle hands reached for her head. "I'll ride back and get Agnes. I don't think you should ride with a damaged ankle and a concussion."

"What? No, Lianna, I'll be fine on the back of your horse," Evelin protested.

"Don't be ridiculous! You wait here with Trys and I'll get Agnes. She can heal you and we can all head back."

"Maybe I should go and get Agnes, Li?" Trystan offered.

"Trys, all joking aside, I am the fastest rider. Eve is soaked. We don't want her having to wait any longer than necessary and we're both terrible at healing. Let's just sit her in the temple and I'll be back before you know it."

Lianna grasped Evelin and glowered at Trystan. He gently but firmly placed his hand around her other arm, allowing her to brace against him. Pain seared through her leg as she hobbled in the direction of the temple, trying hard not to lean too much on Trystan. The scent of him was almost overwhelming in it's intensity: a combination of beeswax polish, freshly washed linen, and a lingering hint of vellum and ink.

The temple was mostly derelict, though it hummed with an ancient power. Built of white moonstone, the altar was guarded by six towering pillars, each three times the height of a fully grown fae male. It had been built in the shape of a hexagon, to represent the six children of Igraine and Xoros. Grey-brown vines snaked around each of the pillars and intertwined with each other along the stones that crowned the structure.

Trystan and Lianna placed her down gently on an ice-cold bench, gnarled by the centuries.

"I'll be back soon," Lianna assured them, hurrying off towards her waiting mount.

Trystan nodded as she left, leaning against one of the pillars, one hand resting on the shortsword fixed at his waist.

Evelin slumped back against the bench and stuck her damaged leg out in front of her. Now that they had stopped, she could feel the bitter chill of her soaked clothes and began to shiver. She pulled her cloak tighter around her shoulders, though its sodden bulk did little to warm her.

"Here." Trystan removed his own raven-black cloak.

"Thank you," Evelin replied, her fingers trembling as she attempted to unclasp her cloak, fumbling at the bronze fastening.

Trystan knelt in front of her, softly moving her frozen hands out of the way. "May I?" he asked, waiting for her nod of permission before unlatching the clasp. He pulled the cloak down and swiftly wrapped his own around her.

Evelin kept her eyes trained on her lap as he rubbed her upper arms with his strong hands. Slowly, the shaking subsided, and she risked a quick glance up at the king.

His face was streaked with dirt and blood – hers, Evelin supposed – and his hair had fallen forwards, the ends brushing against his cheekbones. Their eyes met and his gaze burned into her. The concern in it was evident, but there was something else that she couldn't place. Being this physically close again was torturous. Her desire for Trystan had not diminished in any way, and every inch of her skin burned against her wet clothes. A sudden impulse flitted through her mind, a need to peel off her soaking garments and push herself against his warm, solid body.

Ever since that night in the alley, she had felt stupid and rejected, feelings echoed during her first few weeks of marriage to Marcellus. God, she was such an idiot, having feelings for another man who clearly didn't want her.

Evelin forced herself to swallow; there was absolutely no way she would make a fool of herself again. "I'm feeling much warmer now," she managed to get out as she pushed herself backwards.

Trystan coughed, clearing his throat, and rose to his feet. He looked down at her and frowned slightly, before turning back to the forest. They remained silent for a long while, until Evelin's pointed ears pricked at the sound of hooves crunching in the snow.

Thank goodness.

"My lady!" Agnes exclaimed, hurrying up to her. "What on earth were you doing racing through the forest?" The healer glared at Trystan.

Evelin didn't reply to the scolding. In barely any time at all, Agnes had healed her broken ankle and sealed the graze on her head. Although she still felt slightly shaky, Evelin was able to ride pillion behind Lianna back to the palace. It wasn't a long ride, yet she still had trouble keeping her thoughts trained on the bath that awaited her, and not on the handsome king who rode behind.

CHAPTER TWENTY-FIVE

EVELIN

By the time they returned to the palace, the skies were grey and full: the first truly significant snowfall was coming, and would be coming fast.

Evelin's body was aching from the ride and Agnes' swift healing. The servants had already drawn her a long, deep bath, and she let out a slow, controlled breath as she eased herself down into it, the warmth stinging her. She lay there for what felt like hours, allowing her mind to remain blissfully empty, before the sound of small feet skipping lightly across the marble floor drew her attention.

"Mama! Where have you been? Can I get in?" William asked, reaching into the tub to grab a handful of bubbles.

"No, darling, I'm going to get out in a minute. I've just been on a ride with Aunty Lianna and I got a bit cold, but I'm fine now," she explained, smiling softly at her son's inquisitive face.

"Oh! I've got something for you!" he exclaimed, pulling a crumpled note from his trouser pocket and holding it towards her.

It was a short message from Lianna, asking Evelin if she wanted to dine with her that evening. Although she was bone tired, she *was* hungry… and she didn't want to disappoint Lianna.

Mind made up, she eased herself out of the bath and wrapped

one of the wonderfully fluffy towels around her, before dressing in her favourite cerulean gown and making her way down for dinner.

"Sorry I'm late, William got hold of your note somehow, so I only just saw…" Evelin trailed off.

The only person in the oak-panelled room was Trystan, his form silhouetted against the fire. The table was set, but for five, not two.

Evelin frowned. "Evening, Trystan," she said tentatively. "Sorry, I thought I was dining with just Lianna. Who else is joining us tonight?"

Trystan pulled at the neck of his tunic, a rich moss green, fitted snugly to his powerful, lean body. "Lianna mentioned your plans. I've invited Nik and Ceinwyn, if that's alright?"

"Of course! The more the merrier," Evelin reassured him, though after her disastrous ride today, she had been looking forward to a quiet supper with Lianna, not stilted formality with Trystan and his advisors. Ceinwyn had warmed to her over their lessons, but the commander still made her uneasy.

It was as if Nikolas knew she had been thinking about him, for he entered seconds later, swaggering in, wearing a dark tunic and trousers, his hair half tied back. He nodded briefly at Trystan but studiously avoided Evelin's gaze before pouring himself a large measure of liquor from the decanter on the side table.

Just behind him followed the two women. Lianna was wearing a delicate gown of the palest yellow, whilst Ceinwyn wore a silver tunic and trousers. Both radiated beauty and elegance, presenting a sharp contrast to the brutal darkness of Trystan's best friend.

"Shall we sit?" Trystan asked, taking the chair at the head of the table.

The others followed his lead, the commander and Ceinwyn

sitting to Trystan's right, Lianna and Evelin to his left.

"Before we eat, I believe you have news of some importance, Nik," Trystan added, his tone grave.

"Yes. I have finally heard back from our agent in Azmar." His blue eyes shifted from Trystan to Evelin, and his voice lowered a fraction. "Marcellus knows of your escape, princess, and that you are here in Valon. He appears to be unaware of your infant's true nature, but Brigantium has begun to ready its forces. The attack in the old town seems to have just been a warning…"

Fear, undiluted and hideously potent, swept over Evelin. Her pulse raced and the room became intensely warm. She tried to read the commander's expression, but his face was inscrutable.

"I've already told you my thoughts on the matter, Trys, but as commander of your forces I need to know what you want me to do next."

"Ceinwyn, what do you advise?" Trystan asked his chancellor.

Ceinwyn remained silent for what felt like an age, staring at her glass. "If Brigantium is readying for war, we need to make our own preparations. We cannot leave ourselves undefended."

"This is not Parissi's war, Ceinwyn," The commander looked at Trystan beseechingly. "Let me—"

Trystan raised a hand to cut him off. The man fell silent, his face a picture of barely controlled rage. Evelin could feel the anger emanating from him across the table.

"It doesn't matter if Brigantium are preparing their forces. Winter is here," Trystan stated, gesturing to the snow falling past the windows behind. "By tomorrow, all the ports will be frozen, and the mountain pass will become unusable. There is nothing Brigantium can do whilst winter holds. When spring comes, I will arrange to speak with Otto, ruler to ruler. For now, though, we simply prepare our soldiers, and wait."

The commander leaned forward and as if he were about to

respond, but Trystan shot him a glare and he remained silent.

The rest of the dinner passed awkwardly, Lianna trying, and failing, to make small talk. When the final dish had been served, Evelin rose and took her leave.

Back in her rooms, she held Gabriel and read William his new stories. As soon as the boys were in their beds, she crept silently out.

There was something she had to do.

CHAPTER TWENTY-SIX

TRYSTAN

Trystan sat in his study, nursing a glass of strong Parissi spirit. His long legs were propped up on the table and his eyes were closing when Evelin's voice floated through the room.

"Trystan, I know it's late, but may I speak with you for a moment?"

"Yes, of course," he replied, sitting up and gesturing for her to sit next to him on the sofa.

Her skin was paler than usual, and the king watched her fingers tremble as she ran them over the hem of her sleeve.

"What is it?" he asked gently, angling himself towards her.

"Trystan, I really appreciate everything you've done for me and the boys, but I can't stay in Valon any longer. I'm putting you and your whole country at risk. It isn't fair to you or your people. I've spoken to Agnes, and we are going to try to reach her family."

His chest tightened painfully. Without thinking, Trystan reached out and took her hand in his. The sparks he had felt in the old town rippled through him as he gently stroked her upturned palm with his thumb. He stared deeply into her eyes, so wide and earnest.

"You are not going anywhere, Evelin. This is your home for as long as you need it, and there is no way I am going to let you travel with an old woman and two young boys just as winter is setting in."

"But—"

"No," he insisted, pressing down slightly more firmly.

Her eyes were drawn to where he stroked her palm, and he found himself unable to fight the urge to touch more of her. He reached out his other hand and gently cupped her chin, tilting her face up to meet his gaze.

"I don't want you to go, Evelin."

He shifted closer, his eyes drifting down to where her heart pounded in her chest, her breasts rising as her breathing quickened.

This was madness, Trystan knew that. In no sane world should he allow himself to go any further. She was married. Offering Evelin sanctuary was dangerous enough; bedding the wife of Brigantium's commander would be an act of war. His rational self screamed at him to stop, to stand up and leave. But all he could focus on was the rim of onyx around Evelin's eyes. How had he never noticed before?

He watched as she swallowed, and when she parted her lips ever so slightly, Trystan lost all sense of himself.

His palm cupped the back of her head, fingers tangling in her silky hair, as he pulled her mouth against his. Evelin's lips were just as soft and welcoming as he had imagined, and he lost himself in the feel of her, his fingers aching with desire to touch; to explore her body.

His heart thudded in his chest, and as she let out the softest moan, opening her mouth to him, Trystan felt himself strain against his trousers. Her hands moved to the side of his face, pulling him closer. God, he needed her; he needed all of her, now. Leaning back, he began to pull Evelin to straddle him on the sofa before the rational voice in his mind broke through.

What in God's name was he doing?

"We have to stop."

Trystan pulled back and stood abruptly, running his fingers through his hair as he cursed himself for the look of confusion and hurt on Evelin's face. God, all he wanted was to make her pain go away.

"Evelin, please don't mistake my stopping for a lack of desire on my part. If I let myself, I would be peeling off your clothes and exploring every inch of your body." She let out a tiny gasp, which nearly broke his self-control. "But if we continue... you are married, Evelin. To the man who commands the largest army on the continent."

Evelin frowned, the glint of anger in her eyes almost sending him to his knees. "Then what *was* that, Trystan?"

"That was me acting on my baser instincts! God's breath, Evelin, you have to know how much I want you? From the moment you walked through the palace gates I've been holding myself back. I'm trying to be a better man, a better ruler. You and Parissi – you both deserve better than this."

Evelin said nothing in response, her arms folded over her chest.

Eventually, her eyes dimmed, and she let out a weary sigh, one Trystan hated that he had caused.

"You are one of the best men I know, Trystan. Never doubt that." She stood on her tiptoes, planting the softest whisper of a kiss on his cheek, before walking away, exiting his study and closing the door softly behind her.

Trystan grabbed his discarded glass and threw back the spirit, the burning in his throat mirrored by a similar sensation in his fingers, wrapped around the cut crystal. White light had begun to glow from his fingertips, making the glass fluoresce. His brow furrowed as he slowly rotated his hand, mesmerised by the sight.

By the time he had taken another breath, the light had disappeared.

CHAPTER TWENTY-SEVEN

EVELIN

Evelin stood alone in the corridor for some time, replaying the kiss over and over in her mind, pressing her fingertips to her lips to feel where Trystan's had been only moments before.

She had never been kissed like that, with such raw desire. Her most intimate parts ached with an intensity that was entirely new, but Trystan's words echoed through her mind, shattering the illusion.

'You are married, Evelin.'

She wished she had told him the truth about Marcellus and their sham of a marriage, but where would she start? How could she explain without revealing her naïveté? Her foolishness at still allowing Marcellus into her bed? Besides, Trystan was right. What he would be risking, what they would *both* be risking, by acting on their feelings was too great a sacrifice.

Their feelings. Evelin pressed her fingers to her lips in giddy delight. That was enough for now. To know that he wanted her too, that she was desired. Years of marriage to Marcellus had never made Evelin feel this way.

Her heart was still pounding as she paced her sleeping chamber. Adrenaline coursed through her veins, and it was nearly dawn by the time she finally drifted off. Her mind raced for hours, playing out various scenarios of what she would say to the king when they saw each other next, but one thing cut through the chaos: she needed to be honest with Trystan. The idea that he thought she was someone who would break her marriage vows so easily wounded her to the point of insult. She needed him to understand that she wouldn't, not without just cause.

Resolved that she would find him tomorrow and explain, Evelin finally drifted off to sleep.

CHAPTER TWENTY-EIGHT

EVELIN

The fist connected sharply with Trystan's stomach, knocking the air from his lungs. He gasped, thankful that he hadn't eaten breakfast, else he would have vomited all over the training ring. He held up his palm to indicate to Nik that he needed a few more seconds, heart stuttering in his chest.

Nik grinned, but there was no warmth in his smile. "How many times have I told you not to let your guard down, Trys? That's the second time you've fallen for a feint today. You need to be thinking three moves ahead."

"I know, I know," Trystan managed to reply, still bent double. "Pass me the water?"

Nik merely grunted in response, reaching over the side of the ring to the little table where a flask sat. As Nik turned back, Trystan seized the opportunity. He shot upright, shifted his weight forward, and landed a punch squarely on Nik's jaw. The commander's head snapped backwards, and Trystan let out a deep laugh. A cheer rang out from the benches beside the ring; Lianna had insisted on watching their training this morning and was rubbing her hands with glee.

"That was unnecessary, Trystan," Nik said through gritted teeth as he spat blood onto the floor. He glowered at his friend, rubbing his jaw, before launching himself across the ring.

Nik moved like lightning, so fast that Trystan barely saw the attack coming.

The pair fell to the ground, all semblance of skill and precision abandoned. Nik had the king pinned within seconds and aimed punch after punch at his head and chest. Trystan tried in vain to twist over and regain the advantage. They hadn't fought this way since they were boys, when they had inevitably come to blows over one thing or another. He was strong, but Nik was far stronger, and within seconds his friend's fist connected painfully with the side of his ribs, then his nose. Something cracked and pain blinded him.

"Nik, stop!" Lianna shouted.

Her words made Nik pause and sit back, his thighs still pinning Trystan to the mat.

"What the fuck was that for?" Trystan growled, tentatively feeling his nose to see if it was broken.

"You know what," Nik snapped, standing and rubbing his bleeding knuckles. "I saw you in your study last night. You promised. You promised me this wasn't about you trying to bed her, Trystan. Do you have *any* idea the risk we all face because you can't keep your hands off Marcellus' *wife*? Your people depend on you to protect them, not slake your lust with the nearest woman regardless of the consequences. No wonder you can't summon the light; you're not half the man Silas was!" The commander stalked away, knocking over the water table with a roar of sheer frustration.

Lianna ducked under the ropes and ran to the king's side, assessing his injuries. "What was that all about, Trys?" she asked warily.

"It doesn't matter, Li," Trystan muttered, trying to sit up. His head was pounding and blood streamed freely from his nose. He sat for a moment, gathering his breath.

Nik's words had hurt him far more deeply than his fists.

What he'd said about his uncle was exactly what Trystan felt about himself... but to hear it from his best friend?

When he tried to stand, his vision blurred, and for a second he felt an icy jolt through his head. He had felt that sensation before, and it took him a few heartbeats to remember.

"What the hell, Li!" he shouted. "How *dare* you try to enter my mind?"

His friend recoiled, sitting back on her ankles. "I'm sorry, Trys. Truly. I was worried about what Nik's words might have done to you. I didn't think before I reached out." Lianna had enough grace to look ashamed of herself.

Trystan sighed. "I'm sorry for snapping at you, but please stay out of my head. You know as well as I do that my mental wards are weak as hell right now."

Lianna bowed her head in apology. "I won't do it again. But... can I ask about what I saw?" There was a spark of excitement in her eyes.

Trystan nodded briefly, wishing he hadn't as the world span before him.

"Did you really kiss Eve, or was that just a very vivid dream?" she asked, raising an eyebrow.

Trystan hung his head. "Oh God."

Lianna squealed with delight. "I knew it! Was it last night? Tell me everything, I have to know!"

Trystan let out a bitter laugh, feeling a sharp stabbing pain in his ribs, before dutifully recalling what had passed the previous evening; how he had come so close to kissing Evelin after the attack and how he had finally acted last night.

"Well, you would have to be blind not to notice the chemistry between you two, even when we were all at the Academie. I've always wondered why you never acted on it back then," Lianna mused, pausing for a moment before continuing. "Trys...what you said about Eve being married… I completely understand your point about further endangering relations with Brigantium, but you should know that Marcellus… well, let's just say their marriage hasn't been a good one. Eve's practically been locked away in that ancient hunting lodge for years, with only Agnes and the boys for company."

Trystan felt rage bubble beneath his skin as realisation dawned. Evelin had changed since their time at the Academie; she was more reserved now; less sure of herself. He had thought her behaviour was simply just a consequence of the circumstances. After all, he had assumed she hadn't *wanted* to see him; that married life was treating her well and she had grown apart from him by choice. But Lianna's words suggested that Evelin may not have had a choice at all.

"What are you not saying, Li? Why would he do that to her? To his children?"

"It's not my story to tell. But she's been hurt, Trys. That much should be obvious to you. And then of course there's the whole mess with Otto. God, some days I wish I could strangle that brother of hers. He persuaded Eve to marry so that she could produce a string of Brigantian heirs, knowing that he never would himself, given his preferences for male lovers. Marcellus was *his* choice for her, but all along the two of them were carrying on behind Evelin's back. She only found out after the wedding."

Trystan blinked several times, struggling to come to terms with the truth of Evelin's reality. The last he had heard from her before her marriage was that she had met the man of her dreams, a man with no equal. Of course, he had wondered whether there might have been more to her seeking sanctuary than her fear for Gabriel, but he could never have fathomed the twisted relationship she had been trapped into. Had Otto forced Marcellus to bed her, for the sake of the kingdom? Or worse…

had Marcellus forced himself on Evelin? Had their sons been conceived as part of a mutual act of duty? Or one-sided cruelty?

Overwhelmed by emotion, he managed to choke out, "God, all this time?"

Lianna nodded, a pleading look on her face. "Don't tell her I told you, Trys. She would be mortified; you know how proud she is."

Trystan nodded, unable to come up with a response. "I think I had better go ice my face."

Fleeing the training ring without another word, he walked swiftly towards the nearest snowdrift, thrusting his hand into the icy flakes. The cold dimmed the burning pain, though it did not extinguish his heartache.

Packing the snow into a ball, he held it tentatively against his aching nose and winced at the cold. Trystan knew he should go to the court healer, but there was something about pain like this that was addictive. The sting of his injuries took the edge off.

"What are you going to do about Nik?" Lianna asked, appearing by his side.

"I'm not sure. Maybe I'll speak with him later, after he's had a chance to cool down."

Trystan knew he should be furious with his friend for the beating and the cruel words, but he had found himself thinking the same thing himself. Trying to live up to his uncle's memory was an unbearable burden, one he wasn't sure he could carry. Knowing some of what Evelin had faced since they had parted ways all those years ago just made him feel even more pathetic.

Sighing, he resolved to find Nik later and suggest they go for a drink; tempers often flared in the training ring, and he suspected that the commander felt as badly about the fight as he did. Nik had been like a brother to him growing up; a couple of years older than Trystan, he had looked out for him back in

Eskaria. Their mothers had been friends, and the two boys had played together through the long, hot days, splashing in streams, chasing animals, and testing their burgeoning powers. He had been desperately sad when Nik had gone away to complete his military training as soon as he turned eighteen.

Nik's father, Anders, had been an unyielding man who expected nothing but the best from his son, which meant following their family's tradition of shunning further academic study and focusing on their physical skills and magical power through practical application. Nik had adapted well to military life, rising swiftly through the ranks, and Trystan had always looked forward to his letters describing life at Deathhold. He'd made it sound like a huge adventure; days filled with hunting and training, and nights spent carousing with the other officers in the local taverns.

Once Trystan had finished his studies at the Academie, he too had begun his training, though he had found it far more difficult to adapt to life at Deathhold. Four years of easy living at the Academie had softened him, and he'd resented the orders and enforced routines. Throughout it all, though, Nik had been there, pushing him, encouraging him. He could be a complete bastard, but Trystan knew that Nik would never desert him. They were closer than brothers in some ways, and that was exactly why he had made Nik commander of his forces shortly after he had inherited the throne. It didn't hurt that Nik was also the deadliest fighter in Parissi's military. A born warrior with immense powers – Nik was meant to be a leader of men.

Trystan, on the other hand, had never been destined to be king. But the massacre at the palace had wiped out all those in line, and he had been thrust into a role he had not been trained for and never expected to have. Nik's support over the past two years had been invaluable to him. He would not hold a few punches or words spoken in anger against his friend.

With Brigantium readying its forces, he would need his commander now more than ever.

CHAPTER TWENTY-NINE

EVELIN

Eddies of steam rose from the flask cupped in her hands, the tendrils of vapour dancing in the air. Valon was stunning in the summer, but its winter beauty was ethereal. The buttermilk walls of the graceful buildings sparkled with a frosting of ice and the streets were crisp with snow. It was barely mid-afternoon, but daylight was already fading, so the merchants had lit their shops with faelights that glowed through the stained-glass windows. Their light spread out onto the street and Evelin felt as though she was walking across a frozen rainbow as they meandered through the old town. Evelin savoured the warmth as she sipped her drink, the bitter liquid mellowed by the honey liquor that Lianna had spiked it with before they'd set out.

"Thank you," she said, passing the flask to her friend. "Fantastic idea."

"Well, I was bound to have one sooner or later, wasn't I?" Lianna replied, grinning as she pulled Evelin towards a dressmaker's.

The shop was filled with colourful gowns, exquisitely stitched and adorned with gold and silver patterns that were perfect for winter. Yet as Evelin perused the rails, she found herself drawn to a hidden garment at the back of the shop, almost out of sight.

Made from the silk spun by draegonworms, the ivory fabric was unfathomably light and incredibly soft. The bodice was tight with an off-the-shoulder neckline, whilst full skirts rushed to the ground. The neck, sleeves, and hem were stitched a delicate pattern of golden thread, drawing the eye directly to them.

"You *have* to try that on," Lianna insisted, peering over Evelin's shoulder.

"We're here for new winter cloaks, not ballgowns," Evelin argued wistfully.

Turning away from the bewitching gown, she browsed the racks and selected a sensible burgundy woollen cloak with a fur-trimmed hood. Lianna picked its soft grey twin to compliment her rose-gold hair, which today was spun into endless spirals.

Back on the street, Lianna nudged Evelin. "I think I know someone who would like to see you in that gown."

Evelin spun around and gave her friend a hard stare. "What do you mean?"

"I saw Trys this morning," Lianna replied. "Certain events that transpired last night might have come up in conversation…" Lianna left the sentence hanging, clasping her friend's hand at the look of panic on Evelin's face.

"I can't believe he told you."

"He didn't. He got into a fight with Nik this morning at training. Nik apparently saw you two last night and nearly beat Trys senseless over some broken promise. I don't know what's going on with the two of them, but afterwards, well… Trys and I were talking, and I essentially forced the truth out of him. Now, are you going to keep me – your best friend, I might add – in the dark? Or are you going to tell me what happened?"

"*Nothing* happened. I'm sure Trystan will have told you that much. We kissed, and he stopped it, and I understand why. I'm married. Married to someone who could really damage this kingdom. Trystan had the good sense to stop things before we went too far."

Lianna placed a gentle hand on her shoulder. "You deserve happiness too, Eve. You deserve to be loved. I've only met Marcellus a handful of times, but honestly? How much worse could it get? No, don't look at me like that, you know what I mean! You've already fled the kingdom with his children. Do you really think he is going to forgive that? Besides, he doesn't have a leg to stand on even if you *did* sleep with Trys – he's been screwing your own brother for years! You can't keep letting that man control you."

Evelin shook off her arm, trying to organise her thoughts in the aftermath of Lianna's tirade. She was furious, but not with her friend. She knew Lianna was right. She *was* letting Marcellus control her. But her friend didn't understand the crippling fear she felt at every waking moment. If her husband got to them, what would he do? Would he keep William from her forever? What would he do when he found out about Gabriel? Her blood turned cold at the thought. Her duty was to her children, just as Trystan's was to Parissi. How could either of them let any physical attraction, no matter how strong, override that duty?

"What are you thinking, Eve?" Lianna asked softly.

Evelin didn't know how to respond.

What *was* she thinking?

CHAPTER THIRTY

TRYSTAN

Trystan was sprawled in a wing-backed chair, looking out of the bay window of his bedchamber. In summer, the smell of the rose garden would drift up at night, filling his room with a heady aroma, but all the king could smell at the moment was the hazelroot tincture he had applied to his bruises before icing them again.

Night was drawing in lazily, and the pink sky reflected off the snow outside. He had asked the servants to build up the fires, but still he wore a padded doublet to ward off the chill. Suddenly, a tapping at the window caught Trystan's attention. A raven was perched on the sill, a brass ring securing a message to its leg. He opened the window and untied the parchment, the raven flying back out into the night.

The missive was brief.

Return my heirs to me or my armies will destroy everything you hold dear. You can keep the whore, but if I do not get my children back, she will be the first to feel my fury.

Trystan seethed with a white-hot rage tempered by foreboding. A reckoning was coming, he had known that already, but to see it in front of him in black and white made it truly real. Nik had been right. He had drawn them all into danger, and Marcellus already believed he was sleeping with Evelin despite his restraint. Trystan baulked at how naive he had been to assume a diplomatic solution was possible.

There was a tentative knock at the door and Trystan heaved himself up slowly. His sides felt like they had been kicked by a particularly foul-tempered horse. God, Nik was powerful.

He opened the door to find Evelin wrapped in a cloak, with flakes of snow icing her loosely braided hair. Her eyes widened at his bruised face and her mouth fell into a silent 'o' as she paused like a deer who had just heard the crack of a branch in the forest.

Her brow furrowed as she surveyed him. "Trystan, what happened?"

"That doesn't matter right now. There's something you need to see." He passed her the note he had crumpled in anger.

Her eyes darted back and forth, her fingers turning the note this way and that, as if looking for a missing section.

"Oh God," she exhaled, rubbing her temples. "This is what I meant last night. You should have let me go. You don't know Marcellus like I do. Even if he got the boys back, he'd want revenge. I've doomed us all."

Trystan hated to see her like this, broken and defeated; blamed for something she hadn't even done. Fuck Marcellus, and Otto. He was king of Parissi, wasn't he? If he wanted a woman, and she wanted him, who the hell were either of them to stop him?

And *God*, he wanted her. The Brigantian commander already thought he was bedding her anyway. What was stopping him now?

Fuck it.

Trystan grasped Evelin firmly by her shoulders and pushed her against the wall of his bedchamber. His body was pressed to hers and he could feel the swell of her breasts against him.

"Trystan, what are you doing?" she asked breathlessly.

His hands glided up her face and neck as he whispered in her ear. "You know full well what I'm doing." Carefully, he bit down gently on her lobe, and felt her shiver as his breath caressed her neck.

"We shouldn't…"

Trystan's lips grazed Evelin's neck and her eyelashes fluttered closed.

"Why not?" he breathed as he placed a featherlight kiss on her collarbone. "Tell me to stop and I will."

Evelin's eyes opened and they mirrored his own desire. "Don't stop."

With Evelin having given him permission, he kissed her, his mouth desperate for her, his tongue insistent as he slid it between her lips. Moving his hands downwards, he brushed his thumbs along the sides of her breasts. Her hands grasped at his shoulders, his back, and he hissed as she pressed a little too tightly against his injured rib.

Evelin's eyes flew open at the realisation that she had caused him pain. Her hands went to his chest and she pushed him away from her. Reluctantly, Trystan pulled back, but only a fraction. They were still breathing the same breath, the force between them still palpable.

"Trystan, just… stop for a second." Her eyes whipped back and forth across his face. "What *did* happen to you?"

"This is nothing, you should see the other guy."

"Don't be flippant. Tell me what happened."

Trystan exhaled, biding his time. He wasn't sure how much to tell her. He took a slight step back, pulling away from the temptation of her body. "Apparently Nik saw us together in my study last night."

Evelin merely nodded. She must have already spoken with

Lianna. "I'm sorry, Trystan. I know I've put you in a difficult position, and I know he doesn't want me here. But I still can't believe your own commander would do that to you."

"He isn't just my commander, he's my best friend."

"And that is how your *best friend* treats you? Why on earth would you excuse this behaviour? You are his king, Trystan. For God's sake! How can you let him get away with this?"

Trystan sank back within himself, closing his eyes. He knew Nik's actions should not go unpunished, but he also knew his friend felt betrayed. Deep down, Trystan could not blame him. He felt embarrassed, trying to excuse Nik's actions, but to fully explain them to Evelin would be worse. He didn't want her to see his weakness.

Trystan opened his eyes to find Evelin standing before him, mere inches away from his mouth.

"I'm sorry, Trystan. I'm not angry at you. I just want to understand," she said quietly.

Taking her hands in his own, he admired her quiet beauty. The snow had now melted into her hair, curling it into waves and freeing it from her braid. Her cheeks were flushed from their embrace and her eyes shone fiercely. God, she was exquisite.

Evelin gently pulled her hands out of his grasp to reach forward and touch his face with the greatest care, her fingers tracing soft circles over the bruises and abrasions. His skin was still numb from the hazelroot, but as she leaned forward, he could feel the press of her against him and his body began to respond. Trystan reached his hands around to Evelin's back, fighting an overwhelming urge to press down on her shoulders and move her mouth downwards. He needed to control himself, but seeing her there in front of him was too much.

Just as his hands came to rest on her shoulders, she pulled back and stepped to the side.

He grabbed at her, a move that was anything but controlled. She was already two paces away, though, and he didn't dare embarrass himself by grasping at her again.

"I think you need your rest. Perhaps you should see a healer before we do anything more. I'm having supper with the boys tonight, but I'll see you tomorrow?"

"Tomorrow," he agreed, swallowing hard.

Evelin felt like her core was on fire as she made her way back to her own rooms. She ached to be held by Trystan again, to feel his body pressed up against hers, but seeing him injured had only compounded the disgust she held for his commander. The sound of her boots clacking on the stone floor of the corridor harmonised with the blood pounding through her, the two beats in syncope.

Where was she? Evelin stopped in her tracks, finding herself in part of the palace she hadn't ventured to before. The corridor was spartan, dimly lit by the odd faelight, and bereft of any decoration or furnishing. Her mind had been in such disarray that she hadn't focused on where she was going.

She walked forwards slowly, trying to get her bearings, when a door creaked open behind her. There was the commander, leaning with provoking casualness against a doorframe. A half-smile curved at one corner of his mouth.

"Princess, to what do I owe this unexpected pleasure?"

The feigned politeness, laced with arrogance, infuriated her. Before she knew what she was doing, she had stormed down the corridor towards him. Nikolas towered above her and looked down through his dark lashes, giving her a predatory glance. His audacity finally broke what self-control remained.

"You bastard!" she spat at him.

The words shocked even her.

He opened his mouth to respond, but before he could, Evelin continued, fuelled with the rage of seeing her friend so hurt.

"I have no idea why Trystan even keeps you around. Never mind the fact that he is your king, how could you treat your *friend* like that? You might not like me being here, and that is fair enough, but you are supposed to be the commander of his armies, yet you show no discipline over your own actions? You are not worthy to have command if that is how you treat people. You are not worthy to be his friend."

Evelin paused, but she knew that her features still showed the disgust she felt for the man standing across from her.

His expression was inscrutable as he took a slow breath, before removing his arm from the doorframe and standing upright. "I will not be lectured to by someone who knows nothing of the dangers Parissi faces." Nikolas spoke in a terrifyingly quiet tone. His blue eyes revealed a cold danger as he leaned in towards her. "I think you had better return to your chambers, *princess.*"

The commander didn't give her a second look as he strode back into his office and slammed the door behind him. Evelin was left standing alone in the corridor, her heart racing, palms sweaty. She struggled to regain her composure, regretting speaking so freely and at the same time revelling in the feeling of no longer allowing a man to do as he wished to the people she cared for. The commander's self-satisfied, proud nature reminded her so much of Marcellus, and she'd had enough.

She had been meek and subservient for far too long. Being back in Valon was helping her to remember her own strength, she would not be cowed any longer.

CHAPTER THIRTY-TWO
TRYSTAN

Trystan was having a quiet supper with Ceinwyn, enjoying the last of the Eskarian cheese his mother had sent a few months ago. The snow continued to fall relentlessly outside, and the pair were sitting in companionable silence when a servant entered with a note. He bowed to Trystan, who took it with a nod of thanks, before ripping it open and reading the brief message a few times.

He frowned deeply and passed it to his chancellor.

Trystan,

I am leaving within the next hour for Deathhold. The training of the new recruits will require my personal supervision over the winter if we are to face the full force of our southern neighbours in the spring.

Unless I hear from you otherwise, I will return after the first thaw.

Nikolas

For a woman who was rarely surprised, astonishment was written over Ceinwyn's face.

She took a deep drink and sighed. "You are both still so young."

"I am only a few years your junior, Ceinwyn. Nik even less

so."

"That may be true, but you are still acting like boys, my king."

"And what, pray, would you have me do? Summon him back? Remove him from his position? Arrest him?"

"No, Trystan. I would have you talk to him." Ceinwyn leaned towards him with an intense stare. "It has barely been two years since you were both thrust into these roles. You changed overnight from being friends and Nikolas being your commanding officer, to you being his king. You laugh and joke together, you hunt animals and chase women, but you never *talk*." She shook her head, her short ebony hair catching the faelights.

Trystan let out a dry laugh. "Have *you* ever succeeded in getting Nik to sit and talk about his feelings?"

"Well, it seems like you've both managed to avoid doing precisely that for the next couple of months at least," Ceinwyn retorted.

"Yes, it seems we have. At least I have you for these warming heart-to-hearts, Ceinwyn." He gave her a mocking smile.

"And I wouldn't change that for the world," Ceinwyn replied, raising her glass. "Nikolas is right about the threat in the spring, though. We need to be ready."

Trystan yanked off a hunk of bread with more force than necessary and slathered it with butter. "I've been thinking about that. Would you go to the Academie in the next few days and speak to the Fellows about strengthening the wards on Valon? If Marcellus attacks, the city seems like the most obvious choice, and I want us to be ready."

"Of course, but you know Brigantium's military might. If they attack before the troops arrive from Deathhold, it is unlikely the wards will hold them for long."

"Perhaps we need to start training the city militia?"

"Hm, I do not think it wise to send out such orders to the people of the city. To do so would only cause panic. I will go to the Academie tomorrow. The longer they have to work on the wards, the better."

The grey sky was thick with snow, casting a gloomy light into Evelin's rooms. Despite it still being early, the morning had already been fraught. William had been particularly stubborn about completing his lessons, wailing that he wanted to play in the snow instead. Only the promise of a hot chocolate and an icy walk in the afternoon had settled him.

"You mustn't be frustrated with him, my lady," Agnes said, her voice soothing, as Evelin plumped up the pillows on her bed with unnecessary vigour. The older woman poured them a hot drink, her blue and white patterned dress a mirror for the design on the porcelain cups. "He's in a new place, having formal lessons for the first time, and doesn't get as much of your attention as he used to."

"I can't help that, Agnes. I'm trying!" Evelin protested.

She felt Agnes' hands on her shoulders, rubbing them gently.

"My lady, you are doing a wonderful job with him. William is a loving and intelligent child, but children push boundaries. All I'm saying is that you shouldn't blame him."

Evelin exhaled slowly through her nose. "Sorry. Sometimes I just feel that I can't do right for doing wrong."

"I've never had children of my own, but I believe that is a fairly common feeling," Agnes chuckled, releasing her grip and passing Evelin a steaming mug. "Gabriel is having his morning nap and the nurse is watching over him. Why don't you take five minutes to yourself before you go to see Ceinwyn? Maybe stop fussing with the bedding? You are aware the servants are going to strip the sheets anyway?"

Evelin set down the pillow she had been holding, a sheepish expression on her face. "Thank you, Agnes," she replied, going to sit on the window seat.

The set of rooms Trystan had provided them with were beautiful, with three sleeping chambers, a private washroom, and a sitting room. They were all tastefully decorated, with high ceilings and large windows allowing as much light as possible to enter. Her sleeping quarters were dominated by a huge four-poster bed, carved from a dark oak. The mattress was cloudlike and covered with soft woollen blankets and masses of pillows, which helped to ward off the chill that seeped through the palace at night. Light green drapes edged with gold hung at the windows, framing the view that Evelin was currently inspecting.

Her bedroom faced out towards the docks, eerily subdued now that winter's grip had taken such a firm hold of Valon. The sea was a frozen wasteland, encasing the city. Wooden ships that had once tossed in the ocean's grasp were now frozen in the port, icicles hanging from the masts and rigging. When her window was open, Evelin could sometimes hear the ghostly sound of the timbers straining against their icy prison.

A beam of sunlight broke through the thick clouds, its light sparkling off the frozen sea. She sat there for a while, sipping her drink and enjoying the stillness, before heading to her tutorial with Ceinwyn.

The Chancellor had been doing the same thing as her. When Evelin entered the office, Ceinwyn was sitting with her feet on a stool, drinking deeply from a mug. Her jaw-length black hair was slicked back severely today. On someone else, the effect might look reminiscent of a skeleton, but it only served to emphasise Ceinwyn's statuesque beauty. The smile she gave Evelin brought warmth to her carved features.

"Good morning. Are you well-rested?"

Evelin's eyes broke away from Ceinwyn's piercing gaze. There was no way she could tell her that she had been lying awake most of the night in that huge bed; that she hadn't been able to sleep for hours as she let herself imagine what it would be like to have Trystan in those sheets with her.

"Enough," she replied, clearing her throat with a slight cough.

"Hm, well, let's make a start." Ceinwyn shot Evelin an exposing look. "We're going to look at something today that I usually only cover with my post-graduate students. It's called the fading glamour. Have you heard of it?"

A spark of recollection flickered in Evelin's mind. "Is that when someone who has seen a glamoured object forgets what they have seen?"

"Almost. It can be an object or person. Anything, in fact, depending on the skill of the spellcaster. The further someone is from the glamour, the less they can remember. It is particularly useful if you want to hide something, or someone, more thoroughly. Any person who has seen it would not even be able to describe the glamour, let alone the real object or person hidden beneath."

"Do you think I could cast that on Gabriel?" Evelin asked, excitement building.

"It will take *a lot* of practice and effort, but with your skill, it should be possible eventually," Ceinwyn conceded. "I think the best way to start is to show you. Tell me, what colour was the dress Agnes was wearing this morning?"

Evelin tilted her head to the side as she racked her brains.

She clearly remembered the two of them being together in her bedchamber, seeing Agnes pouring a warm drink. Her hands balled in frustration as she struggled to recall the colour of the gown.

"I have absolutely no idea," she said, her eyes widening as a smile brightened her face. "My God, Ceinwyn, that's brilliant! When did you do it?"

Ceinwyn nodded, a glimmer of pride and pleasure on her face. "At first light. I sent a note to Agnes last night, asking her to see me this morning. She was only too happy to help with your teaching."

"This would be the perfect protection for Gabriel. Where do we begin?"

"With the theory, as always. However, you must remember that if this glamour is performed incorrectly, it could break entirely. We will need to work extremely hard to get this right."

"Of course. I understand. Which books do we need?" Evelin asked, crossing to the wall of shelves that lined one side of the office, eager to start.

☙

"Can we skate on it, Mama?" William asked, hugging his flask of cocoa as they looked out onto the lake.

The vast expanse of ice was at the furthest boundary of the palace grounds. Not intended for fishing or sailing, it was simply ornamental; the fae-made water wasn't deep and was sure to be frozen solid if the port was.

Evelin tested it circumspectly with her foot, just in case. "Perhaps, darling, but we don't have any skates. We will have to ask Trystan when we get back to the palace."

"That's no fun!" William pouted.

Evelin knelt down and brushed his gently curling locks back off his face and behind his pointed ears. Sometimes she struggled to see herself in his features; his hair was the same vibrant auburn as Otto's and his eyes were a deep brown, the twins of his father's, but she hoped that his temperament would never mirror theirs. She reminded herself of how sweet her boy had been with Gabriel this morning, allowing the memory to calm her anxious mind.

She gave him a calming smile. "I know. I would love to go skating with you, but we can't do it without skates, darling. We would end up slipping over, and we wouldn't want that, would we?"

"No, Mama," William agreed, resigned, before his eyes shot to his right, lighting up with excitement.

Evelin twisted to see what had caught his attention. Trystan was strolling up to them, easy confidence in his movements. He was dressed in a sumptuous grey doublet with a long burgundy cape, no doubt made of the finest material, which emphasised the broadness of his chest. His expression was warm but slightly wary as he approached the pair, stopping a respectable distance from them.

"Good afternoon to you both," he said, a slight spark in his eyes as he met her gaze, before he turned to William. "Lord Ashburner, how are you today?"

A slight twinge of pain pricked at Evelin's heart. She hated how his name linked William in such a proprietary way to his father, and just hearing it made the threats of Marcellus' letter seem far more tangible. She wasn't sure if William noticed her expression change, but she hoped not; she didn't want him to see her fear.

William bowed neatly to Trystan. "Sire, do you have any skates we may borrow, please? I would like to go skating on the lake."

Trystan seemed uncomfortable with the question, his eyes searching Evelin's face for the right answer. She nodded slightly, indicating her approval.

"I think we do, but I will have to check with the groundskeeper. He is visiting an ill relative at the moment, but maybe in a day or two..."

William looked frustrated but nodded and ran off after something that had caught his eye in the snow.

"Thank you," Evelin said.

Trystan shrugged, taking half a step towards her. "No matter at all."

The increased proximity sent Evelin's heart racing, and goosebumps raised on her arms that had nothing to do with the cold.

"Are you free tonight? There's something I think you might enjoy in the old town." There was a quiet confidence in Trystan's smile.

"I'll check with Agnes, but I'm sure I can be. That sounds lovely."

The king took her hand and pressed a light kiss to her glove, looking up at her through his long lashes. "I look forward to it."

CHAPTER THIRTY-FOUR

EVELIN

The streets of the old town were relatively quiet as they walked together. Evelin kept a tight hold of her skirts, lifting them out of the trampled snow that dotted the cobblestone pathways; she was anxious for them not to be soaked through before they arrived at their destination.

She had chosen one of the gowns Trystan had ordered for her from the dressmaker, made of olive-coloured silk with a delicately boned, structured bodice. The draped wrap top was cut lower than she would normally wear, and despite the long sleeves, Evelin was grateful for the fur-lined woollen cloak she wore over it. Agnes had pinned her hair up, with thin tendrils floating around her face, and her subtle make-up enhanced the natural rose colours in her cheeks and lips. She hadn't bothered to put a glamour on herself. Marcellus knew where she was now; it didn't matter if any of his agents saw her.

Evelin thought back to the efforts she had gone to when dressing for their outing. She had tried on numerous dresses and fussed over her make-up, re-doing it when she thought it was too much. 'I want to look like myself, just better,' she had told Agnes, who had chuckled at her repeated attempts.

The look Trystan had given her when she'd descended the marble stairs to meet him in the foyer suggested that she had been successful.

"Where are we going?" Evelin asked, trying to avoid one of the larger mounds of snow.

"Telling you would ruin the surprise," Trystan replied, shooting her a playful grin.

She was about to fish for more information when an older man stopped in their path, staring at Trystan. His eyes widened in recognition before he dropped to one knee, bowing his head.

"My king."

The tips of Trystan's ears reddened and he beckoned for the man to stand. "Please, rise."

The man did so and reached into his pocket. At once, three of the guards who had been trailing them lunged forward, drawing their swords.

The old man's face turned pallid. "No, no! I mean no harm to the king. I just wanted to show him these papers. I was sent a raven from one of my suppliers in Brigantium who has told me that he won't be sending any more stock in the spring. Two other merchants have been told the same. I wanted to ask if the king knew if there was any reason why."

Trystan raised a hand and the guards stepped back, sheathing their swords. He sighed and rubbed a hand along his jaw. "I'm afraid that I am on my way to an engagement. However, I am holding my supplicant meetings tomorrow. Tell the captain your name and he will ensure that you are on the list."

"Thank you, sire, thank you," the man said, bowing so low that his nose almost touched the snow.

"It's my fault, isn't it?" Evelin murmured as they continued their walk. She knew the threat her presence posed, but seeing it impact the lives of Valon's citizens was painful.

"It's no one's fault but Brigantium's," Trystan replied gruffly. "They will do as much damage to their own people as ours if they insist on halting trade. Let's not allow it to spoil our night.

Here we are."

They had stopped in front of a large building with two sets of gilded doors, reached by a small flight of steps. Groups of fae filed past them into the building, some staring at Trystan, but none seeming brave enough to try to get past the ring of guards that surrounded them. Trystan was apparently taking no chances after the attack the last time they had been in the old town.

"I remembered how much you enjoyed the theatre," Trystan explained. "I hope tonight's play won't disappoint."

God, she could have flung her arms around him. It had been so long since she had seen a performance. She had loved going to the many theatres Valon boasted whilst she had been studying at the Academie. To be able to lose herself in the story, the costumes, the music, and the lights for a few hours had been absolute bliss.

Evelin smiled broadly at him. "This is perfect, thank you."

The front of house manager personally escorted them up a wide set of stairs carpeted in deepest red, to the royal box. Two comfortable, high-backed chairs sat close beside each other, overlooking the stage.

Evelin stepped towards the balcony, peering down on the orchestra below. They were warming up, so she couldn't quite hear what Trystan was saying to the manager and guards behind them.

Finally, they were alone, save the captain, who stood stony-faced against the wall.

Trystan stood behind her, and his breath caressed Evelin's neck as he unclasped her cloak. His fingers lingered on her shoulders as he removed it in a fluid motion before pulling out a chair for her. She sat, smoothing out her skirts and wondering what on earth to do with her hands. Luckily, she didn't have to wonder for too long, as the manager returned with two programmes and a chilled bottle of sparkling wine. He poured them each a glass before hurrying away.

"To a night of entertainment," Trystan said, clinking her glass. His eyes never left hers.

Evelin took a small sip, savouring the bubbles that tickled her mouth and throat. The programme told her that the play was a new telling of an old story – the tale of Raphael and his two great loves. Raphael, the son of Igraine and Xoros, was married to Asha. Blessed with the power of healing, he came across an injured woman one day, Seraphina. She stole his heart the moment he laid eyes on her, and he spent his life torn between the two women.

The play was beautifully performed, and the music celestial. Evelin's eyes brimmed with tears. She was so transfixed the entire time that she forgot that Trystan was sitting beside her, apart from once, when their knees brushed, sending tingles through her.

"What do you make of it?" the king asked, refilling her glass during the interval.

"It's marvellous! The woman who plays Seraphina has the most exquisite voice, don't you think? And the lighting is so clever! How they capture the mood, the time of day… Thank you so much for bringing me." Evelin felt giddy from the evening and the wine.

"I'm glad you're enjoying it." Trystan smiled, placing his hand on hers as the lights dimmed once more.

Evelin found it painfully hard to focus on the second half of the play as Trystan lightly stroked her hand, drawing small circles on her skin, before interlacing their fingers. Her chest tightened at the intimacy of the touch, and she couldn't help but imagine his fingers elsewhere on her body. When the curtains finally lowered after several encores, Trystan leaned over and whispered in her ear.

"Let's go home."

CHAPTER THIRTY-FIVE

EVELIN

The walk back to the palace was nearly too much to bear.

Trystan had taken Evelin's arm to help her navigate the streets, which had become slippery from the snow that had fallen during the performance, and the heat of him through their clothes made it difficult to concentrate on not falling over.

When they reached the palace, Trystan signalled to the guards and they discreetly glided off.

He turned to her and pushed back her hood. "I'm going to my chambers and I would like you to join me, but the choice is yours," he said in a low voice, his hazel eyes gleaming.

Evelin swallowed, any ability to form words suddenly gone. She nodded quickly.

He gave her a look that burned straight through her, and took her hand once more, leading her to his rooms.

Once inside, Trystan poured them each a glass of an amber spirit, before stoking the fire. Its pops and crackles were abnormally loud. Evelin held the glass in trembling hands, her eyes darting towards the largest bed she had ever seen, the frame carved from a dark wood, with sheets of midnight blue. The faelights were dim, and all Evelin could think was how practised this all was.

It wasn't that she minded the fact that Trystan had been with so many women before her, it was just that, in the moment, she felt woefully unprepared. Marcellus was the only man that she had ever lain with, and being with him had been functional at best, so she had no idea how to proceed.

Trystan moved towards her and she froze as he planted a gentle kiss on the side of her neck, brushing back some loose tendrils with his long fingers.

Every part of her body hummed. "Trystan, I…"

He paused, looking at her with a mixture of tenderness and desire. "What is it?"

"I know this is going to sound ridiculous. I've done this before, but it was never… I never…"

Trystan pulled away slightly and she felt her stomach sink. Of course he didn't want someone as inexperienced and insecure as she was. Evelin felt like an idiot.

To her surprise, he took her hands in his. She squeezed them tight in her own, running her thumb over a raised scar on his left palm.

"Are you sure you want to do this?" he asked.

"Yes, but…"

He kissed her so gently that the touch was barely there. "Let me take the lead. Tell me to stop at any time if I am going too fast or you don't like what I'm doing… but I hope you will like it very much," he whispered, leaning in once more to kiss her neck. "I know I will."

Trystan tilted her chin up towards him and he kissed her, gently at first, teasing, his teeth grazing against her bottom lip. His tongue flicked into her mouth as his hands caressed her back. Evelin had never needed anyone or anything so badly. It was impossible to stop herself as she reached up and wrapped her arms around his neck, standing on her tiptoes to kiss him back more deeply. His hold on her tightened and he cupped her backside, pulling her in closer towards him. Even through their clothes she could feel the hardness of him pushing against her.

Trystan's mouth moved downwards, kissing her neck, the day's stubble on his sharp jawline scraping her delicate skin. Her nipples hardened against her bodice as his kisses moved to her collarbones, desperate for him to continue downwards, but he pulled away and gazed at her, eyes heavy with lust.

"I think we are both wearing a few too many clothes for what I have in mind," he said, gently turning her around and kissing the back of her neck as his hands made quick work of the lace of her dress.

The gown fell to the floor in a pool of silky green fabric, leaving her in only a short ivory slip. Her nipples peaked under the thin fabric, and she suddenly became conscious of her body – two children had not left her unchanged – and she folded her arms across herself.

"Don't," Trystan interjected, turning her back around. "God, you are breathtaking. Every inch of you is perfect, and I intend to spend the next few hours worshipping every… single… part of you," he murmured, punctuating his words with kisses. "Perhaps this will make you a little more comfortable."
Leading her gently towards the bed, Trystan pulled back the sheets and gestured for her to get in. Evelin's heart was racing as if she had been running for hours. How on earth did anyone focus when they felt like this?

She eased herself back onto the bed, pulling the sheet over herself. He unbuttoned his doublet, shaking it onto the floor, and yanked his loose white shirt over his head. She let out a small sigh as he stood there in just his black trousers. His body was even more beautiful than Evelin had imagined. God help her, she ached to run her hands, her tongue, all over it.

From here, the size of his shaft was all too visible, even constrained by his trousers. He followed where her eyes went and smiled. "Not yet. I've not finished worshipping you."

He slid under the sheet, gently but firmly moving her legs apart, and slid his hand up to just above her knee before lying down next to her.

"Lie back," he murmured, and she obliged, sinking into the feather pillows.

As she did so, he planted a soft kiss on her right nipple, prompting a small moan to escape her lips.

"Would you like more of that?" he asked, his fingers teasing at the neckline of her slip.

"Yes," Evelin whimpered.

He kissed her other peak through the fabric, before pulling the slip down, exposing her breasts and placing his mouth fully around one of her nipples. Pure pleasure flooded through her as he licked and sucked.

Her hands moved to his back, feeling the muscles beneath her fingers.

"God, your breasts," Trystan muttered, reaching a hand down between her legs.

He paused, a question in his eyes, and Evelin opened her legs wider, eager for the feel of him. His hand ran up her thigh, squeezing the soft flesh, before moving up to her centre. He stroked her once, twice, her eyes shooting open at the sheer pleasure of his touch.

"May I continue?" he asked, pausing, waiting for her consent.

"Please," she gasped.

His thumb flicked over the bundle of nerves between her legs, her body spasming in response. Evelin felt his finger at her entrance, pushing in gently and moving slowly within. Her breaths had become ragged and she dug her fingers into his back, desperate for more.

"Patience, love. Let me take my time," he chided as she thrust her pelvis towards him.

She needed to feel more of him, immediately. Moving her hands from above her head, she felt for his shaft, now a prominent ridge in his trousers, and began stroking him through the fabric. Trystan groaned, pushing himself towards her hand. She grabbed at the laces on his trousers, pulling at the knot, as his fingers sped up inside of her. The ties finally gave out when a knock sounded at the door.

"Ignore it," Evelin pleaded, reaching her hand into his trousers.

"I intend to," he murmured as her hand wrapped around the iron hardness of his cock.

He let out a guttural moan and flicked his thumb back and forth over her centre.

The knocking began again, louder and more insistent.

"Hellfire!" Trystan spat. "Do *not* move a muscle," he commanded, pushing himself out of the bed and heading for the door.

"What do you want?" he barked, opening it an inch.

Evelin couldn't see beyond the door, but recognised the voice of the guard who had shown her to Trystan's study when she'd first arrived in Valon.

"Sire, my apologies for disturbing you so late, but the Chancellor has requested your immediate presence," the guard said apologetically.

"Tell the Chancellor that I am otherwise engaged," Trystan snapped.

"I'm afraid she said that it is imperative that you go to the Academie at once, sire."

Trystan let out a snort of rage before slamming the door and walked swiftly back to the bed. "I have to go… You have no idea how sorry I am to be leaving," he said softly, his eyes devouring her. "Do not go anywhere. I will be back as soon as possible, I promise."

Evelin nodded, resigned, leaning into him as he kissed her deeply before tearing himself away with a growl.

CHAPTER THIRTY-SIX

TRSYTAN

"This had better be important, Ceinwyn," Trystan grumbled as he strode into the Dean's office.

The room was uncomfortably warm; a fire was raging in the hearth and the Dean must have cast some sort of enchantment, amplifying the heat, which did little to improve Trystan's mood. He had practically ran to the Academie, adrenaline coursing through his veins. All he wanted was the matter sorted as quickly as possible, so he could return to the woman in his bed. He could still smell Evelin's scent on him, making it incredibly difficult to focus. He scowled at Ceinwyn and the Dean, waiting for some sort of response to justify them hauling him out of bed at such an hour.

"It is, Trystan," she replied gravely. "Master Draxus has been attacked."

"What? What happened? How is he?"

"It's not good. Whoever it was has hurt him badly. He's with the healers now, but I don't think they hold much hope," Ceinwyn explained.

The Dean made his way from the desk towards Trystan, his thin hands clasped together. "My liege, I thought it imperative that you be informed straight away. After your rather... unexpected visit with the Master, I felt this matter would be of interest to you, so I reached out to the Chancellor at once," he said, his eyes searching Trystan's face.

Trystan had always felt a visceral dislike towards the Dean and didn't trust him as far as he could throw him; the man was obsequious, calculating, and far too self-interested.

Trystan set his jaw. "An attack of any of my citizens would be of interest to me, Dean." He turned to Ceinwyn, determined to avoid any more conversation with the odious man. "May I see him?"

Ceinwyn nodded.

The Academie's infirmary was a large, airy room with high vaulted ceilings. Large arched windows allowed clear views of one of the quads in the daytime, and there were two rows of beds along each of the longer walls. Trystan had ended up here a few times whilst at the Academie, usually after getting into some sort of drunken scrape or fight in his first year.

The atmosphere was hushed. A group of white-robed healers were crowded around the bed furthest from the door. From the blue light bouncing off the ceiling, it was clear they were hard at work. Trystan stood back, determined not to interrupt the process. After a few minutes, the healers stepped aside, visibly drained from their efforts. Their faces had lost all colour and they were drenched with sweat. It was then that Trystan saw Master Draxus for the first time.

The old man was porcelain white; his eyes were closed, and his black robes shone with blood. As Trystan stepped forwards, the Master's eyes fluttered open and widened upon seeing him.

"How are you, Master?" he asked softly.

One of the healers turned to him, his face grave. "I'm afraid the attack has left him unable to speak, sire. It appears he was tortured for some time."

Rage and nausea roiled in Trystan's stomach. He knelt down beside the bed and clasped the Master's hand in his own. It was terribly cold and clammy, but the old man gave him a reassuring squeeze. Draxus tried to lift his head, gargling as he did so, before dropping back onto the pillows, gasping for breath.

"Ceinwyn, can you send for Lianna?" Trystan asked.

A slight cough sounded from behind him. "Lianna Ogunjimi? We have far more experienced telepaths here, sire. Let me send for Master—"

"No," Trystan cut the Dean off. "Send for Lianna please, Ceinwyn."

"Of course," she replied, exiting the infirmary quickly.

Trystan stayed there for a while, still kneeling beside the Master in a silent vigil, keeping what he hoped was a comforting grip on his hand. The whole time, the Dean lingered by the bedside, trying to lure him into conversation. Trystan's stilted responses finally had an effect, and by the time Lianna arrived, a tense silence had developed.

"Oh God! Master Draxus!"

"Dean, would you give us the room?" Trystan asked.

"I think I had better stay. The Master is one of my Fellows, after all," he protested.

"That will not be necessary. Thank you for your services tonight, Dean."

With the king's curt dismissal, the Dean left, his expression indignant.

"Ceinwyn told me about the attack. What can I do?" Lianna asked.

Trystan straightened and rubbed his thighs, trying to get some feeling back in them. "I want to know who attacked him. Can you get inside his mind and see? Find out what was said?

Li… please, go gently. I don't want to cause him any more discomfort."

"Of course," she said quietly, closing her eyes.

Trystan paced the length of the infirmary for a painfully long time, lost in his thoughts. The attack on Draxus brought back the feelings of weakness and despair he had felt after the massacre at the palace. He knew he was to blame, and cursed himself for bringing Evelin to see the Master.

God, Evelin! He hadn't sent word to her. What must she be thinking? He rubbed his eyes and shook his head.

A hand came to rest on his shoulder.

"Trys, I've tried, but I couldn't get much. I'm so sorry. I have no idea what was said or what happened," Lianna explained, tears spilling down her face. "I can push further, but I'm afraid that it might be too much for him."

"No. Leave him to rest. Did you get anything at all that may be of use?"

She nodded, "An image of a face. It was half-hidden by a low hood, but it might be something."

"Can you show me?" Trystan asked. Anything was better than nothing.

Lianna placed her long fingers gently on his temples and closed her eyes. Trystan's vision went white as a picture of a man slowly came into focus. The brow and eyes were obscured by a black hood, but just below he could make out a broad nose, a straw-coloured short beard, and reddish skin. As soon as it was formed, the image faded.

Lianna sagged before him, her eyes sunken. "Sorry, Trys. That's everything."

He gripped her arm in thanks and walked out into the quad. He had seen that face before. Trystan scoured his mind for who it might be. It was so familiar, yet he couldn't place it; even their name evaded him, dancing like a wisp in the corners of his mind.

It was only as he turned the corner and entered the cloisters that the realisation dawned upon him. Lianna might not have recognised him, she had barely spent any time with the man, but Trystan had. He knew exactly who had attacked Master Draxus and by God, he would pay for his crimes.

CHAPTER THIRTY-SEVEN

TRYSTAN

The first faint light of dawn was flickering into his chambers by the time Trystan returned. He closed the door behind him quietly and walked softly to the bed. Evelin was fast asleep, bundled up in the sheets and blankets, her red hair spilling out across the pillows. He stared at her for a few moments, enjoying the sight of her in his bed, before gently stroking her back.

"Evelin," he said softly.

She stirred, rubbing the sleep from her eyes as she blinked up at him. A gentle smile crept across her face, and she pushed herself up to sit.

"I'm sorry I took so long. There is something I need to tell you about."

Her face screwed up with concern as he recounted the night's events, and he knew that she felt the same rage and guilt as he did.

"Oh, Trystan, I can't believe it. How is he doing? Is there anything I can do?"

Trystan shook his head. "Draxus won't be with us for much longer, but Lianna did find something. She saw the face of the person who attacked him. Evelin… I recognised him. Do you remember Bryce from the Academie?"

"Yes, of course. He was one of your friends." She paused for a moment, the implication of his words sinking in. "Trystan, you don't mean…"

He stood up and walked across to the window. "That's exactly what I mean. It was him, I'm certain of it."

Evelin wrapped her arms around his waist and pressed her cheek to his back. The tension in his neck and shoulders eased slightly, the intimacy soothing. He wanted nothing more than to take her back to bed, but he knew there were more important things they had to consider now.

"I've made arrangements for you and the boys to leave the city."

Evelin pulled away, turning him around to face her "What do you mean?"

He turned and stroked her arms tenderly. "The guards searched all night but they haven't been able to find Bryce. All we know is that he attacked Master Draxus shortly after we spoke to him. It cannot be a coincidence. Perhaps he is in the pay of Marcellus, perhaps he has just gone mad. Either way, it could be you he comes for next. The only thing I can do until he is found is keep you safe. I will not let him hurt you."

Evelin frowned. "But surely I am safe here? In the palace, surrounded by your guards?"

"Dozens of people enter and leave this place every day. There is a house further inland that can be more easily protected. I will send a detachment of guards and they will protect you and the boys until the threat has been eliminated."

"And what if he comes for you?" Evelin retorted.

"I can protect myself."

"And I can't?"

"No, you can't. Not from him. Please, Evelin, just do as I ask. Go now and pack some things. A carriage will be ready to take you shortly."

She glared at him with a fury he had never encountered from

her before, her fists balled tight. "Fine," she said curtly. "I had better go." She dropped the sheet that had been wrapped around her and grabbed her gown from where it still lay on the floor.

Watching her begin to pull it over her head, Trystan stepped forward to help her with the laces.

"I can do it myself," she snapped, shrugging him off, and waltzed from the room, the back of her dress flapping behind her. The slam of the door echoed through the room.

Why was Evelin fighting him on this? Hadn't she asked what she could do to help? All Trystan was trying to do, all he had ever tried to do, was protect her and her children. Surely, she understood that?

CHAPTER THIRTY-EIGHT

EVELIN

"And where is this house?" Agnes asked.

"I don't know. Somewhere inland," Evelin snapped, gathering up her clothes and the boys' belongings.

She was finding it hard to concentrate on what they needed to take. William was running around, asking a never-ending list of questions, and Gabriel was gurgling happily to himself. She stuffed things haphazardly into the trunks Trystan had sent and instructed the servants on which larger items they would require, such as the crib. They darted in and out, fetching things and laying out a small breakfast for the group.

"Come now, my lady. We'll be back here before you know it. The king is right, the safest place for you and the boys is outside of Valon until all this is settled."

Evelin let out a long exhale. "I know, I know. I just… we've just settled here. But you're right, we will manage. As long as he doesn't send that awful commander with us."

Agnes cocked her head. "You've not heard?"

"Heard what?" Evelin asked as she pushed the final things into the trunks.

"The commander left for Deathhold two days ago. The servants were all gossiping about his unexpected departure. Apparently, he is working with the new recruits. He doesn't intend to return until the spring."

This news soothed the blow of being sent away; at least when she returned to Valon, she wouldn't have to deal with him.

The further he was from Trystan, the better.

CHAPTER THIRTY-NINE

TRYSTAN

Trystan jolted awake. The golden clock on his wall, sculpted to resemble the sun with dozens of thin spears of various lengths shooting out from the centre, read midday.

He groaned. Evelin would have left by now. He had wanted to say goodbye; to leave things on a better note.

Damn.

His stomach panged with hunger, but he needed to seek out the captain of the guards. The deputy had been sent with Evelin, along with a company of twenty men.

As he entered the guardhouse, the captain clicked his heels to attention and gave a smart salute.

"At ease, Captain," Trystan said, looking around the room.

Unlike most of the main floors of the palace, the guardhouse was spartanly furnished. The walls were unpainted and the furniture simply functional. There wasn't even a proper fireplace in the room, merely a cast iron stove upon which a kettle was being heated. The smell was musty – smoke, sweat, and leather curdling together.

Trystan sat on one of the oak chairs and indicated for the captain to do the same.

"Have the searches yielded any results?"

"No, sire. The man is a ghost. We have already spoken to everyone you suggested. His mother hasn't heard from him in several years, and his associates from his Academie days deny any contact."

"We keep going. Order door to door searches if necessary. He will be found and brought to justice."

"Yes, sire. Should we contact the commander, perhaps? He might be able to make contact with some of our agents."

Trystan rubbed the back of his neck. "No, that will not be necessary. The commander will still be making his way to Deathhold. I trust your men are able to deal with this?"

The captain nodded and Trystan took his leave. He didn't want to summon Nik back. If he was being honest with himself, he was still pissed off by his abrupt departure and their fight. He would prove he was capable of leading and of quashing any threat to Parissi's safety on his own.

After leaving the guardhouse, the king summoned two of the men to accompany him. He wanted to return to the Academie to check on Master Draxus. The sight of the old man bleeding and weak in an infirmary bed swam through his mind.

The city was unusually quiet, with few people out and about. A couple of patrons tumbled out of the Crossed Swords Inn as he passed, slapping each other on the back and roaring with laughter. It was jarring to hear people enjoying themselves.

Upon entering the Academie, Trystan went directly to the infirmary. He couldn't stand to be in the company of the Dean for another second, listening to his ingratiating twaddle. Outside the doors was a group of students speaking in hushed voices. When they saw him, they quickly moved away, bowing low, shooting curious looks in his direction.

Various smells sat heavily in the air inside the room: predominantly lavender, sage, and frankincense. The outcome was a potent aroma that made his eyes water. He blinked rapidly, clearing his vision. The Master's bed was empty.

A servant passed, eyes low, carrying a bundle of clean linens.

"The Master?" Trystan asked, his voice catching in his throat.

The woman kept her gaze trained on the spotless dark wood floor, but said nothing, apparently frozen in place.

"Master Draxus passed away earlier this morning, Trystan," Ceinwyn said from behind him. "I only found out a few minutes ago when I came to inquire about the state of Valon's wards."

Trystan's whole body tensed. "Bryce will pay for this."

"We need to find him first."

CHAPTER FORTY

EVELIN

It had been eight days since they had arrived at the house. Constructed of limestone worn down by age, the manor was far more comfortable than it appeared to be from the outside. The southern facade was cloaked with ivy and opened out onto acres of ornamental gardens. The interiors were plushly furnished and far warmer than the Summer Palace in Valon. Rich velvets and damasks covered the sofas and chairs, whilst large fires burned in the hearths. The stone floors were carpeted in rugs from Suryadesh, and the walls boasted artworks from all over the continent. All in all, it was a warm and luxurious place to stay.

Evelin was able to appreciate all of it, but the luxury of their surroundings did little to soothe the wrath that simmered within her. A day after her arrival, she had received a brief note from Trystan informing her of Master Draxus' passing and asking if everything was suitable for their stay. She had replied tersely, despite a scolding from Agnes, merely stating that they had arrived safely. The news of the Master's death had rocked her; she knew that she bore a great measure of responsibility, but it was far easier to focus on her anger towards Trystan than her own guilt.

The guards were at least subtle in the performance of their duties, no more than a lingering presence on the edges of their lives. Still, Evelin felt the same frustration, the same powerlessness she had felt during all those years cloistered in the hunting lodge in Brigantium. After enjoying the relative freedom of life in the Summer Palace, of being able to go out riding and exploring with Lianna, this new reality was a particularly hard potion to swallow.

She tried to use her time wisely, reading through the books Ceinwyn had lent her and practising creating a fading glamour. Evelin loved any chance to exercise her mind and powers, so this provided a good measure of relief. William had also started to take an interest in what she was doing, and she caught him copying her arm movements in the bedroom mirror. To her surprise, flickers of pastel green light blossomed under his palms, before dissolving as soon as he brought his hands down. Not knowing she was watching him, William performed the movement again, and this time the light stayed for a fraction of a second longer.

At only five years old, it was very early for him to be able to control his abilities. Most fae began to exert some influence over their powers around the age of eleven or twelve. Before this, anything they did was usually by accident, or a brief flash brought on by intense emotions. Evelin beamed with maternal pride at her son, but under the surface she felt a small measure of apprehension. What was the extent of his powers? She knew little about Marcellus' family, and would not be writing to ask him.

"Did you see, Mama?" he asked excitedly, finally catching her reflection in the mirror.

"Yes, darling! It was amazing, you are so clever," she praised, ruffling his hair. "Have you been learning about this with your tutor?"

"No, all he does is boring letters and numbers. I just saw you and wanted to try."

Evelin caught the frown before it crossed her face. Perhaps

the best thing would be to help him to use his powers properly. "Would you like me to teach you? It *will* involve books as well, I'm afraid."

"Yes please! Thank you, Mama," he said, flinging his tiny arms around her.

Evelin spent the next few mornings teaching William about the different powers the fae possessed and how each fae tended to have an aptitude for one over the others.

"So, all children are born with the ability to use most powers, but as they reach adulthood, their abilities stop developing unless they are properly trained," she explained.

William nodded at her, his face serious. "But you're going to train me, aren't you, Mama?"

Evelin nodded, smiling tenderly.

Teaching William was absolutely joyous, sharing her knowledge and watching him test his burgeoning skills. It was clear that he loved having something special that was just theirs. Yet Evelin's joy was tinged with pain. In the evenings, as she rocked Gabriel to sleep in her arms, she thought about how she would never experience this with her youngest child. She would never be able to teach him how to use his powers, as most parents did with their children. God, she would outlive him by decades. This was not how it was supposed to be. Every time she looked at her baby, she felt such happiness alongside tremendous grief.

Still, a small ember of hope burned within her. Perhaps her aunt would provide answers, maybe even a cure? Maybe she would see him grow and play with his powers like the other fae children. Maybe she wouldn't have to watch him grow old and die before her eyes.

Maybe.

CHAPTER FORTY-ONE

TRYSTAN

The parchment caught light quickly in his study's fire, its corners blackening and curling. It was the third attempt that Trystan had thrown into the flames this morning. He had absolutely no idea what to say to Evelin. It had been nearly two weeks since he'd sent her to the manor house, and he had little news to impart. She was evidently still furious with him as she had not written in a week, and honestly, he was chafed by her ingratitude. Yet he longed to speak to her, to read her words, to tell her that he was trying everything to make it safe for her to return to Valon… to him.

But the words wouldn't come.

He had just poured himself a measure of liquor from a bottle on the ornate cart that sat by the window when a sharp knock sounded. The visitor didn't wait for a response before the door opened and the captain entered, his hair and clothes in disarray, cheeks red.

"We've apprehended him, sire."

Trystan downed the drink and grabbed Lightwielder, gripping its hilt firmly, before following the captain down to the cells.

All prisoners were kept in the dungeons, which were even deeper down than the basement office Ceinwyn occupied. It was a rarity for anyone to be in custody for longer than a few days.

Valon was generally peaceful, its citizens living in harmony with each other for the most part. The small number of those who were arrested tended to be prolific thieves or constant brawlers. These fae were given the choice of a hefty fine or service in the king's armies. Most chose the military option; a regular paycheck and decent food was, for many, too good an opportunity to miss out on.

That being said, there had been more violent, dangerous criminals from time to time. If they could not be trusted in the army or their crimes were too unspeakable, a swift execution would follow. There had only been one such offender in the years since Trystan had been king. He had beheaded the man with his own sword, his stomach had turned to acid, and he had barely made it back to his chambers before vomiting. Despite this, Trystan knew he was ultimately responsible for maintaining law and order in Parissi, and would never expect anyone else to carry out such a sentence on his behalf.

The cell in which Bryce was kept was one of the larger ones. Darkly cold with bare stone walls and floors, it was a gloomy place. Trystan ducked his head as he entered through the low door frame. The man was secured to a chair with tight bindings around his torso. He was broad and powerfully built, but not particularly tall.

Once his eyes had adjusted to the darkness, the prisoner's face came into view. Trystan's whole body went rigid, the muscles on his forearm twitching and growing taut. He stared into the face of his former friend.

"Hello Bryce," he said.

The captive said nothing in reply, but simply glared at him, his grey eyes burning into Trystan.

"We're going to have a little chat, maybe several little chats, and I will get answers. Starting with why you attacked Master

Draxus."

Bryce eyed Trystan with disgust and spat at his boots. "Go fuck yourself, Trys."

Any control the king had hoped to exercise over himself disappeared. Before he knew what he was doing, he backhanded Bryce across the face, sending his head jolting to the side. Blood began to drip from a split lip, but Bryce simply licked it and laughed.

"Nothing you do to me will make me speak, *my king.*"

Trystan breathed deeply, trying to master himself. This was no good. Letting his anger get the best of him would not improve matters.

"Perhaps you don't have to speak at all, Bryce," he uttered darkly, before walking quickly out of the cell, his boots ringing against the cobbled floors.

Lianna's light, graceful beauty was at complete odds with her surroundings. Her pink-tinged locks fell in hundreds of spiralling curls all around her face, catching the one faelight in the cell.

She leaned in close towards Bryce, exuding calm and focus as he looked lasciviously at her chest. Yet, within seconds, Bryce shook his head like an animal plagued by flies as she reached her hands towards his face. Lianna raised her eyebrows at the guard, who gripped Bryce's head in a firm lock, exerting a little too much pressure on his throat. She tried again, closing her eyes once she had made contact.

"Your efforts won't work," Bryce grunted.

In response, Lianna leaned in closer and screwed her eyes tightly shut. Minutes passed, the two locked in a battle for supremacy, before Lianna stepped away, breaking the connection.

"I can't get through his wards, Trys. They're too strong. I'm sorry," she said, her face drawn and disappointed.

He gripped her shoulder. "Thank you for trying, Li. Maybe a few days down here without food might weaken them."

Trystan had just knocked for the guards to open the cell door when a gurgling sound came from behind him. Bryce was straining against his bindings, feet thrashing. His face was turning puce and spittle flicked out of his mouth. In the middle of his throat, a red light glowed brightly from Bryce's own hand, which was wrapped tightly around it. Before Trystan could even move, the light slid downwards towards Bryce's chest, vanishing from sight.

Trystan grabbed his knife and sliced through the ropes with one quick slash, then lowered Bryce to the floor. Lianna knelt over him and ripped open Bryce's shirt, searching for the vanished red light. His former friend's eyes were bulging, and his tongue had swollen so much that it lolled out of his mouth. Bryce's body spasmed, arms and legs flailing uncontrollably.

"What do we do?" Lianna exclaimed.

Before Trystan could reply, Bryce's head fell to one side, eyes wide and unblinking.

Lianna reached out, feeling his neck for a pulse. "He's dead, Trys. How? What *was* that?"

"I have absolutely no idea. I've never seen magic used like that."

"Neither have I," Lianna replied, still staring wide-eyed at Bryce's body. "At least the threat has gone now. Bryce got no more than he deserved."

Trystan said nothing. Bryce's lifeless body lay motionless on the cold stone floor. He had been a friend once, never close like Evelin, Lianna, or Nik, but a friend. Now he was dead, killed by his own hand. Yet there was no pity in his heart for Bryce; all

Trystan felt was disgust for what his former friend had done. He had taken the life of someone who had tried to help Evelin, and Trystan still had no idea if Bryce had found out about the baby. If so, had he told anyone else? The man's death simply left him with more unanswered questions.

"Trys?" Lianna's voice broke through his spiralling thoughts.

"Hm?"

"I said, are you going to tell Evelin she can come back now?"

Trystan considered his options. On the one hand, he still did not know if Bryce had been working alone, or if the danger had truly passed. On the other, he knew that Evelin would be happy to leave the manor, even if she wasn't particularly thrilled to see him again. He rubbed his temples. Why was his life just a series of impossible decisions? The weight of his crown felt heavier every day.

"You write to her, Li. Tell her it's safe to come back," he said, hoping that he spoke the truth.

CHAPTER FORTY-TWO

EVELIN

The journey back to Valon felt much longer than it actually was. The countryside was empty, devoid of life, and glazed with snow and ice. They passed the occasional village, no more than huddles of houses positioned around a stone church, spirals of smoke floating up into the sky from the chimneys. It was a bitterly cold day, so Evelin supposed everyone was warming themselves inside. The windows of the carriage were edged with frost, and though the sun shone, its beams were too weak to melt it fully.

Evelin was wrapped in two cloaks with an extra blanket over herself and the baby in her arms. Agnes and William had snuggled up together on the bench opposite, the boy's head laid on Agnes' lap. He had been so excited to be going back to Valon, eager to see if Trystan would keep his promise about skating on the lake.

Evelin's stomach did a little flip every time she thought about Trystan, a mixture of anger and excitement passing through her. She still resented being sent away, not being given a choice, but she also remembered being together the night before she left. How it felt to be wanted, to want him.

She shook her head, trying to clear those images, focusing instead on what she intended to say to him when she saw him again.

By the time the carriage pulled up in front of the grand entrance, dusk had already taken hold of the city. It was a clear night and the first stars had already emerged, glittering pinpricks in the dark fabric of the sky. Trystan wasn't there to greet them and Evelin wasn't sure if she was relieved or annoyed by his absence. The two women carried the boys gently to their beds and laid them down.

Evelin took a few moments to freshen up, tying back her hair into a braid and splashing some water on her face. She was wearing a warm gown sewn from crimson velvet, with sleeves that cut away to reveal flashes of white. The bottom was damp from the snow outside, but she decided against changing. She wanted to see Trystan before dinner. It would be better to speak alone; there was much that needed to be said.

She twirled her hair nervously on the walk across the palace to his rooms. When she reached his door, Evelin paused. She could do this. Closing her eyes, she rapped sharply twice on the door. No reply came. She tried again. Still no response.

Damn it.

She spent the next half an hour or so wandering the palace, trying Trystan's study, the library, and his rooms again, but to no avail. There was nothing for it but to face him at dinner. She could have asked for food to be brought to her rooms, but she had set her mind to see him tonight, and she would not be cowed back into seclusion, even for the evening.

Trystan, Ceinwyn, and Lianna were already sitting at the table, enjoying a glass of wine in the informal dining room when Evelin entered. She purposefully avoided Trystan's eyes and sat down next to the Chancellor, smiled at Lianna, and poured herself a drink.

"No Agnes tonight?" Lianna asked.

Evelin shook her head. "No, she was tired from the journey and wanted to get an early night."

An uncomfortable silence lay thick in the air. Evelin wished the food had already been served, to give her something to do.

Lianna scraped a hand through her hair. "How did your hunt go earlier, Trys?" she asked, her voice deliberately light.

"Poorly," he replied, not offering any more. He rolled his knife between his fingers, its steel catching the glow of the candles and sending beams of light shooting across the room.

There had been a similarly tense dinner a year before she had entered the Academie.

Her aunt, Katyana, had been visiting, and Evelin had spent the day wandering the grounds of Azmar with her. Katyana was a stunning woman. Slender, and with hair of the lightest blonde, she had the air of the mystical about her. She had the same soft singsong accent of her mother and told the most wonderful tales of growing up in Caledon.

They laughed together and reminisced about old times. Her father never spoke much about her mother, so Evelin had relished the chance to hear about what she had been like. When they'd sat down to eat, Evelin had felt lighter than she had in a long time. The sensation, however, was not to last long.

Just after the first course had been served, her aunt had clattered down her cutlery. 'Titus, surely, as her closest female relative, I know what is best for Evie. You must stop all this nonsense about her joining the Academie. She should come to Elysara and train as a priestess. You know she would be well cared for. She has a touch of the divine about her, don't you think?'

Her father's face had been thunderous. He'd eyed Katyana through his piercing blue eyes set deep under dark bushy brows. 'She's going to the Academie. It has been decided.'

Katyana had sighed theatrically. 'But Titus, it's such a waste of her natural gifts! Izzy would have wanted—'

Titus had slammed his silver goblet down, droplets of wine splattering the tablecloth. Evelin remembered thinking it resembled blood as it seeped into the linen.

'Do not presume to tell me what my wife would have wanted. My daughter has many talents, and she will be trained properly at the Academie, by people of science.'

The discussion clearly over, the dinner had continued awkwardly. Otto had made various inane contributions, needling their father further. Whilst Katyana had made becoming a priestess sound truly magical, attending the Academie had always been Evelin's dearest wish. To be able to study and to improve herself was all she'd wanted. She was grateful that her father had stood his ground.

By the time she yanked herself back to the present, Ceinwyn was saying something about wards to Trystan. Lianna tried valiantly to keep the conversation going, and Ceinwyn appeared oblivious to the tension, but Evelin's contributions were brief, and she only spoke when absolutely necessary. Every time she glanced at Trystan, the same seething anger began to seep slowly through her veins, so she focused on her food, avoiding the king's gaze wherever possible.

By the time the final course was finished, Evelin was desperate to return to her rooms, all ideas of confronting Trystan forgotten.

"Ceinwyn, Lianna, would you give us the room?" Trystan asked, just as she was about to stand. "Evelin and I have things to discuss."

Ceinwyn stood immediately and left with a swift goodbye, but Lianna paused. She looked to Evelin, her eyes asking if she should stay. Evelin shook her head and gave her a small smile through pursed lips. She was truly blessed to have such a loyal friend, especially one who would defy a king's wishes for her.

On the way out of the room, Lianna kissed her on the cheek and shot a look at Trystan that would have made a weaker man shrink under the table, but he said nothing and simply refilled his glass.

Once alone, Trystan pushed his chair back from the table and went to sit in a padded one by the fire, cradling his drink. "Are you going to sit there all night or are you going to come and talk to me?" he asked, his voice carefully measured.

Evelin clenched her fists, running her thumbs over her knuckles. She wanted to storm out, but she refused to give him the satisfaction. With a deep breath, she stood up and sat in the furthest chair from him, looking into the leaping flames.

"Shall I start, then?" Trystan asked.

All Evelin could see of him were his long legs, stretched out before him as he lounged in his chair.

When she gave no response, he sighed. "Honestly, I cannot understand why you are so angry, Evelin. You know full well that I only asked you to leave Valon for your own protection. As soon as the threat was neutralised, I informed you and you were able to return. I fail to see why you are still sulking."

"Sulking?" She dug her fingers into the velvet arms of the chair, leaning forward. "You truly have no idea, do you? Don't sit there saying that you *asked me* to leave. You *sent* me away, Trystan."

He rubbed absentmindedly at his chest. "You are picking over details there. Does it matter?"

She took a deep breath, her nostrils flaring. How was he incapable of understanding this? "Of course it matters! You treated me just like Marcellus did. Another man sending me away, keeping me away from court, away from my friends – my life! You may be king of Parissi, but you do *not* command me."

Evelin stood, unable to resist the urge to move. She walked closer to the fire, running her hands through her hair.

Trystan exhaled deeply behind her. "I merely wanted to keep you safe. I'm truly sorry if I have caused you pain. That was never my intention."

Out of the corner of her eye, she saw him stand, and before she could comment, he stalked over to her and gripped her shoulders tightly.

His eyes seared into her, as if daring her to speak, to challenge him. "Damn it, Evelin. Every moment you weren't here was the most horrendous kind of torture. Not being able to talk to you, to touch you…" He ran his hand lightly down her arm, sending sparks shooting through her. "You must know that I would never do that lightly."

She closed her eyes, forcing down the anger that had now dampened to a glowing ember. "I know," she admitted. "I'm sorry too. I shouldn't have said that. It was wrong of me. I know you're not like Marcellus."

Her heart galloped as the warm glow of the fire reflected off the king's hazel irises. No one had ever looked at her like Trystan did, as if she was the only person in the entire world that mattered. Suddenly, her hands were in his hair, pulling his mouth towards her. She kissed him firmly, insistently, as his hands stroked down her back. It felt like all the rage she had held for days had instantaneously transformed into pure, burning desire. Every part of her longed to touch him, to be held by him.

He kissed her back, matching her pressure, before pulling away.

"My rooms, now."

CHAPTER FORTY-THREE

EVELIN

Evelin's nerves bubbled up once again as Trystan gently pushed her back onto his bed. Nervous laughter built as he stood before her, and when Trystan began to unbutton his golden doublet, a giggle leapt from her lips. She covered her mouth, mumbling an apology, hoping he might laugh too.

He didn't.

Instead, he pulled her to her feet and placed her hands on the buttons. "You do it."

Her fingers trembled as she wrestled with the tiny hooks and the solid gold studs. It didn't help that Trystan was tracing his hands ever so lightly over her neck, her shoulders, moving down to her clavicle. He ran them along the neckline of her dress, stroking her chest with the barest touch, before sliding them ever so slightly underneath the fabric. She couldn't help but let out a small moan as the tip of his forefinger caught her nipple.

The sound broke whatever self-control Trystan had been attempting to exert and he pushed her hands aside, yanking off both his doublet and shirt in one swift move. He kissed her ear, his teeth nipping at her lobe, as he unlaced the back of her crimson gown with practised hands. He pulled it down her arms, and she was very conscious that she wore nothing underneath and was standing there in front of him completely naked.

The king took a half-step back and let his eyes roam over her, his expression greedy. "You are just as beautiful as I imagined," he murmured. "Now, lie down."

Evelin did as bid, biting back the desire to tell him that he still didn't command her. As he moved over her, all she could think was that, in this moment, he *could* command her. She would do whatever he wanted as long as he kept looking at her like that.

Trystan moved closer to kiss her and his bare chest pressed against her own, setting every inch of her on fire. She stroked her hands up his strong arms, pulling him closer as the kiss deepened, their tongues intertwining. He continued his attentions with his mouth, moving down towards her breasts, his kisses light and teasing. When he reached her nipples, he placed one featherlight kiss on each, before gently sucking, grazing them with his teeth.

"Oh God, Trystan," Evelin moaned, pushing her hips up towards him.

His hand reached down and stroked her gently between her legs, sending jolts of pleasure through her. His finger moved slowly round her entrance as he licked her nipple, his eyes burning into her.

"You like this, don't you?"

"Yes," she panted as he pushed his finger into her.

Desire built within her, a tight knot of longing, desperate for more. But all too soon he withdrew and knelt up. He began to unlace his trousers, revealing the long hardness of his cock.

"Are you ready?" Trystan asked, and she nodded, unable to form words.

Carefully, he guided himself to her entrance and pushed inside her. Everything else melted away. All Evelin could focus on was the feeling of him filling her, moving within her.

As her walls tightened around him, Trystan began to move, thrusting in and out, slowly at first, then faster. Her hands were everywhere, running over his heated skin as his movements became more urgent, synchronising with her desperate cries of pleasure.

"Fuck, you feel so good," he moaned in her ear.

The sound of his words alone brought her to the edge. He moved his hand over her breast, and she felt herself explode, clenching around him.

Trystan let out a guttural cry as he found his release, before collapsing on top of her, utterly spent.

They lay together, limbs wrapped around one another for what felt like hours, but was likely only minutes, before Evelin drifted off into a dreamless slumber.

Dawn's faint light had begun to creep into the room when Evelin woke. For a few moments she had no idea where she was, but there was Trystan, lying beside her. He blinked the sleep from his eyes and smiled at her languidly.

"Come here," he murmured, pulling her against him and stroking his hand down the curves of her side.

She felt his shaft harden against her as his hand reached round and cupped her breast. Within seconds, he was above her again, pushing into her. It was slower this time, less urgent but no less pleasurable.

Afterwards, she rested her head on his chest and he gently stroked her back, until she began to shiver from the cold of the morning.

"You're cold." Trystan stood from the bed and grabbed a thick fur from the dresser, pulling it over them both and rubbing her arms to warm her.

Evelin nestled into his side. "Can I ask you something?"

"Anything."

"Why do you remain in the Summer Palace over winter? I thought your uncle always moved his court to the Winter Palace before the first frost."

Trystan didn't say anything for some time, and Evelin began kicking herself for asking at all.

"I can't leave the Summer Palace," he said softly. "I won't leave it. I've not left since I became king. I just… I can't. I wasn't here when… when the attack happened. I swore to myself that I wouldn't leave again until I could be sure of its safety. Besides, it's still too soon after for me to leave. The people of Valon look to me, and if I left, they would see it as weakness. They wouldn't feel safe in their own city. I have to put up with a bit of a chilly home in the winter, but there are worse things in the world."

"I'm sorry for asking—"

"Don't apologise. You're my friend, Evelin. I want you to feel free to ask me anything."

Evelin felt her whole body freeze. *Friend.* She had naively thought that last night, what had gone on between them over the past few weeks, had made them more than that. She cringed inwardly. This was Trystan. She knew what he was like. She knew that he didn't *do* relationships.

Easing herself from the bed, she began gathering her things. "I'd better get back to my rooms before the boys wake up. I should have gone back to check on them last night, and I have a lesson with Ceinwyn today."

Trystan sat up in bed, as if he might protest, but then simply nodded. "Perhaps I could see you again this evening?" he asked, giving her a roguish smile.

"Yes," she said, just a fraction too quickly. "That would be wonderful."

CHAPTER FORTY-FOUR

TRYSTAN

Trystan walked to his supplicants meeting feeling lighter than he had in weeks; in months. Last night had been exactly what he had needed, and a grin spread across his face at the memory.

Strolling past the line of citizens waiting patiently for an audience, he spotted the trader from the night at the theatre. Guilt needled at him as he settled himself in the reception chamber.

The room, like many in the Summer Palace, had walls and floors crafted of marble, with swathes of royal blue fabric draped at the windows. Upon the dais was a throne, which was slightly too ornate for Trystan's taste, but tradition dictated that this was the seat from where he would receive his supplicants. It was carved from wood and gilded with gold, with a sapphire velvet seat. He had no idea why his ancestors had favoured it – the damned thing was hideously uncomfortable.

The morning passed relatively quickly; most of the issues brought to him were easy to deal with, or could be delegated to someone with more expertise in the matter.

As the familiar trader stepped before him, Trystan apologised profusely for the last two supplicant meetings being cancelled due to urgent matters, and the trader's bluster evaporated. To Trystan's relief, the old man accepted his assurances that he would ask the Chancellor to reach out to the Brigantian king.

It was simple enough to shake away the niggle that plagued his conscience as Trystan continued with his audience. No one would be any better off if the state of diplomatic relations with their neighbours became widely known. No, it was far better that calm persisted. After all, the people would never judge him for taking in a woman and her children who asked for sanctuary. Valon prided itself on being a city that welcomed all, and that pride must remain sacred.

Trystan's head was pounding by the time the afternoon's meetings were over. The captain had wanted to discuss the city patrols and resource allocation in tremendous detail. Next, his emissary to Eskaria had demanded that he pour over the minutiae of a new trade agreement, which was predominantly concerned with the proper ageing of cheese. Following that tedium, Ceinwyn had gone into lengthy explanations of the theory behind the new wards created to protect the city. By the time she had finished talking, Trystan was rubbing his temples, eyes half-closed.

"I trust our plans meet with your satisfaction?" Ceinwyn asked, stepping away from the chalkboard she had dragged over for the meeting. Its dusty face was covered in squiggly lines and symbols that had lost all meaning to him hours ago.

He nodded wearily. "Yes, thank you for meeting with the Fellows," he said, standing and stretching his stiff muscles.

"There's one more thing," Ceinwyn added as he turned to leave.

He raised his eyebrows in a silent question.

"I know it is still relatively early in the winter, but I thought we should discuss Luminara. The festival will be upon us in a matter of weeks."

Trystan sighed and pinched the bridge of his nose. The day had been a trying one, and this was the last thing he wanted to talk about. What he *wanted* was a stiff drink and to see Evelin again. The image of her in his bed, moving beneath him, had plagued his mind all day, constantly threatening to break his concentration. No wonder he had a headache from the effort of focusing on the business of state.

"Do we have to talk about this now?"

"I think we do," she replied firmly. "We did not hold the lightgiving ceremony the last two winters. The people of the city have been understanding, but I don't think that will stretch to another missed festival. With the trading issues between us and Brigantium, I believe a return to some sort of normality is called for." There was a watchfulness in her eyes as she spoke, as if she might spook him.

Luminara was the high point of the winter months, especially for a port city surrounded by ice after the weather turned. It was celebrated on the last full moon preceding the end of Valon's hard winter, shortly before the first thaw began. Under King Silas' reign, and all of Trystan's ancestors', the festival was marked by three days of feasting and revelry. Balls and masques would be held at the palace, poets would give recitations, and musicians would perform their newest pieces. The festivities culminated with the lightgiving ceremony on the final evening. The king would cast his magic out over the city from the balcony of the Summer Palace, a symbol of the light and warmth that would soon return to Valon.

Since the massacre, the festival had been unmarked. The streets of the city had remained quiet and subdued, with none of the usual balls or feasts. Trystan knew that no one had expected any celebrations that first winter, only months after the death and destruction that had been wrought upon the city. However, there had been murmurings of discontent last year, and with the concern about trade with Brigantium, he too wasn't sure if the citizens' patience would hold.

"Then we will have to mark Luminara," Trystan conceded, slumping back into his chair. "The people may have their parties and feasts, but there will be no celebrations in the palace."

Although he hadn't been at the ball when Silas and the countless others had died, he had heard about the aftermath from the guards who had finally broken in. They had recounted in grim detail the horrors they had found. He had no stomach for hosting another ball right now. It felt disrespectful and slightly like tempting fate at a time of such international danger.

Ceinwyn tilted her head to the side, the faelights illuminating the magpie blues in her hair. "And the lightgiving ceremony?"

"The ceremony will be held as usual," Trystan said, trying hard to disguise the slight increase in pitch of his voice.

Ceinwyn gathered together the papers she had brought, not looking at him. "I will send out orders to start the preparations."

Bowing shallowly, she turned to take her leave.

He was trying to be better at this, to be better at a job he had never asked for nor expected, but it was so damned hard. His uncle had made it look so easy, but it was just one fucking thing after another at the moment.

He would not be cowed by this.

"Ceinwyn?" Trystan's words stopped her just as she reached the door.

"Yes?"

"I... I need your help. With summoning the light. I... I haven't been able to since my coronation, and even that was... well, it wasn't as I intended. If I'm going to perform the ceremony, I can't make a mistake. The people cannot see me falter."

His chancellor gave him one of her rare smiles; it was small and over in the blink of an eye, but it softened her words. "Coming to me for assistance with light magic won't do you much good, Trystan. You know that it is one of my weakest gifts. Why don't you speak with one of the other Fellows, Master Kramer, perhaps?"

He shook his head, "No, I can't have news of this leaving the palace. The Fellows are a load of old gossips, Ceinwyn. That Dean will use any such knowledge to his own advantage."

"Well, perhaps you should speak with Evelin? She performs light magic adequately and, if I remember correctly, is one of the few people whose tutelage you seemed to take on board."

"Mm," Trystan hummed noncommittally. "I'll think on it."

God, the last thing he wanted was to admit to the woman he had just bedded that he couldn't summon his own powers. But that wasn't something he could say to Ceinwyn.

"You should," she said, opening the door to leave, pausing in the doorway to give him a knowing look. "She's good for you, you know."

The Chancellor left without another word, and Trystan sat for a few moments, thinking over what she had said. He had never been in any doubt that Evelin was good for him.

Whether he was good for her was another matter entirely.

CHAPTER FORTY-FIVE

TRYSTAN

Later that night, Trystan lay next to Evelin in his bed, tracing his hands lazily down her bare back, enjoying the sight of her smiling at him. Whoever said that sleeping with a friend was a mistake was obviously an idiot.

"I'm going to have to go in a minute," she murmured, wriggling as his fingers grazed a particularly sensitive patch at the base of her spine.

"Are you sure I can't tempt you to stay?" he asked, moving his hand a fraction lower.

She sucked in a sharp breath, before rolling away, tugging the sheet with her. "No, I really have to get back to the boys."

He shook his head as she reached for her dress. He was always amazed by her self-control, knowing full well that he did not possess the same virtue. Ceinwyn was right, Evelin was excellent at mastering herself.

"Before you go, may I ask you a favour?" Trystan stayed where he was in the bed, propping his head up on one arm.

"Of course," Evelin replied distractedly as she hunted for some item of clothing that had been cast off earlier.

He chuckled silently to himself. He hadn't been particularly careful when relieving her of her clothes. He half-wanted to stop her, to get her full attention, but then again, maybe it would be easier to admit his weakness if she wasn't looking at him.

"Do you remember how much fun we had when you tutored me in second year?" he asked, running his free hand through his hair and grinning at her. *Yes, keep it light. Keep it easy.*

"Hm, I remember that you were a particularly reluctant tutee most of the time," Evelin replied, pulling on a translucent stocking in a highly distracting way.

"Well, I was wondering if I might, um… beg for your services again?" He tried hard to sound casual. "It's been a while since I've used my light magic, and with all the busyness of ruling, I'm afraid I've gotten a bit rusty. Do you think you could possibly work with me on it? I would repay you in ways that I know you enjoy…"

Evelin paused, touching the base of her neck. She opened her mouth to say something, then closed it quickly. "Of course. It will be fun to have a study partner again."

"Thank you," he said, relieved. "Are you sure you can't stay a bit longer, so I can thank you properly?"

The pillow hit him in the face before he even knew it was coming.

"Well, that was unnecessary." Trystan laughed and flung it gently back at her.

"You are incorrigible! I told you, I need to go. I'll see you tomorrow. For studying," she added with a smirk.

He sank back into the soft warmth of the bed. She truly was a remarkable woman.

Sleep claimed him quickly that night, and soon, visions of dancing lights taunted him in his dreams. He was on the balcony, and before he could even summon the light, buzzing little balls of it flew around his head. They got closer and closer, multiplying until his vision was blinded by the brightness and he had to hold up his arms to shield himself.

When he awoke the next morning, he felt more tired than

before he had gone to sleep. Plenty of caffeine would be needed if he was to be a functioning adult today, let alone a king.

CHAPTER FORTY-SIX

EVELIN

The next few weeks passed in a blur. Evelin's days were filled with snowy walks with Agnes and the boys, punishingly intense lessons with Ceinwyn, and cosy chats with Lianna. After dinner, her nights were spent working with Trystan on his light magic, before more often than not winding up in his bed. She felt like a student at the Academie again during those evenings with Trystan; the strain of trying to raise her children in foreign court, the constant worry in the back of her mind about Gabriel… all of it faded away when she was sat with him, laughing and working on their magic.

His command of the light was improving, but progress was slow, and it didn't help that he was easily distracted and far more eager to retreat to the bed than to put in the hours required studying. When they started their sessions, he had barely been able to summon the light for more than a split second. With time though, and at least *some* study, he was now able to perform basic light spells with ease. He could light and dim the faelights adeptly and create balls of light that danced at his command, but the more complex spells eluded him.

Those in full control of light magic could do many various and wondrous things: use the light to find those telling the truth, illuminate the correct path to a hidden destination, or even temporarily blind any would-be attackers. The spell needed for the lightgiving ceremony was not intricate, but it did require a tremendous amount of power. The ruler of Valon would cast their light out to the crowd, lighting up the city for hours, whilst the population danced and revelled in the streets. Evelin knew that Trystan would once have been able to perform the spell with ease, but he would need to continue with his studies if he was to acquit himself well come the festival of Luminara.

Training with Trystan was more enjoyable than she had expected. He sometimes frustrated her with his lack of focus and desire to take more breaks than necessary, but he was excellent company. It was so good to feel useful, to have a bigger purpose again, and to spend time with her friend. The only thing that continued to trouble her was the fact they hadn't spoken about the nature of their relationship, nor what they were to each other. If Evelin was being honest, the uncertainty made her uneasy, but she didn't want to mess up whatever was going on between them. It was so nice to feel desired and to act upon her own desires, that she pushed the thoughts down and tried to focus on being in the moment.

An unspoken rule had developed between them; after their lessons, they didn't talk of anything serious, and though they might spend hours in Trystan's bed, she never slept next to him. She told herself that maintaining some kind of separation was sensible, and would ensure that she didn't do anything to jeopardise the intimacy between them that she spent her days waiting for. But every time she left him, it felt like a part of her heart splintered off, never to be mended.

CHAPTER FORTY-SEVEN

TRYSTAN

It was only two weeks until Luminara, yet Trystan still hadn't been able to make the spell hold longer than twenty minutes, and its reach was nowhere great enough to light up the city.

The panic was building inside of him, and he would often wake suddenly in the middle of the night, drenched with sweat, his heart pounding. Barely a day passed where he didn't make up his mind to tell Ceinwyn to cancel the ceremony; surely it was better to disappoint a few partygoers than to reveal himself as the fraud he was? Yet, by the evening, after he had trained with Evelin, he felt more in control, as though he might be able to manage the spell.

It crossed Trystan's mind to write to Nik, too. The last time he had felt this woefully unprepared for something had been during the first weeks of his military training. It had been Nik who had helped him get through the gruelling physical exertions. Every morning, the recruits had been woken by a loud bell before dawn. Before being allowed breakfast, they had been forced to run five miles out of the settlement, place a stone with their name carved into it on a mile marker, and return. The mornings were spent running obstacle courses and doing punishing aerobic workouts, while the afternoons were consumed by weapons practice.

Each year, a handful of recruits were selected by the sergeant to join the Ironforged – an elite group of soldiers who were taught how to channel their magic into their own weapons. They were honed into the deadliest legion in the fae realms. Nik was among the best of them, but Trystan had never been selected, though he had eventually managed to acquit himself well enough in training, with a lot of help from Nik. His friend was the reason he had managed to survive that first year.

But Trystan couldn't bring himself to draft a letter. No, he would leave Nik to stew at Deathhold. If he wanted to be a sulky little prick, he could go ahead.

CHAPTER FORTY-EIGHT

EVELIN

"Check." Trystan sat back with a smug smile on his face. He had persuaded her to take yet another break from studying and play a game.

Evelin picked up a piece, but before she could place it down, he cut in.

"You don't want to do that—"

"Don't tell me what I want to do, Trystan."

He leaned forward and kissed the inside of her wrist. The piece nearly dropped right out of her hand.

"It's not very gentlemanly to attempt to distract me," she argued, breathing a little faster.

"Come now," he said, looking at her intensely. "Surely an expert player like yourself would not be distracted by one small kiss?"

"Hm." She tried desperately to focus on her next move. Though she would never admit it, he had derailed her train of thought. *Damn.* Maybe two could play at this game. "Did you know Master Draxus gave me a potion when we visited him at the Academie?"

Trystan sat bolt upright and frowned. "No, you never said. What is it?"

"I honestly have no idea. I'd forgotten I even had it until William found it earlier when he was building a den in my room."

"Why would he give you a potion? Do you think it has something to do with Gabriel?"

"I doubt it… I'm sure if it did, he would have said. I'm reluctant to ask anyone at the Academie, though, just in case."

Trystan didn't reply. Good. She needed time to think, to ponder her next move.

Ah! "Check mate." She leaned back in her chair and smiled.

He rubbed his forehead. "Well, it appears you have won. What would the victor like as her prize?" he murmured, leaning over and kissing her neck.

"Mm… I know what I *really* want."

"You only have to ask," Trystan promised as he slipped her dress down off her shoulder.

"Two more hours of studying," she said with a chuckle and pushed him away. "Now, try the incantation again."

CHAPTER FORTY-NINE

TRYSTAN

Trystan was sparring with one of the guards in the training ring, trying to shake off some of the nervous energy coursing through him, when a servant arrived, carrying a message. He paused and unravelled the straps from his knuckles before tearing open the seal. It was a message from one of Parissi's few remaining agents in Brigantium; with Nik away, they now reported directly to him.

The missive contained little information, merely confirmation that Brigantium continued to prepare its troops but had made no move towards the border. It was barely worth the paper it was written on, but at least Trystan didn't have to deal with anything further on *that* particular front.

Trystan returned to his efforts in the ring, but his mind was no longer focused. The guard – who was called Owen – landed a few punches that he should have avoided easily. Owen's face contorted with fear and regret after each blow, which only served to frustrate Trystan further.

"I'm terribly sorry, sire. Are you alright?" he asked, passing the king a nearby towel.

"Of course. Let's continue," Trystan responded briskly. Having to reassure the young man that he was perfectly fine after every slight knock was getting wearisome.

The two continued for a few more rounds before Trystan

made his excuses and returned to the palace.

He had barely stepped into the foyer when Ceinwyn accosted him.

"How is your training for the ceremony going?" She was wearing her old Fellow robes and had her short hair slicked back.

"It's going," he replied. "Off to the Academie tonight?"

"Yes, the Dean is presiding over a service for the Fellows in memory of Master Draxus," she explained. "Evelin tells me you're making progress."

Trystan bristled slightly. She was pushing for information and he didn't like the thought of the two of them talking about him behind his back. "Some, but it seems that you don't need me to keep you abreast of that."

Ceinwyn arched an eyebrow and pursed her lips. "No, I do not." She swept her cloak around her slim shoulders and descended the steps into the early evening.

Trystan balled his fists and strode purposefully back to his chambers. While a servant drew him a bath, he wrote a short note to Evelin, telling her that he was feeling under the weather and would not be up to any studying tonight. Sinking into the tub, he drew in a sharp breath. The sting of the scalding water on his aching limbs felt sublime.

He lay his head back against the hard copper edge of the bath and inhaled the scent of eucalyptus that was drifting up from the water. The tension began to leave his body, but his mind still whirred. He needed to be able to perform the spell, but he just couldn't face any more practice tonight. Perhaps a couple of his old friends from the Academie might be amenable to some drinks and cards?

Yes, an evening of distraction might be in order.

"Who would have thought it?" the man laughed, spraying ale from his mouth.

"Not me!" his companion chortled, slapping his knee.

"She is *not* my betrothed," Trystan said and knocked back his drink. "I knew I shouldn't have said anything to you two. We are merely friends with some additional… privileges."

"I wouldn't mind getting some privileges from her," the first man sniggered with a crude gesture.

The Crossed Swords was thrumming with people. Lively music was playing, and the place was packed. The three men occupying Trystan's usual booth had been keeping the barmaid busy with their orders.

"Are you going to play your hand or not?" Trystan asked. He was losing patience. The two men were old friends from the Academie and were usually excellent company, but something about them grated on him tonight. Perhaps it was his conscience telling him that he should be back home studying with Evelin.

"Khaim!" the man replied, slapping down his cards with a flourish.

"We're not playing Khaim, you idiot!" Trystan groaned, though even in his frustration he couldn't stop a snort of laughter. "Should we call it a night?"

"What? The night is still young! Anyway, a couple of friends said they would join us in a little while…"

"Yes, come on Tryst… Trysthhhh… Treestan," the other man whined. "There's no better wingman than a king."

"Yes! And you owe us for ignoring us for so long."

Trystan sighed. It was true – he hadn't been the best of friends recently. "Fine. One more hour. Then I am going home."

CHAPTER FIFTY

EVELIN

The sun was fully risen before Evelin dared to visit Trystan. The potion in her hand was still warm from the palace healer – a simple draught of lanfire root and witchbane to ward off whatever sickness was ailing her friend.

Agnes had given her a questioning look when she hadn't left after the boys had gone to bed last night, but Evelin had enjoyed an evening of easy conversation with her companion. She had been feeling guilty recently about leaving Agnes on her own so much. Last night had been a good way to make up for her absence, and Agnes had also managed to identify the potion given to her by Master Draxus. Evelin was sure Trystan would be interested to hear what it was.

She knocked softly on the door to Trystan's private chambers, but when no answer came after a good minute, she turned the handle slowly and let herself in, as she did most evenings. The drapes were still drawn and the faelights were dim, so it took a few heartbeats for her eyes to adjust to the gloom.

The room was in total disarray. Chairs were overturned and empty glasses lay strewn across every surface. A man of about thirty years old lay on the floor snoring loudly, his clothes dishevelled. Another man was curled around a slim female, both lying on one of the sofas. The room stunk of stale liquor and sweat.

What on earth had happened?

Picking her way across the room, Evelin attempted to avoid the various pieces of clothing and glasses dotted around the wooden floor, and halted. There, on the bed, was a tangle of bodies. Two beautiful women, wearing nothing but their slips, lay sleeping, and between them was Trystan. He was propped up slightly on the pillows, the women lying on either side of him, one with an arm draped over his bare chest.

Evelin froze. What on earth was she looking at? Should she scream in rage or run from the room? Did she have any right to? Before she could decide, Trystan's eyes shot open and darted straight to her. He pushed himself upright, brushing the arm from his chest.

"Evelin, I… it's not what it looks like," he started, moving across the gigantic bed towards her. His feet tangled in the sheets as he tried to stand.

"Trys, what are you doing? Shut up, it's too early," the woman with gold-blonde hair muttered.

The king ignored her and walked up to Evelin, taking her face in his hands. He looked down at her with a blurry intensity, his eyes bloodshot.

"What did you do?" she managed to whisper, pulling away from his touch.

"Nothing. Nothing happened," he said, stepping towards her as she withdrew further. "I went out for a couple of drinks with some friends. They wanted to come back here and so I said they could stay over."

Did he think she was an idiot? That she could be lied to so easily? Cold rage built in her. "In your bed?"

Trystan glanced away for a second. "Nothing happened," he repeated, his voice earnest. "Trust me on this. I know this doesn't look good, but they are just friends."

Evelin raised an eyebrow a fraction. "Aren't we *just friends*?"

Trystan's features shifted from pleading to confusion, his eyes scanning her face. Why did he seem perplexed by her question?

"Yes… no… we're…."

"We're done is what we are." Evelin's eyes prickled with angry tears, and before one could fall, she spun on her heels and ran from the room, leaving Trystan standing half-dressed and surrounded by the wreckage of the previous night's debauchery.

CHAPTER FIFTY-ONE

TRYSTAN

Ceinwyn took over the role of tutor without comment, only giving the king a severely raised eyebrow and slight shake of the head.

Training with her was far less pleasant than with Evelin, Trystan reflected, as his chancellor drilled him on theory for another interminable hour.

After his fight with Evelin, he had almost thrown in the towel and cancelled the lightgiving ceremony. But after spending that morning nursing the worst hangover he had experienced in years, and wallowing in self-pity, the memory of his uncle's eternal disappointment had spurred him into action. He had cleared out his fellow revellers and taken an ice-cold bath, before marching down to Evelin's rooms.

It was Lianna who had greeted him at the door.

"Trys, you need to piss off. She doesn't want to talk to you and neither do I." Lianna had attempted to shut the door, but Trystan thrust his foot into the gap, grimacing as he held it open.

"Li, come on. You know I'm not like that. I wouldn't do that to Evelin. Just let me talk to her, or at least let me show you the truth."

"No. Evelin showed me already. I don't need to see any more. You promised me you wouldn't hurt her! You've fucked up and you need to deal with the consequences. Now move your damned foot."

He had backed away, stung by the words. He knew it had looked bad, he could admit that, but his friends were blowing it out of all proportion. Well, damn them. If they wanted to think the worst of him, so be it. He had known that blurring the lines of friendship with Evelin was stupid, and he cursed himself for thinking with his cock. God, he truly was living up to his reputation as King Silas' irresponsible nephew if that's what they thought of him.

Trystan would prove them wrong. That wasn't him. He would not embarrass himself further in front of his people, nor would he disappoint them by calling off the ceremony. He had gone straight to Ceinwyn, begging her to help prepare him, and for the past fortnight he had spent every waking moment, when not engaged in state business, honing his power.

His exertions sapped every ounce of his energy and, by the end of each day, he fell into a deep slumber. But his dreams were haunted by visions of Evelin, in his arms, in his bed, her long red hair fanning over the pillows. Her laugh echoed in his ears each night, and Trystan woke, no longer in panicked sweats, but rather with a feeling of abject loneliness.

He had barely laid eyes on her in the past two weeks, and on the one occasion he had, whilst she was speaking with Ceinwyn in the library, she had made her excuses and left immediately, not even looking at him.

A battle raged inside him; he wanted to plead with her for forgiveness one minute, then yell at her for questioning him the next. Instead, he had done nothing, her silence wounding him more than Nik's beating all those weeks ago.

"Shall we finalise the arrangements for tomorrow?" Ceinwyn's words broke his thoughts.

"Yes, of course."

CHAPTER FIFTY-TWO

EVELIN

"And you will be attending the ceremony, of course," Ceinwyn added as Evelin stood to leave their session. The Chancellor's expression did not bely any hint of question.

Evelin paused, twisting her hair around her fingers. "I don't think my presence is necessary?" she half-asked, half-stated.

Ceinwyn continued to look through the papers she was holding and pursed her lips, saying nothing in reply. The awkwardness of the silence was heavy in the air.

"I'm not a member of the court," Evelin protested, panic clear in her voice. "And I haven't spoken to Trystan in two weeks. He doesn't want me there, anyway."

Ceinwyn sighed and laid the papers on her lap, turning to Evelin. "That man doesn't know what he wants, but you *will* be there, Evelin. As a show of respect to the kingdom that has given you and your children refuge, if nothing else. You know the rumours that are circling about relations between Parissi and Brigantium. Seeing the Brigantian Princess Royal standing on the palace balcony may ease concerns."

"But what if…"

Ceinwyn cut her off with a wave of her hand. "I will see you this evening. Good day, princess," she said, before turning back to her documents.

Evelin's face glowed red as she left Ceinwyn's office, a sigh escaping her. Apparently, she *would* be attending the ceremony after all.

CHAPTER FIFTY-THREE

TRYSTAN

Trystan spent most of the afternoon in the training ring, working out the excess energy pumping through him. Despite the chill, he was stripped down to just his trousers and working up a sweat. He was practising punches on a dummy, fists blasting into it time and time again. Owen had excused himself an hour before, the captain having summoned all of the guards for a briefing.

Tonight's festivities would be the first large gathering in the city since the massacre, and Trystan knew the captain wanted to make sure that everything went smoothly. There would be guards stationed throughout the city, as well as a cohort keeping the line between the crowds and the steps to the palace. The main gates would be thrown open and the people of Valon would be able to wander the grounds of the palace, enjoying the final night of Luminara. In the past, a grand ball would be held after the ceremony, with dignitaries from the city, the Academie, and the other fae kingdoms invited to share in the celebrations. But not tonight. Tonight, would be as short and simple as possible.

Footsteps sounded on the wooden floor, and Lianna entered, dressed in a stunning gown of pale pink silk, her hair coiled around her head.

She glowered at him. "Ceinwyn sent me to fetch you."

"And there was no one else?" Trystan asked, puzzled.

"The servants are all busy preparing food parcels to go out

to the families in the Stacks," she explained, tapping her foot impatiently.

Another prickle of guilt plagued him. The Stacks was the poorest area in Valon; he should be doing more to help the people who lived there. Valon was generally affluent, but there were still pockets of poverty, much to his shame.

"Are you coming or not?" Lianna snapped. "Ceinwyn said I wasn't to leave without bringing you back in. If you don't hurry up, you won't have time to change… unless you're intending to go dressed like that?"

Trystan sighed. "I'm coming," he said, unwrapping the straps from his reddened knuckles. As he dropped the wrappings to the floor, he paused. "Li, you know I didn't sleep with those women, don't you?"

Her eyes were cold. "No, I don't."

Trystan ducked under the ropes and came to stand in front of her. "Please Li, let me prove it to you. Enter my mind – you will see that what I say is the truth."

"Trystan, I don't think that's a good idea… Evelin already showed me what she saw."

"Please. Am I not your friend as well?"

Lianna frowned, but reached forward and placed her hands lightly on his temples. Trystan felt a shiver run down his spine as she delved into his memories. He had been working on his mental wards as well as his light magic, but dropped them as she probed.

After a few minutes, she stepped back, a slightly sheepish smile on her face. "I'm sorry I didn't believe you, Trys."

"It's alright, I understand why. It looked bad, I know that, and I shouldn't have lied to Evelin about going out."

"And you probably shouldn't have let that crowd back up to your room," Lianna added. "Don't you have about a hundred spare bedrooms in this place?"

He laughed bitterly. "No, I shouldn't have let them come in. I was an idiot."

"Yeah, you were." She nudged him with her shoulder. "You can't treat Eve like that though, Trys. She's not one of your usual conquests. She might appear controlled, but underneath it all she's vulnerable. You do know how much you mean to her, don't you?"

Trystan didn't say anything. What could he say?

"Come on," Lianna prompted. "Let's get you presentable for the ceremony. Although… if you turn up looking like that, a large section of the city will think all their Luminaras have come at once."

Trystan grunted, a faint blush colouring his cheeks. "I think formal attire would be more appropriate. Let's go."

CHAPTER FIFTY-FOUR

TRYSTAN

An inky darkness had fallen on the city by the time Trystan stepped onto the balcony. He tugged at the neck of his white shirt, which peeked out from beneath a royal blue tunic. A stiff collar, edged with gold, brushed irritatingly at his freshly shaved jaw. Blood pounded in his ears and he fought to keep his breathing even as he set eyes on the huge crowd assembled below. The entire city had come out for the occasion.

Stepping slowly towards the edge of the balcony, he gripped the cold stone railings, and excited murmurings rippled through the crowd. A cough sounded behind him; he wasn't the only one standing on the balcony. Hovering by the windows was the Dean, bouncing on his heels expectantly.

"Shall I call for silence, sire?" he asked, bowing his head.

Trystan didn't reply as he cast his eyes over the rest of the small group; Ceinwyn wore the official scarlet robes of her chancellorship, Lianna was next to her, and there, at the back, was Evelin. She took his breath away. Dressed in an ivory gown that fell off her alabaster shoulders, a circlet of gold plaited into her hair, she was a vision of royal perfection. His gaze returned to her face; she was smiling softly at him. Relief washed over him. Whatever happened tonight, seeing her smile at him once more made everything worth it.

The dry, obnoxious cough barked again.

He turned to the Dean. "Thank you, yes."

The Dean strode forward, his black velvet robes billowing behind him. He raised one arm to the crowd and, twisting his hand slowly, brought it rapidly back down to his side. The people knew the sign and fell into an eager hush.

Trystan returned to the edge of the balcony, his mind whirring. He looked down at his arms, straining to command them to rise, to perform the spell, but they hung there, numb and impotent at his side. He swallowed. He was going to fail at this too, and the whole city would see how weak their king truly was.

A soft, slightly cold hand settled over his own.

He turned to find Evelin at his shoulder, waving gracefully to the crowd.

"Just breathe. You can do this," she whispered, her thumb rubbing the back of his hand as her eyes remained fixed on the crowd.

Evelin's words unleashed something within him. Dropping her hand, he thrust his arms outwards, casting the spell. Golden spheres of light shot from his palms and out into the night sky. Their paths curved and swirled above the heads of the citizens below, leaving trails of glowing embers in their wake. The crowd oooed and ahhed as they followed the path of the light, their eyes wide with wonder. The dark of winter had been banished, and Valon glowed.

Warmth filled Trystan's chest. He had done it. The light had spread far and wide, glowing brighter than he had ever managed before; somehow he knew it would hold, burning through the night until dawn broke and the last remaining revellers stumbled to their beds.

He tore his eyes away from the sight. Evelin's pale hands grasped the ledge as she leant forward. Lips parted and eyes wide, she was taking in every second. The spell illuminated the strands of her hair and her eyes burned bright, reflecting the light.

She turned to him. "It's so beautiful, Trystan. I knew you could do it."

He smiled tenderly and inclined his head towards the open door, subtly raising his eyebrows. She nodded briefly and followed him back inside the palace. Once out of view from the people outside, he took her hand and led her back to his chambers, looking around every few seconds to check that she was still there. When the door closed behind them, he took her in his arms and kissed her deeply.

"Trystan..." Evelin broke away from his embrace for a second. "I'm so sorry I didn't believe you, I—"

"No," he interjected, brushing a loose strand of hair off her face. "*I* am sorry. I shouldn't have lied about feeling unwell. I shouldn't have let them back up to my room, especially when I'd had so much to drink. I didn't even realise they had climbed into bed with me—"

"It doesn't matter," she said, planting a soft kiss on his jaw.

The sensation sent shockwaves through his body. God, he had missed this. He had missed *her*.

"You were brilliant tonight. I knew you would master the light."

"I think you were the only one," he replied softly, as she trailed kisses down his neck.

Her eyes were bright. "I wish you could have seen what I saw."

Her expression was so open, so fervent, that he couldn't stand not having her closer. Trystan pulled her in, pressing his chest against hers, and kissed her with a fiery intensity. Her hands grasped at his tunic, releasing the clasps before she peeled it off him. He ran his mouth down her neck as he tore at the lace of her bodice. The gown fell to the floor, leaving her once again in just a slip.

Trystan's hands cupped her backside and lifted her off her feet as she wrapped her legs around him. He carried Evelin towards his bed and laid her down, before stripping off the rest of his clothes. The scent of her – lavender and some sort of spice – made his head spin.

"Please," Evelin begged.

"Are you ready?" he asked, running his finger between her legs.

She writhed under his touch, a whimper escaping her lips. "Yes. Now. *Please.*"

Trystan pushed her legs apart and guided himself inside her, pressing in just an inch. She grabbed at his shoulders, pulling him towards her.

"Do you want more?" he asked, one corner of his mouth curling upwards. He loved seeing how much Evelin wanted him, how she needed him.

She raised her hips towards him, desperate.

"Be patient," he whispered in her ear. She moaned, her frustration building. "That's it. Good girl."

He was determined to take his time, to savour every moment. Not being with her the past two weeks had been a particular kind of torture, and he would not be rushed. He entered her a little more, moving back and forth, just a fraction. The feeling of being inside her was almost too much.

"Please," she murmured in his ear, and his self-restraint finally buckled.

He thrust into her, feeling her clench around him.

"God, I love this," he murmured. "I love you."

Evelin's eyes flickered open, searching his face, and he paused, hardly daring to move in fear of ruining everything yet again.

"Do you mean that?" she asked, her voice trembling.

"Yes. I love you. I love you, Evelin. You don't have to—"

"I love you too," she whispered, her eyes sparkling.

Those words freed him in so many ways, and he lowered himself inside her again, his gaze never leaving her own as he made love to her. There was no barrier between them now, no pretence of mere friendship. His soul was hers, and he gave it gladly.

Once they were finally sated, Trystan rolled back next to Evelin, pulling her close to him. The scent of her hair, rosemary and lemon, wafted towards him as he kissed her forehead softly.

"Thank you," he whispered.

"What for?"

"For everything. For believing in me, even when I didn't believe in myself. For making me a better man." He paused. He needed to say more, to explain. "I'm not sure we have ever just been friends, Evelin, but when you asked me, I didn't know how to answer. You are, and will always be, first and foremost my friend, and I never want to lose that. But to never be able to kiss you, hold you, be intimate with you ever again is a far worse prospect."

Trystan felt Evelin's mouth curve into a smile against his chest.

"Yes, we wouldn't want that," she murmured, sleepily.

He ran his hand down the curve of her side and pulled the sheets over them. His eyes felt heavy and he hugged her close, enjoying the sensation of her bare leg nestling between his.

As he drifted off to sleep, he reflected that, if he believed in it, he would swear this must be what heaven felt like.

CHAPTER FIFTY-FIVE

EVELIN

A faint tapping woke Evelin from her slumber. It was still dark; she hadn't meant to fall asleep. Easing herself from the bed, she took care not to wake Trystan. The noise grew louder and more insistent. Where was the sound coming from? Her mind was addled with sleep. Then she saw it – a raven at the window.

Evelin gently pushed up the sash and goosebumps rose all over her body as an icy blast rushed into the room. The raven held out its leg obligingly and she untied the message. Its duty done, the bird hopped onto the window ledge and soared into the dark night. The note was addressed to her.

My dear Evie,

Thank you for your note and for reaching out. All is well with me. In fact, we have had a particularly good winter. Our three new novices are all performing their duties with great care. I believe I have done particularly well in their selection. They are kind and respectful girls who bring much credit to our order – and me, of course!

Our order is thriving, but I still always feel a twinge of sadness when I think about how happy you would have been among us. What a Priestess of Igraine you would have made, Evie! Maybe you would have even risen to be my successor one day. Still, I thank God and Igraine

Evelin's hands shook as she reread the message. Wray Keep was at least a week's ride away, possibly even more before the winter eased. It would also mean crossing into Brigantium. Would the Stertborg Pass even be crossable yet?

Trystan was lying in the twisted sheets, his gorgeous golden-brown hair rumpled across his face. If she told him, he would never let her go. She had forgiven him for sending her away to the manor, but she knew that his first thought would be to protect her; to keep her here, where she was safe.

Evelin understood his concerns. Going into Brigantium would be a huge risk, but she needed answers. She had to know what was wrong with Gabriel. If there was a chance that she could help her baby, she must take it. Trystan would only stop her, or talk her into waiting. This was the only way.

With only the briefest of backwards glances, she gathered her things and left.

The sun was rising and the last spheres of light glimmered faintly in the sky as Evelin pulled her brown, hooded cloak up over her head. She had picked a simple, grey woollen dress for the journey; it was warm, and shorter than her usual gowns, just skimming the tops of her riding boots.

The corridors of the palace were empty and silent – the servants always enjoyed a day off after the lightgiving ceremony, and everyone else was still asleep. Evelin tried to step lightly to disguise the sound of her boots clacking on the floor of the back atrium. Everyone might be in bed, but she didn't want to draw any more attention than necessary.

Two guards were stationed outside, leaning against the pillars that framed the back entrance to the palace. They shot to attention, hands reaching for the swords strapped to their side. Evelin pushed the door wider with her foot, a large basket in her arms.

"I have the final food parcel for one of the families in the Stacks," she said, giving them a tight smile. "Cook said I had to drop it off first thing."

"Not much of a day off for you, is it?" the nearest guard chuckled.

"No," she replied, hugging the basket tight to her chest. "But I'll be able to go back to bed soon if I hurry."

"Fancy some company when you get back?" the guard asked, giving her a lascivious look.

"I may have to take you up on that offer," she said, looking up at him through her lashes. "But I've got to hurry now. Maybe I will see you later?"

The guard stepped aside and gave her an overly dramatic bow. As she stepped past him, she felt a large hand squeeze her bottom, making her jump. She pushed down the desire to strike the man, to scold him for daring to touch her, but she had to be quick. Why did so many men think that women were no more than objects to be handled at will? Now was not the time for this fight, she reminded herself, but one day…

"Cheeky!" she said instead, giving him a wink as she stepped lightly down the steps.

There were still a few revellers wandering the palace grounds as Evelin made her way to the stables. The horses were quiet, enjoying their breakfast in the warmth of their stalls. Placing her basket down, she pulled back the cover. Inside was a bulging saddle bag, packed with the provisions she would need for the journey.

A grey mare poked her head over her stall door and nickered at Evelin. She stroked the beast's long nose and began tacking her up. Once the saddle bag had been strapped on, Evelin led the gentle mare out and mounted quickly, before guiding them calmly out of the grounds and through the gates, still wide open for the festivities that were finally ending.

She turned away from the docks and headed inland, towards the forest that stretched nearly to the Brigantian border. In no time at all, the trees began to grow thicker, and Evelin felt a small measure of relief. She had made it out.

CHAPTER FIFTY-SIX

TRYSTAN

Trystan reached his arm across the sheets, feeling for Evelin's warm body, but the bed was regretfully empty. He rubbed his eyes; daylight was streaming in through a gap in the curtains. He had hoped that Evelin might've stayed. He wanted to have her again. Those weeks without her had felt like years. God, he wanted to have her every minute of the day. She must have gone back to the boys. No matter, he would see her later.

The room was cold. No servant had been in to light the fire, so he would remain where he was for a while longer. Lying there, Trystan felt perfectly at ease for the first time in years. Sleep soon claimed him once again, and by the time he woke, he was ravenous.

Wrapping a soft robe around himself, he went to pull back the curtains, stretching his neck from side to side. He squinted, adjusting to the brightness outside. The palace grounds were finally empty, but he could see the debris of the previous night's festivities scattered through the rose garden. The icicles hanging from the window frame were dripping sporadically onto the ground below. The thaw had started.

His earlier calm began to fade as reality dawned on him. If the winter was easing here, it would be happening in Brigantium even faster. If Marcellus did attack, it could be sooner than they had expected.

He needed to send a raven.

Trystan spent the remainder of the day in meetings with Ceinwyn and the captain of the guard. He paced his study during their discussions, throwing questions and scenarios at them in quick succession, and by the evening, his mind was so full of plans and remaining problems that he could barely function.

The informal dining room was quiet. Ceinwyn and Lianna were both reading in companionable silence by the fire.

Lianna looked up at him as he walked towards them. "I've managed to rustle up some things from the kitchen."

She gestured towards the strange selection of food on the low table in front of her. A thin slice of pie, some bread, cheese, and a few sad looking vegetables lay haphazardly on a board.

"Looks delicious," Trystan said with a hint of sarcasm.

"Yes, it's not the best dinner I've ever had," she replied, tutting slightly. "However, I did find plenty of wine. I think it pairs wonderfully." She poured him a glass as he sat down next to her.

Trystan took a deep swig. "Where's Evelin?" he asked, looking around.

"Not hiding behind the curtains," Ceinwyn commented, as he turned back to face her.

"Don't start," Trystan sighed, tearing off a chunk of bread. "It's been a long day."

"I've not seen her today. The nursemaid will be having the day off, so she's probably just with the boys," Lianna reassured him. "Anything I can do to help, Trys?"

Trystan chewed his food, staring into the jumping flames of the fire. "Maybe, just not yet."

After he had eaten as much as his stomach could handle, he took his leave and headed for Evelin's chambers. He ached to set eyes on her after such a long and difficult day. Besides, after what they had admitted to each other last night, calling in on her surely wasn't overstepping?

Trystan knocked firmly on the door and waited.

Agnes answered, her hair in disarray and her expression severe.

"Hello, Agnes," he started, giving her a broad smile. "Is Evelin here?"

"Sire, I have *just* got the boys to sleep, please would you be a little quieter." Agnes stepped into the corridor and pulled the door to behind her.

"Ah, yes. Of course. Sorry," he apologised, not feeling as confident. Something about Agnes had always unsettled him slightly; her sharp eyes tore through any bravado and saw the uncertain boy that so often lurked beneath. "May I speak with Evelin, please?"

Agnes rubbed her left wrist, wincing as she did so. "Sorry, sire. My ageing joints are aching tonight. I had better get to bed." She turned to re-enter the room.

"May I speak with Evelin?" Trystan repeated. The old woman was clearly going senile. How old *was* she? He would have to speak to Evelin, maybe get a healer to take a look at her.

"Ah, sorry, sire. The princess is resting and asked not to be disturbed," Agnes said, stepping into the room. "But I can wake her, if you require her presence?" She shot him another severe look.

Trystan sighed. "No, that will not be necessary. Thank you anyway," he replied, taking his leave and returning quickly to his own rooms.

When Evelin didn't send word in the morning and wasn't at dinner the next night, Trystan went straight to her chambers before he had even finished the first course, knocking softly this time. When Agnes answered the door, he spoke first.

"Agnes, I must speak with Evelin. Let me in, please," he ordered, stepping towards her.

"Sire, I don't think that is wise. It is chaotic here. The little lord is refusing to go to bed and—"

"I can handle a little chaos. Let me in," he repeated, frustration growing.

When Agnes didn't respond, he brushed past her into the rooms. A nursemaid was pleading with William to get into his night clothes whilst he bounced on one of the couches. The cacophony of sounds assailed the king's ears, but Evelin wasn't there. Nor was she in the main sleeping chamber.

"Where is she?" he demanded.

Agnes drew herself up. "She's not here, sire."

"Then where the hell is she?"

Agnes' gaze shot to William, struggling into his night clothes. "She's gone, sire," she whispered.

The words didn't make sense. "Gone? Gone where?"

Agnes moved with surprising grace and speed across the room and passed him a crumpled note. "She left this for you, sire."

Trystan read it and re-read it, not taking the words in. "She's gone back to Brigantium?"

Agnes swallowed. "Yes, sire. She contacted her aunt many weeks ago after your visit to the Academie. The princess only recently heard back from her."

He gripped Agnes by the arm. "When did she leave?" he

asked, tightness coiling through his chest.

Agnes flinched under his grip. "Yesterday, at first light," she said, not meeting his stare.

"Damn it!" Trystán swore, releasing Agnes and storming from the room.

Why hadn't Evelin come to him? There was no reason for her to travel alone; he had guards aplenty. Alone, she had no way to protect herself from any danger. He balled his fists, trying to control the panic rising inside him.

Brigantium might be Evelin's home, but Marcellus had been clear about what he would do to her if he found her. Grey spots buzzed around the edges of his vision. He blinked rapidly, trying to clear them. He had to think. He had to figure out how to get her back.

The wind howled through the trees, snagging at branches and kicking up detritus. Evelin tried her best to make herself comfortable, nestled against the roots of a large silver-oak. The ground was damp below and there were drifts of snow around her. Perhaps this hadn't been the best idea.

She pulled her cloak tight, shivering into its folds. She had set a small fire, but she didn't want to risk a larger one and draw unwanted attention. Her arms and legs trembled with cold and she drew her knees up to her chest, hugging them for warmth. Gabriel. She was doing this for Gabriel, she repeated to herself, trying to block out her physical discomfort. If Katyana had answers as to why he was a fae-borne human, maybe there was a solution. Maybe she could have the life she envisaged; maybe he could too…

A branch cracked and woke her from her slumber. Evelin's eyes shot open and scanned the forest. Her breath quickened, and she reached for the knife that she had shoved down her boot, holding it out in front of her. Her pointed ears were alert, sensitive to the smallest sound. The wind had died down and there was just the gentlest rustle of overhanging branches. Her own heartbeat was the loudest thing in the forest. She tried desperately to master her breathing, to instil calm.

Just when Evelin had managed to convince herself that the

noise was nothing, she smelled it. Sickly sweet with death and decay.

A mournwraith.

Mists swirled between the trees, coalescing and forming a shape as she pushed herself further back against the trunk. The knife shook and an icy panic took hold of her. Evelin had never seen a mournwraith, but she had read about them and the scent that accompanied them when she was a child; there could be no mistaking it. Mournwraiths were perhaps the most feared of all the dangers lurking in the borderlands. Few had seen them and lived to tell the tale, so descriptions of them were often vague. What *was* known was that they appeared to travellers, took the form of a deceased loved one, and lured them back to their nest to feast upon them.

She couldn't do this; she wasn't strong enough. Why had she come on her own? Why hadn't she asked for help? She was going to die. The boys would be left all alone, just because she hadn't wanted to be held back. What kind of a mother was she?

The mists began to gather from the ground up. They eddied and spiralled, twisting into shape. The hem of a gown appeared, two feet peeking out from under its grey folds.

"No," Evelin croaked, her mouth dry.

She knew the form the creature was going to take. Evelin closed her eyes against the vision, but she was well aware that no strength of will would stop it. The creature would lure her back. It would know the words to say to get her to look it in the eyes and follow it willingly. *Think, Evelin.*

The potion.

Slipping a hand inside the pocket of her dress, she fished around for it. Among the collection of special leaves William had given her and various notes she had put in her pocket to read later, she found it. With shaking hands, she removed the stopper slowly, careful not to make a noise, and swallowed the vial's contents in one.

The pearlescent silver liquid burned like the fires of hell as it slipped down her throat. It stole her breath and her eyes filled with tears that stung, but she fought hard not to gasp out loud. The corners of her vision blurred. Was this supposed to happen? What if Agnes had been wrong? Her chest constricted and it became hard to breathe, but something changed. The air in front of her rippled and around her some sort of translucent casing developed.

It had worked.

Thank you, she mouthed silently, and closed her eyes against the coalescing shape.

The bottle Master Draxus had pushed into her hands had been a shielding potion. One that would conceal the identity, even the whereabouts, of the person who took it. She had packed it in case she came across someone who might do her harm in Brigantium. It was dangerous to be a lone traveller on the roads these days, especially being a woman. However, whether it would work against a mournwraith was another matter entirely.

Evelin opened her right eye a fraction. Before her stood a woman of immense beauty. Long, wavy hair cascaded down her shoulders. She had a light and easy smile, and her eyes darted around her.

"Evie, darling. Where are you hiding? Come to Mama."

Tears pooled in Evelin's eyes as she heard her mother's voice for the first time in decades, her chest wracked with silent sobs as she held her hands over her mouth, stifling her cries. She wanted nothing more in that moment than to run into her mother's arms.

The mournwraith glided through the clearing, looking around. It couldn't find her; it couldn't lock eyes with her because of the potion.

"It's bedtime now, sweetheart, let's go and read a story," the siren voice of the mournwraith called out to her. Because that is what it was – a wraith. It wasn't her mother. Evelin's mother had been dead for years, and if she followed it, she would meet the same fate.

It wasn't her.

It wasn't her.

Evelin held her nerve and closed her eyes. She didn't want to lose the image of her mother. Her father had taken down every portrait of her mother in Azmar, and she had no idea where they'd gone. This might be her last chance to look at her mother's face… but she had her own children now, and what good was she to them if she was dead?

She kept her eyes tightly shut for goodness knows how long, until the voice faded. Finally, when she braved looking once more, the clearing was empty, though her heart was hollow.

It felt like she had lost her mother all over again, but Evelin was still alive, still breathing. All she had to do now was make it until dawn.

CHAPTER FIFTY-EIGHT

TRYSTAN

Trystan stalked through the wide corridors of the Summer Palace, the smack of his boots reverberating off the walls. He was sick of everything being so damned difficult all the time. Growing up, he had assumed that being king would be immensely freeing; that a monarch would have the power to do as they wished and bend everyone to their will. The reality couldn't have been more different. Rules not of his making constricted him at every turn. Impossible situations kept presenting themselves, and *he* was expected to find a solution that would please everyone.

Evelin's presence in Valon hadn't made his reign any easier, pushing his country to the brink of war, and now her absence had him considering what he wouldn't give up just to see her again. Physical pain prickled through his chest at the thought of her alone in Brigantium. Damn the woman to hell, he would give up nearly anything for her.

Trystan let out a bellow of rage and slammed open the door of his chambers, spending the rest of the evening wallowing, quite literally, in a deep bath, knocking back liquor.

It was nearly midnight when Lianna burst into the room.

"I'm assuming she didn't tell you about leaving either?" she asked, paying no heed to the fact that the king was completely naked in the water without any remaining bubbles to cover him.

"For God's sake, Li! You could have knocked!"

She gave him an exasperated look and threw him a robe. "I'll avert my eyes to protect your royal modesty," she said sarcastically, turning with an exaggerated flourish.

Trystan pushed himself up, water dripping from his body as he shook the water from his hair. It needed a cut, and he needed a shave.

Once dressed, he turned to Lianna. "Of course she didn't tell me. Do you think I'm such an idiot that I would let her go into Brigantium alone? If it wasn't tantamount to an act of war, I'd march over the fucking border and bring her back myself. That woman does whatever the hell she pleases; it's not the first time she's run away in the middle of the night, is it?"

Lianna turned to him, a concerned expression on her face. "I'm sorry, Trys. I know you're hurting. But that's not exactly fair, is it? You can't compare her fleeing from Marcellus to her trying to find answers about Gabriel's condition."

Trystan sagged onto the bed, head in hands. "I can't believe she left without telling me. This is why relationships shouldn't last more than a few nights. At least, mine shouldn't."

"For God's sake, Trys, stop with this tedious self-pity. You know why she's gone. Not everything is always about you," Lianna snapped, her hands waving violently. "Evelin's a mother before she's your... whatever she is. She's doing what she thinks is right."

"And it's right to leave her children here? Alone?" Trystan's ire was up. He had been certain that Lianna would have at least offered some sympathy. She had to be worried about her best friend too.

"They are fine with Agnes." She paused, softening her tone. "Listen, I agree. Eve shouldn't have gone out alone, but perhaps there is another option. I could go after her."

Trystan raised his head. "What?"

"I'm not a citizen of Parissi, so it won't cause an international incident if I'm spotted. I'm used to travelling alone, and I've visited Brigantium many times, as you know." Lianna knelt in front of him and stroked his hands softly. Her pink curls fell across her face, her eyes earnest. "Let me find her."

Trystan squeezed her hands in his own, an ember of hope glowing within him, warming the icy claws that gripped his heart. As angry as he was with Evelin, all he wanted was for her to be back here, safe with him.

"As long as you're sure."

"I'm sure," Lianna confirmed, standing.

"Pay a visit to the armoury before you go."

She grinned. "Oh, I intend to."

CHAPTER FIFTY-NINE

EVELIN

Across the pass, the Brigantian side of the mountain range was an arid landscape, and Evelin had been glad of the extra water she had packed. Now back at sea level, the terrain was becoming lusher, trees springing up around her.

Evelin knew she wasn't far from the hunting lodge. Every snap of a branch, every small movement, sent panic careening through her, even though she was riding away from it. She detested the fear that her husband had instilled in her, but she no longer had the strength to fight it. She could only try to ignore it as best she could.

When Evelin finally reached the fort at Wray, it was even gloomier than in her recollections. Her aunt had brought her and Otto there for a summer camping trip one year. Even then, she had thought it was odd. Katyana enjoyed her creature comforts, so camping was a strange idea.

Otto had been in his element, running wild through the overgrown forest and throwing stones from one of the crumbling ramparts, but Evelin had been far less enthralled, feeling an intangible sense of unease the entire time. A sensation that hadn't been helped by her aunt's all too vivid stories of past battles seen by the fort, which exuded sadness from its bricks. At least in summer the days had been long and the weather warm, now the grey never lifted and even the most intact rooms were damp, with moss covering the walls.

The date on her aunt's note had told her that, riding at a decent pace, her aunt would be due to meet her in the next few days. Evelin placed her belongings on a nearby table and tried her best to clear a ground floor room of the years of debris. By the time she had finished, it was relatively comfortable, though the walls still whispered their songs of lament. She lit a fire in the old hearth and sat close by it, seeking the light and warmth that pushed away the memories the fort held.

Evelin's eyes felt heavy and her aching muscles were just relaxing when a sharp sound jolted her. Footsteps sounded outside; her aunt must have arrived sooner than expected. Excitement and relief washed over her like the warm summer sea as she stood and brushed down her dress, tucking loose tendrils of hair behind her pointed ears.

A dark, cloaked figure stood in the doorway. Evelin's blood ran cold, her legs failing her. Not breathing, she backed away, her thigh bumping painfully against the table.

The figure spoke with a voice of ice.

"Hello, wife."

CHAPTER SIXTY

EVELIN

"What, no embrace for your husband?" Marcellus asked mockingly as he lowered his hood. His dark hair shone in the firelight, but his skin was sallow, blueish circles curving beneath his eyes. His eyes raked her up and down with a feral intensity. "The climate of Parissi suits you, Evelin. It's a shame you will never see it again."

The moss clinging to the walls felt soft and cold beneath her palms; she pushed herself up against the hard stone, trying to put as much distance between her and Marcellus as possible.

There was only one exit and he was blocking it. She had no means of escape.

The knife! It was still stowed in the bag that rested on the table. Her eyes flicked to it and she lunged, but Marcellus was faster. He brought the hilt of his sword down sharply on her outstretched arm. A sharp, burning pain shot through her wrist and she swore, gripping her bruised arm against her chest.

"Ah, so she does speak," Marcellus snarled.

"What do you want?" she retorted, fighting back a sob.

He stepped forward, the gap between them closing rapidly.

His bony hands gripped Evelin's shoulders painfully and slammed her back against the wall.

"You know what I want, whore."

"You will never get to them!" she hissed, her voice breaking as tears beaded on her eyelashes. "They are safe, and they are protected."

A strange look passed across her husband's face and suddenly, he released her, withdrawing. "We'll see about that," he muttered. "Guards, seize her and strap the bitch to my horse!"

A dense group of soldiers stormed into the room. The one closest to Evelin grabbed her and hauled her off her feet. He threw her over his shoulder, grunting as she struggled and kicked against him. The scent of stale sweat and leather assaulted her nostrils as he held her tight, carrying her out of the doorway.

With men surrounding her, Evelin's struggles were in vain as they tied her wrists and ankles, throwing her body over Marcellus giant stallion and securing her to the beast with rope, the rough fibres cutting into her skin.

Marcellus's men rode painfully fast, and her bones ached to the point she thought they might snap by the time they reached the hunting lodge.

After the first night, she had no longer been tied to Marcellus' horse, but instead had to stomach his arms around her waist as she rode pillion. All through the ride, he had whispered dreadful, dark words into her ears, tormenting her endlessly. Despite the awful memories she held of years of isolation and sadness, she had been glad when the familiar sight of the hunting lodge appeared in the distance.

Upon arrival, Evelin barely had a chance to breathe before she was dragged down off the horse by one of the guards and marched down to the lower level of the lodge. The floor was a mystery to her; she had never been down there before and didn't realise that a labyrinth of rooms lurked beneath. At the end of the longest corridor, they stopped outside a solid wooden door with a grill. The guard opened it and roughly pushed her inside.

"Enjoy your accommodation, *princess,*" he sneered.

The door was shut and bolted with a dull thunk.

Evelin was alone.

The cell was small, barely ten feet across, with a damp-looking straw mattress on the floor and a rickety wooden chair. There was a bucket in the corner, which she assumed, with horror, must be for her toileting needs. It was bitterly cold and almost pitch black. There were no windows or faelights in the room, the only light coming in through the grill from a distant faelight down the corridor.

A wave of dizziness rolled through her and Evelin lay down on the stinking mattress, pulling her cloak tight against the chill. Lying there, she tried to focus on happy thoughts to fight away her despair.

"William, Gabriel, Agnes, Lianna, Ceinwyn," she whispered to herself, repeating their names over and over, like a spell to ward off the darkness.

She couldn't bring herself to say Trystan's name. He would never forgive her for leaving. Everything between them, everything they had fought so hard for, was over.

No, she wouldn't let herself focus on it.

"William, Gabriel, Agnes, Lianna, Ceinwyn," she began again.

Evelin had no idea how long she had been lying there when footsteps sounded in the corridor. A large form blocked the light out at the door and peered inside. The door opened with a creak and Marcellus entered.

"Stand up," he commanded. He was wearing his usual black tunic and trousers, his bony hands encased in dark leather gloves.

Evelin's body was so cold and stiff that she found it hard to move. Before she could even push herself upwards, Marcellus crossed the cell and yanked her to her feet by her arm.

"When I say stand, you fucking stand!" he spat. His eyes

were bloodshot and wild; he had obviously been drinking since their arrival.

"Marcellus, please—"

Her words did nothing but inflame him further.

He lunged at her and grabbed her roughly by the throat, clenching tightly as he pushed her against the wall. Her head slammed back against the cold stone, making her eyes water and sending a blinding pain through her skull.

"Don't. Fucking. Speak. To me," he hissed at her through clenched teeth.

He tightened his hold on her throat, his leather-clad fingers digging into the sides of her neck. Evelin's eyes widened. Every breath was an effort, becoming shallower as he increased the pressure. She began to panic and scratched at his arm, digging her fingernails in hard enough to draw blood. Marcellus's face, screwed up with rage, swam before her as she gasped for air.

She couldn't die like this. She couldn't leave the boys alone. With one ragged breath, she screwed her eyes tight, summoned what little energy remained and shakily raised her arm.

"Lux," she rasped.

A blindingly bright ball of light erupted into the air. Marcellus flinched, letting go for a split second, but it was enough time for Evelin to strike. She brought her knee up sharply between his legs, connecting hard with a dull crunching sound. Marcellus doubled over and Evelin ran for the still-open door. Her feet slipped across the damp stones as she rushed for the exit, gripping at her bruised neck. She had just made it into the dim light of the corridor when her head was yanked back; he had grabbed her braid.

"Bitch!" he spat and pulled her round to face him, wrapping the braid around his hand.

With his free arm, Marcellus landed a sharp blow across the

side of her face, so hard that her knees buckled, but he kept her on her feet by pulling on her hair. Evelin's eyes rolled, unable to focus as she gasped at the pain.

Marcellus released his grip on her hair and shoved her roughly to the floor, before kicking repeatedly at her ribs and stomach. Each blow racked her body with pain. Evelin curled into a ball, whimpering as she tried to protect herself.

Marcellus laughed at the sound. "I'm going now, but rest assured, this is not over."

Evelin kept her eyes shut tight, tears streaming as his boots stomped across the floor and the door clanged shut once more.

Lying on the ground in agony, Evelin was too shaken to move. She had never known such pain, such hatred, directed towards her. She attempted a basic healing spell, but she was far too weak to summon any of her magic.

It must have been the next morning when two guards arrived, pulled Evelin to her feet, and marched her along the corridor.

Her body protested with every step as they dragged her along the damp, fetid passageway. Her mind struggled to keep up with what was going on.

Was this it? Was she was being taken to her death?

Too soon, they arrived in a familiar room. The library was gloomy, with only one window, high up near the ceiling. The walls were lined with shelves, each one holding hundreds of leather-bound volumes.

In her years at the hunting lodge, Evelin had often visited the room; books had been a welcome solace in the evenings after Agnes had retired. She'd lost herself in the stories and in worlds she'd thought she would never see. It had been a place of safety and of adventure, if only in her mind. Today, Marcellus had twisted that sanctuary into a place of terror.

The guards shoved her down roughly into one of the chairs

in the centre of the rectangular room. Two hooded figures stood on the far side of the library. They were silent, and eerily still. She tried to make out their features, but their hoods were pulled low and her face was swollen from the beating, one eye almost shut.

"You look a little tired this morning, princess. Did you not sleep well?" a voice, laced with venom, came from the figure on her right.

Marcellus.

Evelin refused to say a word. She wouldn't respond to his taunting. In the cold depth of the night, shivering and bleeding on the floor of her cell, she had come to a realisation: it didn't matter what she did or said, she was already dead. Marcellus knew where the boys were. The scouts had reported that Brigantium had been amassing its army since before winter. They would invade as soon as spring had arrived in its entirety, and all she could hope for was that Valon's wards and armies would prevail.

Her husband had no possible need to question her. This was all just part of a sick game, and she wouldn't give him the satisfaction of provoking her.

Marcellus crossed to her and removed his hood. He was drawn and tired, his cheeks hollow and eyes watery. "What? No '*Marcellus... please*' today?"

Silence was Evelin's only response, although she was sure he could hear her heart pounding in her chest. He was toying with her. Yet her reticence angered him more.

Marcellus yanked off one of his black leather gloves and threw it to the floor, closing his eyes. A red light began to glow from his palms – blood magic.

Evelin's eyes widened. She had known that Marcellus had a small aptitude for fire magic – he had conjured animals shaped from fire in a show of skill designed to impress her when they first courted – but she had never known about this. Blood magic was an extremely volatile art, which required immense concentration, and sapped away the life force of the user. Few fae had ever heard of it; only through her studies at the Academie had she come across the theory in one of the more arcane texts in the library. It had only one use – the taking of a life.

This was it. This was how she died.

Marcellus raised his hand, the red glow illuminating his face. His features twisted into an expression of unadulterated rage. Evelin closed her eyes, picturing her two boys playing together in the sun. His evil would not be the last thing she saw. She wished she'd had more time with them, that Gabriel might remember her face as he grew up. She sent up a silent prayer that Trystan would keep them safe as a single tear streaked down her face. She had failed them utterly and completely.

"No." The voice was strong and clear. She recognised it. "The king has been clear. You will not kill his sister."

Relief was like a waterfall, washing over Evelin so powerfully that she sagged in her chair. Some small spark of love for her must still burn within Otto. Her eyes burned with tears, but as she opened them, she had to blink repeatedly, unsure of what she was seeing. The figure on the left had walked over to Marcellus, his raised hand still clasped. From beneath the hood, rose gold hair swirled against the dark of the cape.

"Lianna?"

Her friend gave Evelin an imperiously cold glance, before turning back to Marcellus. "You know that Otto wants to avoid war with Parissi. I've seen the Ironforged in training... if you don't keep your head now, there will be war. We need another solution."

Marcellus opened his mouth to retort, but closed it instead and dropped his arm.

What was going on? Why was Lianna here? She had been speaking to Otto? Why was Marcellus doing her bidding?

Marcellus read the confusion in Evelin's face and gave her a smug smile. "Wondering why she's here? You've been played for a fool, Evelin. Lianna is an agent of Brigantium, and has been reporting to me for years."

Evelin didn't want to believe it. She couldn't believe it. Not her best friend.

"Why do you think she stayed so close to you all these years? For your dazzling personality? Did you think it was at your lover's request that she arrived in Valon so shortly after you? Lianna was the one who suggested to me that you might run to Trystan, so she kindly volunteered to go back and keep an eye on you and those degenerates in Parissi. She has been reporting to me on your movements, and those of the Parissi court."

Evelin searched her friend's face for some confirmation that her husband's words were lies, but a different person was looking back at her. The warmth and joy in Lianna's face was all gone – what remained was no more than a ghost to her.

Marcellus turned to Lianna. Evelin could still feel the hatred, the violence, radiating from him.

"If I'm not to kill the bitch, what would you suggest?"

Lianna reached out and stroked him lightly on the shoulder, like a mother pacifying a toddler on the verge of throwing a tantrum. "I read Trystan's thoughts on a number of occasions whilst I was in Valon. He still thinks he can feel it when I breach his mental wards, so he was extremely unguarded around me. He even invited me into his mind himself just before Luminara, in a pathetic attempt to prove his worth." Lianna let out a cruel chuckle as she picked at her manicured blood-red fingernails. "The king of Parissi is weak, immature, and impulsive. He believes himself to be noble and chivalrous, but he cannot control his own emotions and desires. Trystan is in love with your wife. He's only recently admitted it to himself, but it consumes him. It overwhelms any rational thought that goes through that pretty head of his. Reach out to him and let him know that you have her captive; he will be willing to negotiate with you."

"Weak, just like his uncle," Marcellus snarled. "I'll send a raven and arrange a meeting, but I think perhaps I should send proof that I have her in my custody… I wouldn't want him doubting us."

Evelin swallowed hard as Marcellus pulled a silver knife from his belt. He loomed over her, using the blade of his knife to lift her chin to meet his gaze; its cold steel burned against her skin.

"What shall I take?" he murmured.

He twisted slightly and dug the knife into her flesh.

Lianna coughed from behind him. "Your king's command, my lord? His sister was not to be harmed."

Marcellus sighed and withdrew his knife, nicking her skin. A small drop of blood dripped onto the front of Evelin's dress and he smiled, pleased with himself. Swiftly, he grabbed a lock of her hair and sliced through it, dangling it in front of her.

"Let us hope this will suffice," he sneered, walking out of the room.

Lianna pulled up her hood and followed him, not looking once in Evelin's direction. Moments after the two had left, the guards escorted her roughly back to her cell.

Once alone, she sank to the floor and burst into uncontrollable sobs. She had never felt so hopeless.

Trystan had sent raven after raven to Evelin, to Lianna, even one to Evelin's aunt, but no responses came back. The hope that he had felt when Lianna departed to find Evelin had dimmed to a barely lit ember after having heard nothing for so long, but Lianna's forthright words had stuck with him. He would not give in to self-pity. Instead, he would focus on the things within his control.

Work rapidly became a comfort, though as the port thawed, he was dealing with more concerns about Brigantian traders not being willing to sell to Parissi, or hiking up their prices exponentially. Ceinwyn had released a statement to the Merchants' Guild explaining that Trystan was currently in negotiations with Brigantium over a new trade deal, which was making some Brigantian traders a little nervous, but that it would be finalised soon.

The lie made the king uneasy, but at least it seemed to have calmed the nerves of Valon's merchant class.

Trystan wondered if he should approach Otto directly and speak with him man to man, but thought better of it. From what Evelin had told him, Marcellus was the power behind the throne, and he didn't want to risk making things worse by either of them finding out that Evelin had returned to Brigantium.

It was shortly after noon when a servant arrived with a

message from the captain of the Kingsguard, requesting his presence in the guardhouse immediately.

Trystan's senses were assaulted the moment he entered. The barren room was filled with the tang of blood, but he was struck most by the noise. It was oppressive, with people shouting across the space while other secretive conversations took place in voices that were not quite hushed enough. A scout lay on one of the wooden benches. He was young, possibly just out of training, and his blond hair was stuck to his head with sweat. The blue uniform he wore had turned purple-black with blood that oozed from a wound in his side. His breathing was ragged, and flecks of foam gathered at the corners of his mouth.

The young scout's eyes shot to Trystan and he held out a shaking hand clenched around a roll of parchment.

"Sire," he gasped, eyes bulging at the effort.

Trystan stepped over to him and grasped the man's hand tightly in his own.

"A healer?" Trystan shouted, trying to figure out where the blood was coming from.

"On their way, sire," the captain replied, running his hand through his silvering hair.

Trystan was paralysed by his inability to help. There must be something he could do. He looked around desperately for anything that might help, but there was little of any use. Trystan's own abilities as a healer were pitiful, and he feared doing more damage through an attempt. All he could do was stay and keep vigil, hoping the healer would arrive soon, but the scout's breathing slowed, and within a few minutes, he was gone.

"Damn!" Trystan exhaled. He didn't want to let go of the young man's hand, but he couldn't bear to see his eyes remain open like that, the terror in them all too visible. He reached across and gently closed the scout's eyes. "Who is he? What happened to him?" he asked the captain.

"He was attacked whilst on patrol. His name was Gawain Llyndros, sire," the captain replied. "I believe you are acquainted with his older brother, Owen."

Trystan simply nodded in confirmation.

"I will speak with Owen shortly, sire."

"Where was Gawain found?" Trystan asked.

"Close to the Brigantian border."

Trystan closed his eyes and took a deep breath. He clenched his fists and they crunched down on the note that had been thrust into his hand by the scout. Whatever it was, he needed to read it.

"Please let me know when you have spoken with Owen, captain. I would like to speak with him personally when he is ready," Trystan requested, before returning back to his study.

As soon as he closed the door, he rotated the note in his hand and went to break the seal.

He stopped. There was a lock of wavy red hair under the fern green wax.

No.

Please, God, no.

Trystan tugged at his collar as ice ran down the back of his neck. Fingers trembling, he broke open the seal. The contents confirmed his worst fears.

"Get me the Chancellor now!" he bellowed to the servant whom he knew would be hovering outside the room.

Ceinwyn arrived moments later, face red and out of breath, frowning in puzzlement at him.

"What is it?" she asked.

"This was in the possession of a scout who was attacked within our own borders. He's dead." Trystan thrust the note towards her and paced the room, staring out of the window.

"You can't go," Ceinwyn said simply, handing the note back. When he didn't respond, she stepped towards him, frowning. "It is too dangerous. Merely crossing into Brigantium puts you on the backfoot. I don't care if Marcellus has asked to meet with you; it is not worth the risk, Trystan."

He rounded on her. "That is not your decision. I am the king and I *will* be at that meeting." A sob threatened to break free. "I cannot remain here when Marcellus has her, Ceinwyn."

"But would she want you to go? Evelin is an intelligent woman. She knew the risk she was taking when she left."

"It's not just about her. Marcellus threatens war if I do not meet him – would you rather have me call his bluff? Not to mention this blatant act of aggression against one of my own subjects, in my own realm. I must do *something*."

"Are you sure this is the action you wish to take? Surely, there is an alternative that places you in less personal danger?"

The meeting was in three days. It was a hard ride, but it was doable. The location Marcellus had selected was not far across the border. Trystan's heart was galloping, palms clammy. He clenched his fists. The decision was not one that he had taken lightly; he knew what he was risking, but it had to be done. He respected Ceinwyn's counsel, but he was king. The decision rested on his shoulders alone.

He would show no more weakness.

CHAPTER SIXTY-TWO

EVELIN

The sky promised storms as Evelin was lifted ungracefully onto a brown mare. She gripped the leather reins. Could she flee? No one else was mounted… maybe she would get enough of a head start to disappear into the forest? The idea of escape floated around in her mind, but she was paralysed and instead continued to stare down at her dirt-covered hands. The squalid conditions of her cell had only been made bearable by the fact that Marcellus had not returned. She had hoped, and feared, for a visit from Lianna, but she had been left in isolation, not even spoken to by the guard who shoved her daily meal through the slit in the cell door.

She tipped her head back, feeling the first droplets of rain fall on her forehead and slide down her face.

"That won't do anything to wash the stink from you," Marcellus said, swaggering over to her. "Now, just to make sure you don't try any tricks…" He pulled a length of rope from a canvas bag and tied it roughly around her wrists. Once finished, he whispered a few words and cast his hands over the bindings, which glowed orange – a spell to suppress her magic.

Evelin kept staring straight ahead, focusing only on her breathing.

Marcellus mounted a grey stallion with an intricately braided white mane. He had about twenty guards with him, all menacingly built and heavily armed. Out of the corner of her eye, she spied Lianna step forward to join the party. A sharp pain balled in her throat as her former friend nodded at Marcellus and swung onto her own horse with majestic ease. At Marcellus' signal, the group began their journey.

Evelin didn't know where they were going, but whatever awaited her would not be good.

The party halted by the edge of a lake. The waters mirrored the slate grey of the sky; the rain, which hadn't stopped throughout their journey, disrupted its surface. There were no settlements around the lake, but just ahead of them was a boathouse and short dock sticking out into the water. A boatman, who looked as weathered as the rocks on the shore, raised his silver head from where he had been nodding off on a rocking chair. With surprising speed, he scuttled into the boathouse and bolted the door shut.

A wise move.

The sun was setting behind the mountains that loomed in the distance. Marcellus turned in his saddle, but kept a tight grip on the reins, yanking his poor horse's head back and forth.

"Where the fuck is he?" he spat at Lianna.

Lianna was unconcerned, shaking the mass of curls out of face. "If he said he will be here, he will," she responded, and returned to cleaning her nails.

Marcellus snorted and looked out towards the lake. Evelin kept her eyes trained towards the mountains. If Trystan was coming, that was where he would arrive from. Her stomach twisted into knots as she dared to hope that he might come for her, though another part wished he would stay safe in Valon with her boys.

The light was fading as a bundle of dark figures came into view.

Riders.

As they gradually approached, she could clearly make out Trystan, sat bolt upright on his mount, a grey cloak flying behind him. He was flanked by four guards, an unusually small company for such a meeting. Panic rose in Evelin's throat. If Marcellus attacked, Trystan would be outnumbered.

Trystan paused thirty feet across from them. His usually smiling mouth was nothing but a thin line. His eyes darted to her, narrowing as he took in her appearance.

"How kind of you to finally join us," Marcellus sneered. "I trust you have come willing to negotiate?"

Trystan gave the briefest of nods, his upper lip curling into a snarl.

"What do you intend to give me in return for your whore? I must admit, she's a little worse for wear, but I hear you aren't as discerning about your women as some." Marcellus leant across to Evelin and grabbed her lower jaw in his hand, squeezing it painfully. She gasped as he turned her head back and forth.

Trystan's hand went to his sword. "Don't fucking touch her!" he cried out, pausing his fingers an inch from the hilt, clearly remembering himself.

"Be careful how you speak to me, boy," Marcellus hissed, not letting go of his grip on Evelin's face.

Her eyes began to well with tears from the pain. She blinked rapidly. She refused to let Marcellus make her cry. Never again. She strained against the bonds that suppressed her magic, but she was too weak to even test them.

"I have an army ready to invade your poxy little realm," Marcellus continued. "One word from me and your precious

Valon will be ashes."

"I think you ought to speak with your king first. Word has it that he isn't too keen on war with Parissi. Perhaps he has less faith in your military prowess than you do?" Trystan's voice remained surprisingly even. "A diplomatic solution seems to be a far better option all round."

Marcellus finally released his grip, thrusting Evelin to the side with such force she almost fell from her horse. "Make this quick," he spat, glaring at Trystan.

Trystan tilted his face up to the sky and put his fingers between his lips. He let out a short whistle, a single note which echoed across the waters. From a thicket of trees towards the mountains, a large bird soared into the sky – Trystan's braxhawk. It was silhouetted against the setting sun, but it was clearly carrying something in its claws as it swooped down towards them.

Horror dawned on Evelin. It wasn't something, but some*one*.

'No!" she screamed as the bird landed beside Trystan, gently laying its cargo by his horse's feet.

"Mama!" William cried, struggling to his feet, trying to get to her, but Trystan jumped from his horse and grabbed him firmly by the shoulders.

Evelin threw herself off her mount, landing awkwardly without her hands free to catch herself. Luckily, the boggy ground cushioned her fall. She scrambled to her feet and ran to her son. Kneeling before him in the mud, her eyes scanned him for injury. The boy sobbed and flung his arms around her, gripping her with a strength she didn't know he possessed. She buried her face in his neck, soaking in his scent and tried desperately to control her own tears.

Trystan's voice made her pull away. He was still speaking to Marcellus. "Your heir. In return, you will release the princess to me and all hostilities with Parissi will cease."

Evelin recoiled, her eyes widening as she stared up at the king. "No! No, Trystan, you can't do this, please!"

She shuffled on her knees in the mud towards him, William still gripping her tightly, but Trystan kept his eyes trained on Marcellus.

"I believe I have two heirs, boy. Where is the other?" Marcellus asked.

"The oldest will suffice. The baby is too young to leave his mother and will remain in Valon as surety against any incursion from Brigantium. We can review the situation with your youngest heir when he is older," Trystan stated, still not looking at where Evelin knelt in the dirt. "Do we have an accord?"

How could he do this? How could Trystan trade her son like this? Evelin would never have left Valon if she had even suspected that he would use William like a pawn to defend his own realm.

Marcellus rolled his shoulders and exhaled sharply. "Fetch the child, Lianna."

Evelin spun to see her friend, *her best friend,* cross towards them and reach for William's hand.

"Come on, William. Why don't you come with Aunty Li and you can tell me all about what you have been up to? I've missed you," she said, ruffling his hair.

The boy's cheeks were stained with tears. "No, I want to stay with Mama! I don't want to go with him… Mama!"

"Lianna, please!" Evelin begged, staring up at her former friend. "Don't let him take William. Why are you doing this? If you were ever truly my friend you wouldn't do this! He's my son!"

"What the fuck are we waiting for?" Marcellus yelled, making William jump. "Bring him to me, now!"

Lianna turned to Trystan. "Go now," she said softly, before

scooping William up into her arms.

The boy struggled and flung his arms out towards Evelin.

Arms still bound, her magic dimmed, there was little Evelin could do, but that wasn't going to stop her. She tried to push herself upright, her feet catching in the muddy folds of her dress. Baring her teeth, she launched herself at Marcellus. She would kill him, rip him apart if she could just get to him, but before she even made it two steps towards her husband, Trystan grabbed her shoulders and pulled her backwards.

"No! I won't leave without my son! Get off me, get *off!*" she yelled, trying to wrench herself from his grasp.

She kicked Trystan hard at his shins and managed to get one arm free. How could anyone expect her to abandon her son? Why was this happening? She had to stop this. She would never leave him, not while she was still breathing.

"I'm sorry," Trystan whispered as he held a cloth over her mouth. It was damp and smelled of bitter oranges.

Any residual strength dwindled out from her limbs and she suddenly felt woozy.

Oblivion claimed her. The last thing Evelin heard before she fell into unconsciousness was William's sobs.

When Evelin awoke, she found herself lying on a damp cloak in the middle of a forest. It had stopped raining, she thought, blinking, trying to focus. Then she remembered. Fear swept over her.

William.

Evelin thrust herself upright. Trystan was sitting beside her, regarding her watchfully.

"How? How could you?" she croaked. Her voice was dry and

hoarse – it didn't sound like her own.

He looked away from her, into the depths of the dark evergreens surrounding them.

"Answer me!" she screamed.

"It was the only way," he replied sadly, turning back and reaching for her hand.

Evelin recoiled; the thought of him touching her was beyond comprehension. "*The only way?* You should have left me there! My life does not matter, only my sons'. Why would you give William to him?"

"Why?" Trystan's eyes flared. "Because I love you, and I couldn't let Marcellus hurt you. You are *everything*. I couldn't bear to think about what he might do to you if I didn't come to some sort of agreement with him. I couldn't let Brigantium attack Parissi. I couldn't risk the lives of my people any longer. I made the only call I could. Many noble children do not remain in their mother's home for long. This is not that unusual. Marcellus is the boy's father, and as such, he has rights. William will not be hurt; Marcellus has assured me of that, he just won't be with you."

"I will never forgive you for this. *Never.*"

"I'm sorry," Trystan replied, pushing himself to his feet. "But I'm willing to live with that if it keeps you and my country safe."

CHAPTER SIXTY-THREE

EVELIN

Evelin didn't speak a word to Trystan on the ride back to Valon. She had never felt such hatred towards anyone, not even Marcellus. She brooded silently for hours, alternating between anger and fear. The pull she felt in her heart right now, drawing her back to William, was like nothing she had ever experienced before. Every step forward tugged painfully on the thread between them. How could Trystan have given over her child to that monster?

Trystan had always been the best man she had ever known. He was good and kind. How had she never seen this side of him? How could he have been so detached? Evelin knew that he didn't love William like she did, but Trystan loved *her*. Surely that had to mean something? How could he ever have truly loved her if he was willing to break her heart in two like this?

When they arrived back at the Summer Palace, Evelin got down from her horse without a word, passing its reins to a waiting servant. She refused to look at Trystan, so consumed by anger and grief that she didn't trust what she might say. Without so much as a backward glance, she stormed up the steps and practically ran to her rooms.

Agnes stood by the window, the lines on her face more prominent than ever before. "I'm so sorry, my lady. I have failed you. I couldn't stop him taking William." Agnes' voice was frail as she fell to her knees. "Please forgive me."

Evelin ran to Agnes and knelt before her, grasping her hands. "There is nothing to forgive. You do not bear any of the blame here. If Trystan wanted to take William, it would have been impossible to stop him. He is king and commands all here," she said soothingly. "Don't worry, Agnes. I'm going to get him back."

Agnes looked up at her questioningly. "How?"

"I don't know yet," Evelin admitted. "But I am *not* leaving him with Marcellus."

∞

Evelin spent most of the night awake, half-formed plans emerging in her mind, only to be dashed into smoke by logic. By the time dawn began to peek through the curtains, she had made up her mind to go out for a ride to clear her head. She needed some fresh air and to be active; to have something to do to take her mind off the memory of William sobbing for her.

Evelin pulled on a moss green woollen riding dress and a scarlet cloak and headed towards the stables. As she descended the stairs towards the foyer, Trystan came into view. He was speaking with one of the guards, the two of them poring over some papers. He turned to look at her, frowning.

"Where are you going?" he asked, voice firm.

"Out," she replied, walking straight past him.

"Out where?"

"For a ride. Or am I captive here too?"

The king recoiled, wounded by her words, and shook his head. "You're not going alone. It still isn't safe. Owen," he said, turning to the guard, "please would you accompany the princess on her ride? She is not to go too far from the city, no further than the old temple. Make sure you are well-armed."

Evelin was done being dictated to by him and walked purposefully to the back steps leading down to the stables. The guard scurried after her, but she made no attempt to slow down. Pushing open the double doors, the warmth of the early morning sun beat down on her face and she took a deep breath. Her heart was beating rapidly, and she tried to calm it as she crossed the courtyard.

"Princess, would you allow me a moment to change into my riding boots?" the guard asked politely when they reached the stables, bowing slightly. He was hesitant, as if worried that she might decide to ride off on her own instead.

Evelin nodded curtly, pushed open the stable door, and banged straight into someone leaving. The blow winded her with its impact.

"I'm sorry," she said, catching her breath.

It took her a few seconds to recognise the man she had collided with. His dark brown hair had been cut dramatically into a short, textured crop with faded sides and his stubble was now a fairly thick, but neat, beard.

Blue eyes stared down at her with a fiery intensity, then narrowed and darkened.

"Who did this to you?" Nikolas asked in his deep, resonant voice, raising a calloused hand tentatively towards her cheek.

Evelin stepped back and frowned. Ah – the beating from Marcellus. Her reflection in the mirror last night had been startling. Purple-green bruises marked her cheekbone and jaw, a small cut running along her temple. Agnes had offered to heal her, but Evelin had refused. She was being silly, but the ache of her injuries was a reminder of what Marcellus could do and that she must not stop in her quest to retrieve William. She couldn't let her baby boy face a beating like hers.

"My husband's work," she explained briefly, trying to avoid

any further conversation. Evelin went to step around him, but Nikolas moved into her path. "Don't. Not today," she warned, but he would not be deterred. He stood there, an immovable wall. She wanted to hit him, to push him out of her way. Why did all the men in her life insist on blocking her, fencing her in? "Get out of my way, commander," she hissed, shoving down the rage that threatened to erupt.

"Tell me what happened," he said insistently, his expression inscrutable.

Damn him. Damn *all* of them.

Evelin resolved to shove him aside when a sudden realisation dawned upon her. Maybe he wasn't another problem... maybe he was the solution. He was a trained fighter, with men at his disposal. Perhaps he could be prevailed upon to help her? Trystan had said he was a man of honour...

Taking a breath, Evelin told him everything. About the raven from her aunt, about her capture and beating, and finally about the trade Trystan had made for her life. Through it all, Nikolas stood silently, his jaw clenching occasionally, but he made no interjections and kept his expression carefully neutral.

"... so, I intend to get William back," she finished. "But I need help."

"It seems that you do," he agreed, and looked into the stable yard at Owen's approach. "Enjoy your ride, princess."

Nikolas gave her one last look, then strode off in the direction of the palace.

The commander was an arrogant asshole who didn't want her in Valon in the first place. Why had Evelin expected more from him? The bruising on her face had seemed to shock him, but he was probably just curious. After all, no doubt it wasn't every day he collided with a princess sporting such injuries. At least her first impressions of him had been accurate.

CHAPTER SIXTY-FOUR

TRYSTAN

The walls of the study reverberated as the door was flung open with savage force.

"Ah, you're back. How was the journey?" Trystan asked his friend, trying to keep his tone light.

"Long. The thaw hadn't yet arrived at Deathhold when I received your raven, otherwise I would have been here sooner," Nik replied, helping himself to a large glass of liquor before sitting in the chair across from Trystan. "I believe much has happened in my absence."

Trystan sighed; he shouldn't have been surprised that Nik was well-informed. As commander of Parissi's armies, he always had an ear to the ground. "The guards gossip more than the fishwives at the docks," Trystan observed.

"Yes, they do, but I actually ran into the princess this morning. She was very forthcoming."

Trystan raised his eyebrows. Evelin had made no secret of her distaste for the commander, and he was surprised she had even bothered speaking to him.

"You made the right call, Trys," Nik assured him. "For Parissi, at least."

Trystan felt his whole body relax, and he sank back into his chair. "You think so?" he asked, desperate for further confirmation that he wasn't the evil bastard Evelin thought he was.

"You can't risk the lives of millions for one boy. War with Brigantium would devastate our realm," his friend replied, taking a swig of his drink.

"It wasn't just for Parissi, though… I had to get her back," Trystan admitted, shame pricking at him.

"Yes, I heard about your dalliance with the princess."

"It is no mere dalliance… she is more than that," Trystan admitted, getting up to pour himself a drink.

As he passed Nikolas, his friend grasped his forearm tightly and indicated for a refill. He poured them both generous measures and replaced the lid on the crystal decanter carefully.

"How *are* you going to get her son back?"

Trystan contemplated the swirls of amber in his glass, the sun picking out flecks of gold. "I'm not," he said, turning back to Nik and passing him his drink. "As you said, I'm not going to risk the lives of my people. William will be well cared for by his father and uncle. He is Otto's heir, after all. I will write to the king about the boy coming to visit for the summer. I'm sure something can be worked out."

Nik raised an eyebrow but remained silent; Trystan wasn't exactly sure what that look was supposed to mean. Nik had been the one to first warn him to keep his distance from Evelin, to think of his kingdom before all else.

"*You* think I should attempt a rescue?" Trystan asked incredulously.

"I—"

Nik was interrupted by the arrival of Ceinwyn. She was unusually flustered, skin flushed and breathing hard.

"I've just had a raven. You both need to hear this," she huffed, nodding her head towards Nik. "We have confirmation about the group behind the massacre."

Trystan's heart stopped beating as he waited for Ceinwyn to continue.

"They call themselves the Soldiers of Xoros. They're a highly secretive organisation with arms in nearly all of the fae realms. They are rabidly anti-human and are responsible for numerous atrocities against humans and fae-sympathisers across the last couple of centuries. Their structure and hierarchy is murky, but we have discovered the identity of the man who led the attack in Valon." Ceinwyn hesitated, meeting Trystan's eyes with a solemn expression. "It was the Duke of Ashburner."

"Marcellus." Trystan's mind was swimming. Evelin's husband was the one who had killed his uncle? All those innocent people? She had told him of Marcellus's distaste for humans, his violence, but he could never have imagined the man's cruelty would go this far. "And Otto?" he asked. If the king of Brigantium was also behind this, it made the situation far more serious.

"Unknown," Ceinwyn replied, but she wasn't looking at Trystan. Her eyes were fixed on Nikolas. His usually tan skin had drained of all colour.

"When do we leave?" Nik asked, his voice rough.

"We don't," Trystan replied. "We can't march our armies into Brigantium, especially when we don't know the extent of Otto's involvement. We must bide our time and find out more."

"But my reports have told me that Marcellus is still at the hunting lodge. Why wait until he's back in the safety of Azmar? The walls of the capital's fortress haven't been breached in over a thousand years. Let me go now. I can take a small contingent of men, maybe even retrieve the boy at the same time?"

"He might have already left. It's not worth the risk," Trystan argued.

Nik's hands balled into fists. He crossed to where Trystan still stood, by the liquor cabinet. It was true that Nik was taller and broader than Trystan, and far more deadly, but he would not be intimidated. He squared his shoulders, ready to take on any blow Nik dealt, and stared him straight in the eyes.

"Trystan, Nikolas, enough," Ceinwyn said sharply, easing herself between them. She turned to look up at Nik. "Go cool down. Now."

His friend looked at Ceinwyn with such venom that Trystan was surprised she didn't flinch, but the commander said nothing and stalked out of the room, slamming the door behind him.

"Let him go," Ceinwyn said soothingly. "He will calm down soon enough. Nikolas needs to learn not to let his rage control him, and also how to follow his king's commands."

"Maybe I should have approved the mission?" Trystan wondered aloud.

"No. We don't know enough to risk such an incursion into Brigantian territory, especially just after you have negotiated a relatively fragile peace. We bide our time. Your uncle would be proud of the ruler you've become, Trystan."

"A ruler who has lost two of his best friends in the same number of days," he said, bitterly.

"You haven't lost either of them, and your decisions mean that you won't lose your throne," Ceinwyn replied, walking to the door. "Get some rest. You look exhausted."

Trystan *was* exhausted. Days of riding, of replaying every decision in his mind, had worn him down. A short rest might give him the energy he needed to speak to Nik... or even to Evelin.

CHAPTER SIXTY-FIVE

EVELIN

Evelin was dreaming. William was playing with a young boy, about the same age as him. They were running around the rose garden in the grounds of the palace in Valon. It was the height of summer and the sun beat down on them. She tilted her face up to better feel its warmth. Sitting on a bench, a light breeze wafted through her hair.

The boys ran towards her, and, as they approached, Evelin realised that the other boy was Gabriel. But Gabriel was fae. His ears were pointed, he was just as tall as his brother, and in his right hand glowed a ball of white light. She reached her arms out, ready to embrace her children, when suddenly the ground began to shake under her. A giant sinkhole opened, sucking in the rose bushes either side of her into blackness, its diameter growing every second.

"Run!" Evelin screamed to the boys, trying desperately to get to them, but she was stuck to the bench as the ground continued to vibrate.

"Princess," a voice called to her. "Princess, wake up."

Evelin blinked open her eyes. The room was dark, and a man leaned over her bed. She opened her mouth to scream, but a gloved hand shot out, silencing her.

"Princess, don't be alarmed. I need you to get out of bed, now."

The face behind the hand was still in shadow, but Evelin recognised the deep rumbling bass of the voice. The commander. What was he doing here?

He slowly removed his hand from her mouth, watching her reactions apprehensively. "Please don't scream. I have something I must speak to you about. Time is critical."

Confused, Evelin grabbed a robe as he turned away from her to give her some privacy. He put his hands on his hips but was unable to keep still, shifting his weight from one leg to another. She put the robe on quickly and motioned for Nikolas to follow her into the sitting room. The one lit faelight in the room revealed that he was fully dressed in well-worn black fighting leathers, a dark cloak wrapped around his powerful frame.

"Well, what is it?" she asked impatiently, hugging her robe more tightly around herself. The cold stone floor stung her feet. She wished she had put on slippers.

The commander leaned in towards her and Evelin fought the urge to recoil from him. She still couldn't stand him, but she was conscious that Gabriel was asleep and didn't want him speaking any louder than he had to. It had taken hours to get him to sleep and if Nikolas woke him…

She felt his breath, sweet with mint, on her cheek as he whispered in her ear. "There isn't enough time to tell you everything right now, but I am taking a group of my men into Brigantium to apprehend your husband. The duke is wanted for questioning in relation to a matter of great importance, but I thought it might give us a chance to bring your son back with us."

Evelin's heart jolted.

"Marcellus is still residing in the hunting lodge," the commander continued. "However, we've not had time to prepare for this mission and it would make it far less dangerous for my men if we brought someone with us who knows the lodge and how it is guarded. It would make it more likely that we can retrieve William safely, too. You lived there for years. Would you come with us?"

"Yes," Evelin replied without hesitation. "When are we leaving?"

"Now," he replied. "I've got provisions and weapons, just bring what you will need for the next few days... and perhaps some things for your son."

"Give me a few minutes." Evelin paused, a thought stopping her. "Is Trystan coming as well?"

"No... it would be unwise for him to come with us, from a diplomatic position. Trystan needs full deniability, so will remain here," Nikolas explained. "Any *more* questions, or can we get going?"

Evelin wanted to know what was this *matter of great importance* was that had seemingly changed Trystan's mind, but she decided it didn't matter, not if he had ordered this mission to go ahead.

"Where shall I meet you?" she asked, already turning back into her sleeping chamber.

"By the stables. The guards on the rear doors are expecting you," the commander said, before slipping out of the sitting room on strangely silent feet, cloak billowing behind him.

Within less than a quarter of an hour, Evelin was following his path. The guards on watch kept their eyes straight ahead of them as she eased the doors open and hurried down the steps. Outside the stables, a group of about ten men was assembled, each carrying a pack and sporting an assortment of lethal-looking weapons. She didn't recognise any of their faces, but none of them looked to be new recruits. Their heights varied, but all were stocky, and most were easily in their thirties. There was no panic or restlessness among the group either; they were watchful, ready, but conserving their energy. These men had clearly seen their fair share of active service.

The commander appeared from the stables, strapping a sword across his back. As one, the men turned to look at him, awaiting his command.

"We go now," Nikolas ordered, nodding to them and walking towards the east gate.

Evelin hurried after him, struggling to keep up with his pace. "No horses?" she asked. "Surely it will take us too long on foot?"

"There's a boat waiting for us at the docks. One of the smugglers owes me a favour and will take us to a cove not far from the lodge," he explained as they hurried down the silent streets of the city. "Now, hush."

Evelin's eyes narrowed. "Why do we have to be quiet?"

She might not have been able to see it, but she felt his eyes roll. "Because Brigantium has agents in Valon, and I'm sure that if they see a group of armed men boarding a ship in the night, they will report that directly by raven," he whispered.

The docks were less quiet. A pair of drunken sailors staggered along the port, arm in arm, singing a bawdy sea shanty at the top of their lungs. The commander held up a fist and his men stopped in their tracks, hidden by the shadows. Evelin followed their lead and halted just behind the commander. Adrenaline was already coursing through her body and she had to fight hard to keep herself still and silent. She tried to focus on Nikolas' cloak in front of her, so black that it seemed to suck in any nearby light.

As soon as the sailors had passed, he signalled for them to keep going and the group continued onwards, heading straight for a small vessel bobbing gently in the waters.

The captain of the boat was a small, ferrety man, whose

eyes were constantly whipping back and forth. He exchanged a few, tense words with the commander, gesturing wildly. The commander said nothing in return, merely exhaling so deeply it sounded like a growl. He towered over the captain, who recoiled from the intensity of the gaze shooting down at him, before indicating for the rest of the party to board.

The men moved as one, pulling on ropes and unfurling sails without needing to talk to one another. Evelin was shocked by the speed with which they cast off and set out into the open waters.

Soon, Valon was no more than a haze of lights in the distance.

CHAPTER SIXTY-SIX

EVELIN

A large swell threw ocean spray across Evelin's face, waking her from a troubled sleep. She hauled her chilled frame upright from the wooden deck and gripped onto the railing.

"Princess, there's something you should know." Nikolas had joined her, his eyes scanning the night sky, heavy with stars. "Trystan expressly forbade me to go on this mission. He wanted to wait for further intelligence and was concerned about the political ramifications of crossing the border, but I decided to act anyway. Who knows when we would next have been able to get to Marcellus? I stand by my decision, but I am aware that you and Trystan have become… close. I thought you should know that I am acting alone."

Evelin stared at him, wide eyed. She couldn't decide whether to be furious or impressed. "And you waited until *now* to tell me?"

He did not appear to be ashamed of his subterfuge. No, he was biting back a smile. *Damn him.* She wanted to ask him why he was going against his king, but did this information really change anything? Things between her and Trystan were in ruins as it was.

Evelin sighed. "It doesn't surprise me that he forbade the mission. Trystan was clear in his stance about not being willing to risk a rescue. Honestly? Had you told me from the offset, it wouldn't have mattered," Evelin admitted as she followed his gaze heavenwards. "I will take any chance to get William back."

Nikolas' grip on the railings tightened; Evelin could swear the wood groaned under his grasp. "The matter I mentioned before, the one that your husband needs to be questioned regarding… did you know he was a member of the Soldiers of Xoros?"

"The what?" The name was not familiar.

"They are a secretive sect, fuelled by a fundamental hatred of humans and a belief in fae superiority. We believe that a sub-group of this organisation, controlled by your husband, was responsible for the Summer Palace massacre."

Evelin's heart caught in her throat. Unsaid truths flickered into reality, solidifying before her. She didn't want to believe it, but it made sense. Marcellus hated humans, and she had seen him kill before. Nausea roiled in her stomach.

"The information is accurate, I assure you," the commander added, scanning her face. He pulled a scrap of paper from his pocket. "This is for you."

Evelin took the paper from his hand.

Eve,

William is safe. I'm keeping him with me. I will not let Marcellus hurt him. I'm so sorry. I will find a way to bring him back to you.

I love you. Please trust me.

Li xxx

"What is this?" she demanded, the note crumpling between her shaking fingers.

"Lianna has been working as an agent of Parissi for years; she is one of our most valued assets. Her aptitude for telepathy far exceeds anything taught at the Academie. At great personal risk, she has been working inside the Brigantian court for the last two years, gaining your husband's trust. We suspected that Marcellus had information about the massacre, but she has just confirmed that he was the one behind it. Lianna was supposed to get out as soon as she had the confirmation we needed, but she chose to stay." Nikolas looked at her intently, his eyes flicking back and forth across her face.

Her husband was a murderer. An evil monster with a vendetta against humans. A monster who had fathered her human child. Lianna was working for Parissi. She was protecting William. Evelin tried to make sense of everything, but only felt the world shifting beneath her.

"How long until we arrive?" she asked.

"Perhaps another hour."

Evelin watched the inky black coastline and let her mind go blank. She gave herself up to the movement of the sea and simply breathed. Soon, they would be in Brigantium, and she would get her son back.

That was all that mattered right now.

CHAPTER SIXTY-SEVEN

EVELIN

Dusk had fallen by the time the group had crossed the countryside to the hunting lodge. Evelin had always thought 'lodge' was a bit of a misnomer. The building may once have been used as short-term accommodation for the kings of Brigantium during a prolonged hunt, but over the years it had been added to and improved such that now it was more like a fortified manor in the depths of the forest.

The group approached in silence, the commander's men weaving through the forest like spectres. Evelin pointed towards the gate of the walled garden and stepped ahead through the long rustling grass, which was still heavy with the rain that had fallen earlier in the day. She quickly released the spell binding the gate. Its lock glowed blue and swung open on noiseless hinges. The men rushed towards the entrance; swords already drawn as she stepped aside. One man, who was particularly tall, carried an enormous bow. He drew it back effortlessly and a single arrow glowed silver as it flew across the garden, piercing the throat of the guard at the kitchen door. The guard crumpled to the ground, and the group pushed forward.

"It's bolted from the inside," Evelin whispered when Nikolas ran his hand over the door.

"Grayson," he barked, and one of the men stepped forward, holding a dagger.

The soldier whispered words in a language Evelin didn't recognise and gently slid his dagger into the gap between the frame and the door. With a hiss and a small jet of what appeared to be steam, the door eased open.

The group knew the plan. A couple of the men were to remain here, providing cover for when the time came to leave, and the rest were to go with the commander. Their task was simple: find Marcellus and extract him.

Evelin had described the layout of the main floors of the lodge in detail when they had stopped to eat. It was still early enough in the evening that Marcellus should still be awake, eating in the main hall. The hope was that he and his men had been drinking, as was their usual habit, and so would not present too much of a challenge.

Nikolas' men sped off down the corridor, but he paused and turned to Evelin. His body hummed with barely contained energy. The effect, combined with his fighting leathers and long sword gleaming in the faelights, was one of terrifying power.

"We need to get out of here as quickly as possible. Find William and Lianna and get back here. Do not stop for anything else," he said in an undertone. He paused, as though he was going to say more, but instead gave an almost imperceptible shake of his head before following his men.

The corridors were quiet. Evelin hurried through them, hardly daring to breathe. The door to William's room on the first floor was ajar, soft light falling in a wedge onto the floor outside. She peered into the room through the gap; William was lying asleep on his bed, curled into a ball on his side, his auburn hair stuck up at the back. She reached out to push open the door when a strangled cry came from the floor below, followed by a roar of rage. A cacophony of bangs and crashes followed. Marcellus and his men must be putting up a fight.

As she turned back to her son, a blade dug painfully into her ribs.

"Look who's back," her husband muttered into her ear. His breath was warm, damp, and smelled strongly of ale. "You should have stayed at home with your lover, but you never were particularly clever, were you? Lucky for me that you have once again walked into my path. Now I get the pleasure of carving you up."

Marcellus twisted the knife, piercing the wool of Evelin's dress and slicing into her skin. The wound stung and wetness slid down her side. Through the crack in the door, she could still see William, sleeping peacefully.

"He can't know about this. You've already managed to poison him against me," Marcellus grunted, following her line of sight.

He shoved her roughly away from the door and the sudden force made her stumble and trip. She hit the floor hard, her knees slamming into the stone. Evelin twisted, but her legs caught in her skirts and she fell onto her back.

Marcellus loomed above her, snarling. "Don't worry, wife. I'll make it quick."

He raised one fist and closed his eyes as it began to glow red with blood magic.

No. Not like this. She wouldn't die like this.

Evelin pushed herself backwards away from him, her fingers clawing against the cold slabs. Scurrying along the floor, she reached for the knife she had in her boot. Grasping the cool metal hilt of the dagger, she threw it as hard as she could at his leather-clad chest. Her aim was poor; the knife flew past his head without making any impact at all. Now she was left without any weapon – not that she knew how to use one.

Thankfully, the noise of the dagger clattering on the floor distracted Marcellus. He opened his eyes and turned to look at what had made the noise, and his red light flickered and faded.

Seizing the opportunity, Evelin pushed herself upright. Her ears pricked – heavy footsteps were coming up the corner staircase just behind her. Please, God, let it be one of their men. She needed time.

"Why use blood magic, Marcellus?" she asked, her voice half an octave higher than usual. "Why not just kill me with your sword? I know that using it drains a person irreversibly. Surely I'm not worth it?"

Her husband's face contorted with a cruel smile. "It's hardly going to take much to snuff out your pitiful existence, is it?" He stepped towards her, his sword scraping its scabbard as he withdrew the weapon. "But since we're pressed for time—"

"Step the fuck away from her!" The commander's deep voice barrelled down the corridor.

Nikolas pushed her gently to one side as he stepped towards Marcellus. His longsword dripped blood onto the floor and a cut on his forearm flowed freely. His blue eyes were ice cold, all of his former swagger evaporated. What remained was a trained killer.

The sight stole Evelin's breath. He was death made flesh.

The commander paused mere feet from Marcellus, who raked a hand through his black locks and smirked.

"Ah, welcome Commander… Andersson, isn't it?"

Nikolas snarled in response, shifting his weight onto his back leg as he raised his sword.

"I wonder if your king has sanctioned this little foray into our territory? He was all too happy to run back to Parissi with his whore. Though I'm not sure why he would want to keep bedding this one," Marcellus sneered, jerking his head towards Evelin. "The boy king doesn't seem to have your taste for fighting. Perhaps he will grow some balls and pick up a sword when I send him your heads in a sack?"

Throughout Marcellus' speech, Nikolas remained still. Evelin couldn't see his face, but his jaw shifted slightly at the last sentence. With breath-taking speed, he slipped into motion, closing the gap between the two men in less than a heartbeat and stabbing his sword towards Marcellus' chest.

Marcellus parried, using his long, thin knife to block the thrust, and pushed Nikolas' sword away. Pulling another, thicker knife from his belt, Marcellus sliced the blade downwards towards the commander's thigh. Evelin's breath rasped in her throat as Nikolas stepped back a pace and Marcellus switched the knives between his hands, silently gloating at his own skill with the blades.

Nikolas' sword began to glow, just like the weapons his men had wielded earlier that evening.

The commander's movements became more fluid, beautiful in their grace, as he whirled his sword in front of his body. He stepped forwards, chopping the weapon in a complicated series of lightning-fast cuts that forced Marcellus to retreat further down the corridor. The space was narrow, more suited to Marcellus' knives than Nikolas' longsword, but the commander had gained the upper hand. Marcellus was ceding more and more ground as Nikolas cut and slashed forwards.

The two men had almost reached the end of the corridor when Marcellus spat some words that Evelin couldn't quite hear with the ruckus downstairs. Whatever was said made Nikolas pause, and Marcellus jabbed forward with his knife, slicing into Nikolas' thigh. The commander's leg buckled, and he cursed out loud, but when Marcellus went to thrust again, Nikolas lifted up his glowing sword and brought it down with a roar so loud the corridor shook.

Evelin blinked rapidly, not believing what she had just seen.

Nikolas' sword had cut straight through Marcellus' torso, from his right shoulder to his middle. Where her husband had stood mere seconds before, he now lay in pieces.

The commander stood over him, coated in a film of blood, breathing hard.

"Oh God." She wanted to vomit, to run, to cry.

As Evelin swallowed back the bile that had risen in her throat, she remembered herself and ran to William's door. *Please don't let him have seen*, she begged, *please let him be asleep.*

William wasn't at the doorway, at least, and when Evelin gently nudged open the door, she found him still in bed, his covers a tangle around him. She swiftly crossed to him and gently stroked his forehead, savouring the feeling. He shook his head sleepily and gradually opened his eyes.

"Mama!" he exclaimed and flung his thin arms around her, gripping her tightly.

Evelin buried her face in his neck and inhaled the scent of him deeply.

He was finally safe in her arms.

The boat rocked gently on the slate-blue sea. A strong wind filled the sails and soft rain fell, mist-like, soaking through Evelin's cloak. The sun was setting, its orange brilliance a thin line to her right. The crew were down below, sharing an evening meal of hard tack and stew with Nikolas' men; only the bosun remained on deck at the helm. Someone was playing a fiddle below, and the music wafted up to her. It was a plaintive melody, haunting in its beauty.

The salty tang of the sea filled her nostrils, and she tried to process the events of the night before.

Marcellus was dead. She and her boys were finally free of him, but at what price? One of Nikolas' men had been killed in the skirmish at the lodge, and another had a worrying stomach wound. Beyond that, what would her brother make of his lover's death? Would he blame Parissi? Trystan had not sanctioned the raid, and they had initially attempted to take Marcellus alive, but would that matter to Otto?

A deep cough sounded behind her. "I'm sorry to interrupt your solitude," Nikolas said softly. "I wanted to thank you for your assistance getting into the lodge. Without your help with the gate, we would have had to risk a frontal assault, which would have been far riskier." He stared out to sea as he leaned against the railings.

"I am the one who should be thanking you. Marcellus was going to kill me. If you hadn't been there…"

Nikolas kept his eyes trained on the horizon. "He had it coming. It's just a damned shame I didn't manage to bring him back alive. There are a number of people in Valon who would have liked to question him." He sighed. "I trust that your boy is okay?"

"He will be," Evelin assured him, hesitating for a moment. There was something else she needed to know. "May I ask you something?"

The commander turned to her, his expression far softer than she had ever seen on his face before. Something about him was different, more open. She took her chance.

"Marcellus said something to you, just before you… before he…" she faltered, stumbling over her words. "What was it?"

Nikolas frowned, whether at the question or at her impertinence for asking, she wasn't sure.

"Ergh. Did we have to return by boat?" Lianna weaved over to join them, clutching her stomach. Her complexion had taken on a slightly ashen hue and she puffed out her cheeks, exhaling deeply.

"Yes, if you wanted to make it out of Brigantium alive. You were the one who told us that Marcellus was due to be joined by a detachment of the royal guard," Nikolas replied tersely.

"I think this journey might kill me anyway," Lianna muttered as she heaved over the side.

Evelin held back Lianna's hair and leant down to her friend. "It won't be long until we are on dry land. Shall I get you some water?"

"No, thanks. I don't think I could stomach anything right now," Lianna replied and wiped her mouth on her sleeve. She turned to Nikolas. "I hear you came in useful, at least. Well done on killing the bastard; he had powers I've never seen before."

"Yes, my prowess with a sword is quite unmatched, or so I've been told by a number of reliable sources," the commander replied, with a smirk that didn't reach his eyes. "Now, if you ladies would excuse me, I intend to get blinding drunk with my men." The commander sauntered breezily off across the deck, something that seemed impossible considering how much the boat was being tossed on the swells.

Lianna, energy spent, sank down onto the damp wooden boards and huddled into her cloak. Evelin sat down beside her and hugged her knees to her chest.

"I'm sorry I lied to you, Eve," Lianna said hoarsely.

"Why did you?" Evelin asked. "I'm supposed to be your best friend. Didn't you think you could trust me?"

"Of course I knew I could trust you!" Lianna protested. "But I needed to make sure you had full deniability. I was a double agent in your brother's court, gaining intelligence on your husband. Both of them knew how close we were, what if they decided to question you? Otto has other telepaths."

"But why didn't you tell me when I came to Valon? When I told you everything, why didn't you tell me you were working for Parissi? Why did you let me think you had betrayed me when Marcellus captured me?"

Lianna sighed deeply, her shoulders sagging. "I've tried for so long to think two steps ahead and to keep parts of myself hidden, that I think I did the same to you. I should have told you the truth, and I regret it now, but I thought you had enough to deal with, what with Gabriel and everything that was going on with you and Trystan… When Marcellus captured you, he sent word to me. He wanted to use my telepathy skills to find out about Valon's wards from you. I was already in Brigantium looking for you, and knew what he was capable of, so I went straight to the lodge. I only ever wanted to protect you – I never thought Trystan would give up William."

"What *did* you think he would do when Marcellus sent his ultimatum? Surely, you must have suspected that Trystan would agree to it—"

"No! You have to believe me." Lianna gripped her hands firmly. "I thought, perhaps more hoped, that he might delay long enough for the Ironforged to arrive and attempt a rescue. I thought Ceinwyn would counsel caution… Everything went awry when Marcellus captured you. I know that I let you down, Eve, and I am truly sorry. Can you forgive me?"

Lianna wasn't blameless in this, Evelin knew that much, but it was also clear that her friend had been placed in an impossible and dangerous situation.

Evelin nodded. "Of course, but no more secrets from now on, okay?"

"Okay," Lianna replied and rested her head on Evelin's shoulder.

Lianna's apologies and explanations didn't erase the hurt Evelin felt, but what was the point in holding on to that feeling? Good friends were like the stars emerging in the dusk above the ship's sails; whilst not always visible, they were the ever-present constants in one's life, tiny pricks of light that shone through whatever darkness you might face.

It was just after dawn when the boat finally docked in Valon's harbour. After passing on her thanks to the captain, Evelin hurried down the gangplank and walked through the streets of the city. She carried a drowsy William in her arms and was flanked by two of Nikolas' men. Their eyes appeared hollow as they scanned the adjoining alleys on the lookout for any possible threat; the loss of their comrade clung to them and pricked at Evelin too. The group re-entered the palace grounds by the stables, and the two women nodded farewell to their companions before creeping back to their own rooms.

Evelin placed William down gently in his bed and went to watch over a sleeping Gabriel. Pointed ears peeked out from under his woollen hat; Ceinwyn had evidently replenished her glamour whilst she had been away. For a few seconds, Evelin allowed herself to remove the glamour and watch over the true, peaceful form of her human child.

Should it matter that she didn't understand why he had been born like this? She loved him all the same, yet the not knowing still gnawed away at her. Was it her fault? Had she done something to make him like this? She felt like a bad mother for even caring, as if she was failing him by still wanting answers, but she did need answers, and she needed to get them somehow.

She couldn't continue to live like this forever.

CHAPTER SIXTY-NINE

EVELIN

Ceinwyn was in her study, hunched over a thick pile of papers, when Evelin arrived. The Chancellor's face was drawn, but her eyes lit up at Evelin's entrance.

"It is good to see you." She smiled and lay down her pen. "How is William?"

"He's still a little shaken, but he is better than I expected. Thank you for maintaining the glamour on Gabriel whilst I was away."

"I didn't have to – it was strong enough to hold on its own. Your command over glamouring has developed at a highly impressive rate," Ceinwyn praised.

Evelin's cheeks reddened at the compliment, but she felt pride glow inside her. It was wonderful to feel that she was good at something again.

"Actually," Ceinwyn continued. "Since you are here, there is something I need to ask you about. What are your plans now? Do you intend to remain in Valon?"

Evelin paused. She had thought about little else on the journey back. "I know that my coming here has made relations with Brigantium more difficult, so perhaps I should leave… I could always go to my mother's homeland, Caledon, but I worry about what sort of reception I might receive; Caledon is firmly allied with Brigantium, and I still don't know the cause of

Gabriel's condition. I just don't know what the best option is." The enormity of everything was weighing on her heavily.

"Unfortunately, you are not wrong. I fear that war with Brigantium may be closer than ever, but that is not solely down to you. Nikolas was a fool to kill Marcellus, to even attempt to bring him back for questioning. You know your brother far better than I, but I cannot imagine King Otto will take Marcellus' death well." Ceinwyn sighed. "However, I think there may be a way that you can help Parissi. Would you consider remaining in Valon and taking on the role of Vice-Chancellor?"

Evelin frowned, shocked by the offer put to her. "Did Trystan tell you to ask me that?"

"No. The Vice-Chancellorship is not his to offer. This was my idea. He knows that I intended to offer you the post, though. When Trystan appointed me Chancellor, I decided against having a deputy. The kingdom was in disarray after the massacre and I was unsure of whom I could trust. However, the workload has become too great for one person, and I believe that you would acquit yourself well. You are a highly intelligent woman and are capable of great things. You also have an intimate knowledge of Brigantium and are well-versed in the ways of a royal court, which I am not. The palace has been too isolated for too long. Powerful sections of Parissi society are growing restless and the court must function properly again. It will give them an opportunity for their scheming and social climbing, but hopefully in a way that will be of benefit to us. What do you think? Will you stay and take on the role?"

Evelin's face broke into a smile and her stomach twisted with excitement. "Yes. Yes – I would relish the opportunity. Thank you, Ceinwyn. Thank you," she said quickly, her words bumping into one another. She took a deep, calming breath, and tried to slow down.

"Excellent," Ceinwyn replied, picking her pen back up. "I look forward to working with you, Vice-Chancellor."

The morning had not been a pleasant one. Trystan had been woken shortly after dawn by a servant carrying Nik's report of the raid on the hunting lodge. Marcellus had been killed, and one of their own men had been lost in the fighting. The tense peace that had existed between Parissi and Brigantium was surely shattered now.

Trystan had felt fury like never before when he had learned of Nik's failure to follow orders, and when he found out that Evelin had accompanied him, he thought he might implode. He had wanted to charter the fastest ship in the harbour and bring them both back, but Ceinwyn had talked him down. Trystan understood Nik's motives for wanting to apprehend Marcellus; he felt the same desire for revenge eating away at him, tainting anything good that happened with its poison. Yet, his commander had to think of the bigger picture. What use was revenge if it put Parissi in more danger?

Trystan walked briskly down the corridor, and the familiar sound of Nik's voice came from the commander's office. In a haze of anger, he stormed inside. A servant, eyes wide with fear, scuttled out, leaving the two men alone.

His friend was still in his fighting leathers and stank of blood, sweat, and dirt.

"Trystan, I—"

"Give me one good reason not to court-martial you!" Trystan snapped. "You disobeyed your fucking orders and you bungled the entire operation. You are a bloody liability, Nik! Your one job is to protect this realm and your impulsive actions may well destroy us all!"

Nik's jaw tensed and he pulled himself up to his full height. "You should court-martial me, Trystan. I have no excuses." His friend kept his gaze straight ahead, not making eye contact, statue-like.

It was then that Trystan noticed the bloody bandages on Nikolas's forearm; the way that he wasn't putting weight through his left leg.

"You're wounded," he observed.

"Flesh wounds," Nikolas replied dismissively, his leg shaking slightly.

"Sit down, you idiot," Trystan snapped. "I'll send for a healer."

Upon his return to the room, Trystan poured them both a large measure of liquor and sat down opposite his friend, thrusting a drink towards him.

"I probably shouldn't drink this if I am to face trial. I'll need to keep a clear head," Nik commented, the corner of his mouth tugging upwards slightly.

"You know bloody well that I am not going to court-martial you." Trystan sighed. "But you can never do this again."

His friend reached for the knife strapped to his belt and dragged it across his left palm, making a short incision. He held his right hand over the wound. "I promise that I will never again refuse to follow your orders, Trystan." A bright golden light glowed from the cut and sealed it, a livid red scar taking its place.

Trystan swallowed his drink in one go and clunked it down on the desk. "Well, a blood oath was slightly unnecessary. You could have just told me, you know."

"You'll just have to be careful what you order me to do," Nik smirked, downing his own drink. "I'm sorry about the mess I've made. I fucked up by killing the bastard."

"You were protecting Evelin, and honestly, he had it coming." Trystan sighed heavily. "God knows what will happen now."

"War, I suppose." Nik shrugged, running a finger over his new scar. "You will be pleased with the new recruits I trained over winter. Brigantium won't find an attack on us easy."

"That's one positive, I suppose," Trystan murmured, looking up as the healer entered. "We will need to strategize soon, but you'd best rest for now."

War was coming, and there was no better man to lead his armies than Nik.

Now, though, there was one more battle Trystan needed to face.

CHAPTER SEVENTY-ONE

EVELIN

Evelin was in the library, curled up in a cosy chair. She was studying a guide to the noble families of Parissi. Most of them she knew by name already, and many by reputation, but there was no such thing as too much preparation.

There had been so many marriages between the families over the years that she was considering drawing out some family trees, when the door creaked open.

From over the top of the heavy tome, Trystan's tall, lean frame came into focus.

"Evelin, can we talk?" he asked softly, running his hand around the neck of his shirt.

"Sure," she said noncommittally, as she placed the book down on the side table, marking her page with a slip of parchment.

What did the king even have to say that was worth listening to? She kept her eyes trained on the hem of her dress.

Trystan wandered over to her and sat in the chair opposite, pulling it nearer so that they were only two feet apart. Evelin could feel the heat from his body as he leaned towards her. In response, she shoved herself backwards in her seat, trying to keep as much distance between them as possible.

"I need to apologise to you."

Evelin risked a glance upwards, incredulous, but he kept his gaze low, focusing on the floor between them.

"It was unforgivable of me to give up William, and I understand why you are angry with me, but—"

"No," Evelin cut in. Did he truly believe a simple apology would make right what he had done? Her trust in Trystan had been so complete, and now it was shattered. "I don't think you do. William is my *son*, and to me, he will always – *always* – come first. You gave him up without a second thought and forced me to leave him. That is unforgivable, Trystan."

"Marcellus wanted to hurt you, possibly kill you! How could I let you remain with him?" Trystan retorted, raising his head and fixing her with an aggrieved stare.

Why was *he* angry? She was the one whose child had been ripped from her arms. "That should have been *my* choice, Trystan. Mine. Just like you made your choice for your kingdom, I should have stayed with my son."

"For God's sake, Evelin! I know that I fucked up, alright?" His jaw tensed as he took a breath. "Do you have any idea what was going through my mind when I got that letter from Marcellus? When I found out that he had you and what he was threatening to do to you… I lost my mind. I would have done anything to get you back."

"And that *anything* included giving up my son to a mass murderer?"

"I didn't know that he was behind the massacre." He paused and scraped a hand back through his hair. "I will regret what I did for the rest of my life, but I couldn't do anything else."

"Couldn't or wouldn't?"

"I *physically* couldn't." He paused and wrung his hands together. "The night you arrived in Valon with the boys and begged us for sanctuary, I made a blood oath to protect your life at all costs. It meant that no member of my court could override my wishes and scheme to send you back to Brigantium, otherwise my own life would be forfeit."

"You bonded your life to mine," she repeated, a chill washing over her. "Did Ceinwyn and Lianna know about this?"

"No, I didn't tell them or Nik about the oath. It was my trump card to play if they decided that keeping you here was too perilous. As soon as I knew that Marcellus had you and that he was threatening your life, something snapped within me; I was consumed by the desire to find you and it overruled every rational part of me. I had no idea that was how the oath would work. I'd remembered learning about it in our first year at the Academie and thought it would protect you, so I swore to myself that I would never knowingly let you be harmed. I didn't realise that it would hold such sway over me; that I would be unable to do anything but obey my own, earlier command."

"You were a fool to use magic that you don't understand, Trystan." She closed her eyes at his hubris. It was so typical of him.

"I know, and I'm sorry. I tried to fight it. Marcellus had asked for both boys in his demands but I couldn't let him take Gabriel and find out about his humanity." He looked at her intently, reaching for the collar of his white shirt.

"What the hell do you think you're doing?" Evelin hissed as he began to unbutton it.

"Just look, please. I need you to understand."

Trystan's strong hands pulled open the shirt, revealing his chest. On his smooth, lightly tanned skin, over his heart, was a light-grey, intricately swirled pattern about the size of a fist.

Evelin sucked in a sharp breath. Blood oaths were an arcane form of magic, rarely used any more, but they were impossible to disobey. If someone went against the command, they would be racked with excruciating pain, followed by a slow death. She reached a trembling hand to his chest and ran her fingers over the markings. The swirling patterns marked his resistance against the bond; the damage it had done to him when he had tried to disobey.

Trystan's breathing juddered under her touch. "Keeping Gabriel here was all I could do to fight it. I am so sorry I couldn't do more. Giving William to Marcellus was unforgiveable and drugging you… forcing you to leave him… God, I haven't slept. I can't eat. All I can think about is how I betrayed the person I love the most in this whole damned world. You consume me. Loving you is easier than breathing. I have never deserved you, Evelin; you are the most admirable person I have ever met. Your love and faith in me held me together when everything was falling apart, and now I have destroyed it all."

It was like Evelin could finally see the man she had once loved so deeply. He had been a fool to make the oath, but he had fought for her and for Gabriel, undergoing God knows what level of pain. She ran her hand up over his face. He closed his agony-filled eyes and leaned his sharp jaw into her touch.

"You need to release yourself from the oath, Trystan," she said finally, drawing away her hand.

"What?"

"We cannot live with the bond controlling your actions anymore."

His eyes widened a fraction, a spark of hope dancing there. "Does that mean there still is a *we*?"

Evelin swallowed hard. However angry she still was, it didn't erase the fact that she loved him, more than she had ever thought possible. He had hurt her, and it would take time for her to trust him fully again, but now that she understood why, she didn't want to give up on him. On *them*.

Trystan reached out to take her hand and gripped it firmly, as if fearful that if he let go, she would disappear again.

"I love you, Trystan," she said softly. "I can't promise that this will work out, but I want to try."

Trystan looked at her with something akin to wonder. "I love you too," he whispered. "I will go to the Academie with Ceinwyn tomorrow to uncover a solution to the blood oath, and I promise to henceforth do everything in my power to do right by you *and* your boys. Both of them. They are part of you, and I will cherish them as my own."

Tears welled in Evelin's eyes, but before she could respond, there was a brisk knock at the door.

"Excuse me, sire, there is a visitor asking for an audience with the Vice-Chancellor."

A visitor? For her?

"Who is it, please?" Evelin asked.

"The High Priestess Katyana."

EPILOGUE
KATYANA

The journey from Elysara had been treacherous. Katyana was unaccustomed to much travel these days, preferring to stay cloistered with her sisters in the warmth and security of the abbey walls.

Riding through Brigantium had been slow and arduous; she had been so stiff by the end of the first day that she had rested at an inn for a night to ease her aching muscles and enjoy a warm meal. The rest of her passage north had been similarly taxing, and hospitable places to stay had become scarcer as she entered the wilderness of the middle lands. However, the thought of Evie needing her, desperate for her wisdom and guidance, fuelled her. Katyana was certain Evie would understand her being a day or so late to their meeting; her niece had always been such an accommodating and sensible person.

Yet when she reached the fort, there had been no sign of her. The fortress was ghostly quiet. Katyana was no tracker by any stretch of the imagination, but it took little skill to recognise recent prints in the dense mud – horse and fae. Evie's letter hadn't contained large amounts of information, but Katyana suspected what had happened. That awful Marcellus must have been behind this. She weighed her options carefully.

Katyana could go to Azmar and appeal to her nephew, but Otto was still as stubborn and ungrateful as he had been as a child. It was unlikely he would do anything to rein in the duke. Going to Valon might be a better plan. Evie had been staying there with the new king, a friend from the Academie, apparently.

Katyana despised the city; the bustle, the *worldliness,* was so overpowering to her keenly developed sensitivities.

She rubbed the bridge of her nose in an attempt to release some of the pressure building in her sinuses. Really, all of this could have been prevented if Titus had just let her initiate Evelin in the priestesshood. She wouldn't have been pushed into a ridiculous arranged marriage or forced to flee to that Godforsaken Valon.

Men. Always interfering in the lives of women.

Katyana sighed and heaved herself up back onto her horse with a groan.

She had not wanted to risk the mountain pass, so Katyana had ended up waiting days for a boat willing to take her to Valon. She was surprised how so few were sailing now the ports had reopened, but the opportunity to rest and replenish her stores of energy was much welcome. When a fat, sweaty trader, who smelled distinctly of horse, finally agreed to take her last few coins in exchange for passage, Katyana resigned herself to her fate.

She had handled the sea journey admirably, she reflected, as she stepped onto the docks in Valon. Maybe in another life she would have been a sailor – it was far more preferable than travelling by horse, at least.

The strong breeze carried wafts of fish as it whipped at the strands of white-blonde hair loose at her temples. Katyana always wore it in the fashion prescribed by her religious order

– coiled in tight plaits around her head, with two small sections around each ear shaved away. She pulled her hood up. Valon was a particularly irreligious city, and she didn't want to stand out.

The Summer Palace was easy enough to find. The building was so laughably ornate that it stood out like a beacon of excess. The guards on the front gates were obstinate brutes, refusing to let her through and keeping her, *her*, waiting on permission from their captain. After the meaningless wait, Katyana was eventually shown through to a small waiting room.

"I am here to speak to the king about Princess Evelin of Brigantium," she said in her clearest voice to the captain as soon as he stepped foot in the room.

"The princess is en route as we speak," the captain assured her. "I trust you are willing to wait a few minutes longer?"

He raised an eyebrow in a highly disrespectful manner, that was just so typical of a citizen of Valon, before turning on his heel and leaving.

So, Evelin was safe and, apparently, back here in Valon. That was something at least. Katyana closed her eyes and let her neck relax as she waited. Soon, warmed by the fire, she was dozing.

"Aunt Katya," Evie's sweet, soft voice startled her awake.

Katyana's eyes fluttered open to see her beautiful niece leaning over her, gently stroking her arm.

"Oh, my wonderful girl!" Katyana exclaimed, pulling the young woman tight against her.

"Thank you so much for coming. Are you hungry? You must be after journeying all the way here."

Katyana released her hold on her niece. "I wouldn't say no to some bread and water. My stomach cannot tolerate the richness of Parissi food."

Evie nodded and whispered to the servant outside the door, before taking a seat beside her.

"Forgive me Aunt Katya, but I am desperate to find out what you alluded to in your letter. Do you have knowledge about what it means to have a fae-borne human?" Her eyes were wide and she was wringing her long, delicate fingers together. Fear and hope waged a battle for primacy in her words.

"Yes, of course, my darling girl," she said, gripping Evie's hand in her own. "That is why I was so determined to come. It is a rare situation, certainly, but not undocumented. Indeed, I believe one of the most sacred texts held by the sisters of my order may be able to explain the circumstance of Gabriel's birth. It is an ancient text, difficult to translate, but from what I can gather, it states that during the moment when God cursed the first humans to their fate for their greed, the great-great granddaughter of Igraine, a fae woman called Diana, conceived a child with her fae lover, who was made human by God's curse. Stripped of his powers, the father abandoned Diana and settled with the rest of the humans. Diana's child was born fae, but it is said that he carried within him a spark of his father's humanity. Diana's son went on to marry another fae, and that spark was soon forgotten, but it seems that the writer of the scroll believed that, one day, humanity would emerge again from that fae's bloodline. In other words, a fae-borne human would be brought into this world. There is a prophecy associated with this tale, of course – our ancestors loved to prophesise – which states that this fae-borne human child will bring about the destruction of the fae realms and bring them under the dominion of the humans forever."

Evie's skin turned deathly pale.

"Ah, fear not my dear. Such prophecies are almost always fanciful nonsense. You must be thankful, Evie! Your son is a gift from God."

Katyana squeezed her niece's hand but Evie pulled away, her

eyes wide and panicked.

"But what if someone finds out about the prophecy, someone who might want to harm Gabriel? You can't tell anyone else about this, Aunt Katyana. Promise me!"

"My lips are sealed. Continue to glamour the child and try not to worry about the future. You are living under the protection of the king of Parissi, in this heavily guarded palace. Just enjoy every moment you spend with your children, and raise them in God's image," Katyana soothed. "Speaking of your boys, may I see my great-nephews? Goodness, that does make me sound horrendously old!"

"Of course," Evie replied softly.

Katyana could tell that her niece hadn't fully taken on board her words. She was about to try again to allay Evelin's fears when a stunningly handsome man popped his head around the door. His chiselled features and graceful bearing were almost enough to make her regret the oath of celibacy she took upon joining her order.

"I'm sorry for intruding," the man said, giving an apologetic smile. "It is wonderful to meet you, Priestess. Evelin, are you alright?"

His eyes went straight to her niece and looked at her with such concern and love that Katyana was momentarily taken aback.

Evie gave a tiny shake of her head, tears forming in her eyes. The man crossed to her in less than a heartbeat and wrapped his arms around her, holding her tight against his chest as she told him of the prophecy. She sobbed into him, her body shaking.

After a few minutes, the man pulled away and took her face in his hands. "Whatever happens, we will face it together," he soothed, and planted a gentle kiss on her brow. Evie gave him a small smile and nodded weakly. "Who knows what Gabriel will do or be when he grows up? All you can do is love him and guard him as you would any other child. His future is not written."

Katyana knew that Evelin's fears were not unfounded, but her niece had finally found a place of safety and love – a home.

She sniffed. It was just a shame that it was in such an iniquitous place as Valon.

To be continued...

ACKNOWLEDGEMENTS

This book would not exist without the extraordinary generosity of so many people.

I'm grateful to the whole team at Cranthorpe Millner for their work in bringing this book to life. Special thanks to Vicky for edits that always made the story sharper, to Jenna for spotting its potential in the first place, and to Amy for the advice that kept me pointing in the right direction.

Hugh and Lia, thank you for reading this story through and offering thoughtful, honest feedback. And Heather – my best friend forever – you've been my loudest cheerleader from the first word to the last.

To my Mum, Dad and Nan, for always being there from the start with steady encouragement. You have always made me feel like I could do anything.

To my boys – Edward and Peter – you are my everything, my reason, and the brightest part of every day. This story exists because you remind me what matters most.

And to Mark, thank you for your constant support and for making room in our lives for this story to be written.

Finally, to you, the reader – thank you for stepping into this story and giving it life beyond these pages.

ABOUT THE AUTHOR

Fascinated by magical realms since childhood, Jen A. Egerton's passion for tales of court intrigue, epic battles, and complex characters led her to study Modern History at the University of Oxford. Now a mother to two young children, Jen works as a secondary school teacher, using her fleeting spare moments to conjure up fantasy worlds on paper.

Keep up to date on all things the *Fae-Borne* series by following Jen on socials:

Instagram: @jen_a_egerton
TikTok: @jen.a.egerton

www.ingramcontent.com/pod-product-compliance
Lightning Source LLC
Chambersburg PA
CBHW030541190726

48283CB00006B/1965